THE WILLING WAR

THE
WILLING WAR

A NOVEL OF MARYLAND
IN THE AMERICAN REVOLUTION

VOLUME ONE
The Old Line Chronicles

JOHN CONRADIS

FIRESIDE FICTION
2007

FIRESIDE FICTION
AN IMPRINT OF HERITAGE BOOKS, INC.

Books, CDs, and more—Worldwide

For our listing of thousands of titles see our website
at
www.HeritageBooks.com

Published 2007 by
HERITAGE BOOKS, INC.
Publishing Division
65 East Main Street
Westminster, Maryland 21157-5026

Copyright © 2007 John C. Conradis

Cover painting: "Departure of Smallwood's Command from Annapolis, 1776"
by A.W. Thompson
Courtesy Maryland National Guard Museum, Baltimore, Maryland

Cover design and map preparation by Roxanne Carlson
Flintlock Press/roxcarl@verizon.net

International Standard Book Number: 978-0-7884-4380-0

American Liberty, A Poem

Bear me some power as far as winds can blow,
As ships can travel, or as waves can flow,
To some lone isle beyond the southern pole,
Or lands 'round which pacific waters roll,
There should oblivion stop the heaving sigh,
There should I live at least with liberty,
But honour checks my speed and bids me stay,
To try the fortunes of the well fought day,
Resentment for my country's fate I bear,
And mix with thousands for the willing war.

Philip Freneau, 1775

A Map of
Maryland and the
Delaware Counties,
1757

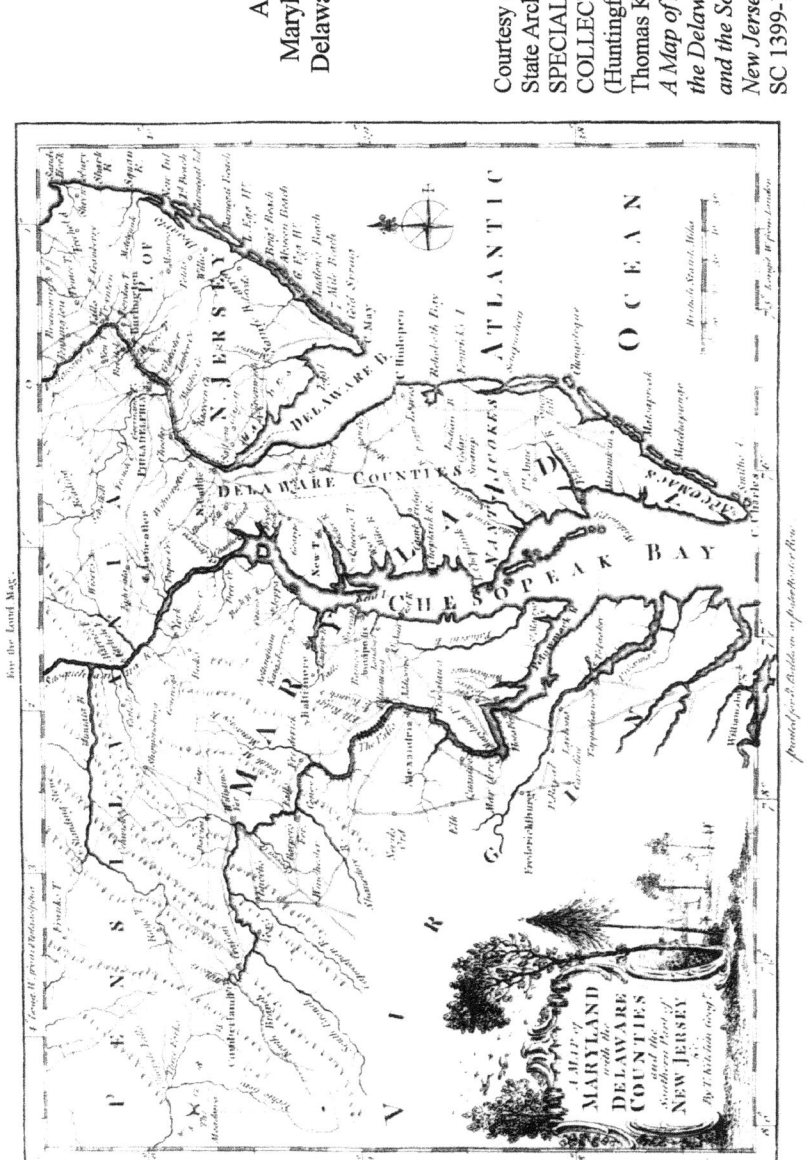

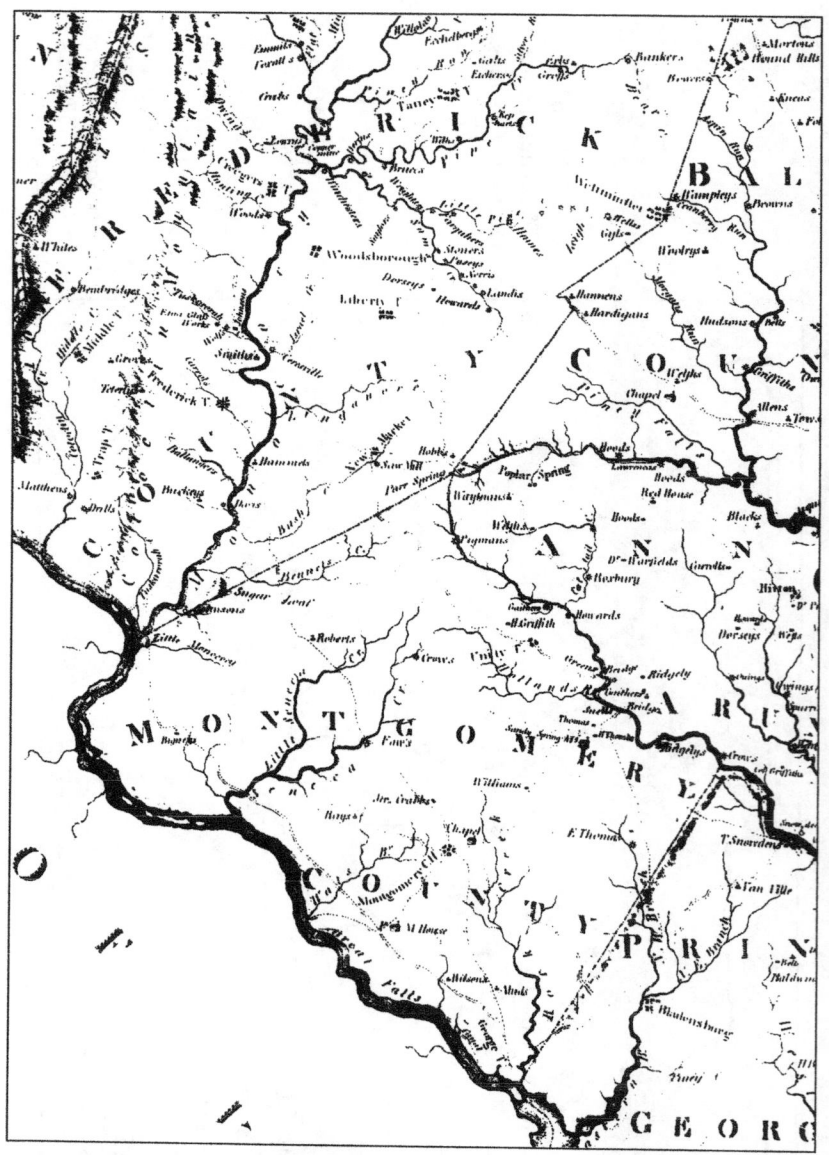

Map of Maryland, c.1776, showing Montgomery County (formerly Lower Frederick County). Hungerford's Tavern became the Montgomery Court House.

Courtesy of the Maryland State Archives SPECIAL COLLECTIONS (Maryland State Law Library Historic Map Collection) Dennis, Griffin, *Map of the State of Maryland*, 1794 [1795]. MSA SC 5459-1

Part One

A Happy and Discontented Country

Whereas, the power, but not the justice; the vengence, but not the wisdom of Great Britain . . . which scourged and exiled our fugitive parents from their native shores, now pursues us, their guiltless children, with unrelenting severity.

Doctor Joseph Warren, 1774

1

THE MISCHIEF THAT WAS COMING

Rock Creek Chapel
Lower Frederick County, Province of Maryland
November 6, 1774

CHRISTOPHER SIMS SIGHED. He had spent the last two years brooding and yearning for a love life. Looking up at a black canopy formed by smudges of trees, he knew that it was going to be a long workday; but he walked with a light step, practically skipping along like a boy going fishing, because he was off to see the woman he loved. The anticipation of what awaited him at the end of the road made him heady. Come to think of it, the road he was now on was clear and easy on the legs. He picked up his pace.

As he walked along the road, between the ruts, on soft grass, he thought about these rare occasions for "courting," if his visits to the Crabbe homestead could be called that. It wasn't so much the miles that kept them apart; it was the awkwardness of pursuing a bound woman as a wedding mate.

This segment of the "Great Road," as it was most commonly called, wound through a stretch of woodland and dense undergrowth. Here the road was hardly more than a path that had to be marked by blazes on trees, barely wide enough to allow the passage of freight wagons and carts, swaying and creaking as they rolled between George Town and Frederick.

Emerging from the woods, Christopher could, in the early light, see a landscape almost devoid of trees. Few people admired the prospect in these parts. "Untidy" was the most apt word to describe it. The view was one of undulating fields irregularly bordered by tangled growths of saplings and brush. During the growing season most of these fields were filled to overflowing with squat, splay-leaf tobacco plants, although some fields, the "old fields," were allowed to lie fallow and revert to brush and scrub pine.

This was the scenery all the way to Hungerford's Tavern, which Christopher saw in the distance as he veered off onto the Baltimore Road, to travel east towards Rock Creek. Soon he came upon the little chapel and what folks referred to as the "rectory," which was a simple log cabin. But call it a cabin or a rectory, this was home to the Reverend Crabbe and his family, and to the bound woman, whose name was Hannah Williams.

As he approached, Christopher saw a man off in the distance emerge from the woods and walk towards the road. He recognized the man as James Murray, a notorious Tory in the lower county whose condemnation of those who opposed government policies in any shape or form had caused him to run afoul of popular sentiment on more than one occasion. In addition, local gossip, for what it was worth, added to Murray's known misdeeds by accusing him of being a Crown spy.

Christopher noted Murray's presence as curious, since the man lived miles from here—but then again, he was carrying a fowler and he might be out hunting for all Christopher knew.

Then to his surprise, as Christopher approached the cabin a few minutes later, he saw the Reverend Crabbe also emerge from the woods and walk towards the cabin.

"Hullo, Reverend," Christopher called out.

"Why, Christopher, I didn't expect ye until later."

"Yes, well, I've a lot of work to do back at the farm, so I decided to get an early start here. Hope that doesn't interfere with your plans."

"Nay—not at all, Christopher. Always appreciate your help."

"Say, wasn't that Jim Murray I saw walkin' out of the woods just before you did?"

"James Murray?—Ye don't say?" A look of concern, like a shadow obstructing the sun, passed over the Reverend's usually placid visage, and just as quickly changed to a theatrical expression of perplexity.

"No, in fact, I didn't see him. Wonder why he didn't stop to say hello." The Reverend gave Christopher a shrug in dismissal.

"I just thought you two might have run into each other since you came outta the woods about the same place—that's all."

The Reverend Crabbe laughed. It seemed somewhat forced.

"Well, that is *odd*, I have to admit, Christopher. But I walk in the woods to mull over my sermons and I'm oblivious to everything around me. Missus Crabbe says a bear could amble right by me and she doubts I'd notice it!"

For some reason Christopher just didn't believe this explanation. Perhaps all those accusations against the Reverend Crabbe *were* true, that he only pretended to believe that a man could be a patriot and still be a loyal subject to the king. That was his argument and a good many people gave him the benefit of the doubt because of it.

Christopher might have worried this more except that Hannah Williams just then came out the door and walked behind the cabin.

She had glanced his way, but made no gesture of recognition; nor did Christopher give any sign that he had been looking forward to this moment for weeks.

In truth, Christopher did not outwardly visit the Crabbe home to court Hannah Williams. This would have been unacceptable behavior. Instead, Christopher contributed free labor to the Reverend Crabbe as part of the community's obligation to lend him and his family a helping hand in return for his services as both neighborhood preacher and schoolmaster. This—and this alone—provided Christopher with the excuse to steal a moment or two with Hannah.

Community support consisted of doing various chores, usually the backbreaking ones, for the Crabbes. Today it was to cut some chestnut trees for fence posts and black walnut for rails to mend the fence around the kitchen garden, which had been breached by pesky deer.

Unfortunately most of Christopher's time would be spent in the woods chopping down trees and there would be no excuse for Hannah to come in close proximity to him while doing that.

It wasn't until he was stacking the cut logs in the shed that Christopher had a chance to be with Hannah.

She rounded the corner of the cabin, a tall young woman, who carried herself well in her hand-me-down calico gown, checked woolen petticoat and red wool shawl, carrying a tankard and trencher.

"Good morning to you, Mister Sims," she said gaily.

"And to you, Missus Williams."

As Hannah came up to him, Christopher felt a little embarrassed. He had tossed his coat to do his chopping and his linen shirt, his best for the occasion, was now wet with sweat and beginning to give off a ripe manly odor.

"Let me get my coat—"

"Chris," and Hannah's smile turned into a little laugh. "I think a hard-workin' man is very attractive." With that, she placed the tankard and trencher on a stump and quickly united with him, trading kisses which seemed so passionate that they might be heard within the cabin.

They separated smiling and satisfied for the moment, but both pitied the other for having to hide their happiness.

After this short but sweet interlude, Christopher did not see Hannah again. As he was about to leave, the Reverend Crabbe came out with a cup of rye whiskey and some small talk, his usual way of saying thanks.

"Reverend, we'll have the fence repaired within the fortnight," Christopher reported.

"That's wonderful, Christopher. Missus Crabbe has been worrying about the deer ravaging our winter vegetables."

They stumbled through the conversation after that. Both men had stated their political differences between each other. There was no sense in expounding on that as long as they wanted to avoid making it personal—which neither of them did. And small talk amongst men could only last so long.

"We'll be seeing ye at services this Sabbath?"

"Aye, ye will indeed, Reverend. Until then...."

"Fare thee well, Christopher."

Christopher set off on his journey home as the Reverend gave a farewell wave and turned towards the house.

2

THE BACKCOUNTRY

Hungerford's Tavern
Lower Frederick County
Mid-December 1774

FOLLOWING DRILL, which was conducted in the cleared field in back of Hungerford's Tavern, the men would tarry a bit to discuss whatever was on their minds. Eventually most would take advantage of these rare community gatherings and have a drink or two with the boys.

Today's was the second drill session held since the Provincial Convention had called for a well-regulated militia, ostensibly to relieve the mother country from the necessity of maintaining any standing army in the province. When this was announced two weeks ago, it caused more than a few questions.

"What's this all about?" they asked.

George Winston couldn't answer that question, but he did volunteer a few enlightening facts. "Now, every one knows there's no standing army in these parts...*and* it's arguable whether there's one in the entire province."

They all agreed that this was probably true. In fact, it had been years since there had been a need to even call out the militia. The only current reason for doing so was for the annual

Militia Day, a spring social event and a day for frolicking and excessive celebration.

Henry Tune, the company lieutenant, offered this: "I heard we're exercising to prevent the Redcoats from plundering our province—like they're doing up there in Massachusetts—if they have that idea in mind."

"What...?"

These *were* troubled times and they did talk about the possibility of someone, somewhere having to maybe fight the regulars. But this was more a curiosity than anything else, to talk about in outraged voices over a cider. None of them could imagine the day would ever come when the regulars would march up the George Town-Frederick Road to threaten their homes and families. What on earth for? It was even hard to imagine the idea of a British attack on the port of George Town.

Feeling no better informed now than before this exchange, Christopher Sims hoped that they would get a straight answer today from their community leaders who had just returned from a meeting in Frederick, the county seat.

Climbing the steps to the porch, he quickly looked over the various news items, advertisements and messages tacked to the tavern's wall, which served as the community notice board. Seeing nothing new, he went into the tavern's long room.

This room was thirty-two by sixteen feet, more or less, with a large fireplace at each end, its interior made murky by a swirling atmosphere of old smoke, raw spirits, cooking food, burnt grease, and ripe body orders. The two windows on each side of the door filtered the natural light through oiled paper so that it penetrated into the room as a dull brown; the fresh outside air which was brought in by the opened door seemed to accentuate a particular interior smell rather than dispel it. The room was full of men, sitting and straddling the benches or standing, all talking loudly and laughing, and the susurrating sound of their conversations made his ears ring. This was a rural tavern at its best.

Hungerford's Tavern was a social hub for the local back-inhabitants, those who lived in isolated rural areas such as this part of Frederick County. The tavern was located on the Great

Road midway between Frederick Town, the county seat and only real town in western Maryland, and George Town, a small river port on the banks of the Potomac. It also sat at a crossroads that led to Baltimore and to Bladensburg, both important centers for the tobacco culture of the region.

There had been an establishment for the public entertainment located in this unnamed hamlet for as long as anyone could remember. Why, in 1755, when the same structure was known as Owen's Ordinary, General Braddock himself had supped here on the way to his epic defeat at the hands of the French and Indians in the meadows near Fort Duquesne, in the far reaches of Pennsylvania.

In more recent times, Charles Hungerford had acquired the license for operating the tavern and had made considerable improvements in both the tavern's appearance and entertainment. The rude building was clad in clapboard to cover its original walls of undressed logs; a plank floor was laid down; the roof pierced by two dormer windows for the upstairs loft, used as sleeping quarters for both the Hungerfords and overnight guests; and a covered porch, running the length of the structure, had been added.

In addition to the cosmetic changes, the tavern offered a fair measure of liquor and surprisingly good fare for a rural inn; it also served as an informal post office for the distribution of mail and news from the outside world, delivered from time to time by James Cavil, the circuit rider from Baltimore.

Christopher entered the room and immediately saw Doctor Wootton, Henry Griffith, and Archibald Orme, three of their representatives who attended the meeting at the courthouse in Frederick, talking to a number of the more comfortable landowners in the lower county. He knew that as soon as this group broke up they would start circulating around the room informing the rest of what had transpired.

In the meantime, he could sure use a drink. He went over to the cask of cider, provided free of charge by the Griffith brothers on each drill day, and, jostling happily with the others, drew a mug. He spotted Jeremy Heynon, friends since they were four years old, with a group of fellow farmers sitting at one of the trestle tables and joined them, forcing room on the crowded bench, which they gave good-naturedly.

As they drank and talked about the crops and the weather, all of them were wondering about the strident talk concerning the mother country and how this might affect them.

Back in June, many of them, Christopher included, had met here at Hungerford's and agreed on a resolution supporting the city of Boston when its harbor was blockaded by an Act of Parliament. They also strongly voiced the need to secure American freedom through every legal and constitutional measure. They even sent their sentiments to Annapolis for insertion in the *Maryland Gazette*.

That was one thing, but since then the anger had grown on both sides, the conflict kept escalating, and the result, of course, had been violence. Just this past October, Marylanders had burned the brig *Peggy Stewart* for attempting to unload a cargo of that scorned commodity, tea. Now there was talk about a well-regulated militia....

Where will this end? Christopher and his neighbors watched their leaders, waiting for the opportunity to question them directly.

Suddenly longing for the callowness of youth, Christopher nudged Jeremy, pointing to one of the tables crowded with younger men and boys, whooping it up, oblivious to their elders concerns. They were more interested in the next frolic or shucking bee, horse racing, and girls. Every one of those young men, Christopher suspected, harbored a boy's passion for the saucey bound girl Sally, who was even then slipping and ducking among the crowd to deliver food and drink. Some of the young men tried to catch Sally's eye, but she had no time for boys who drank only cider which had already been paid for by somebody else. Christopher and Jeremy smiled at each other, remembering their own coming of age experiences at Hungerford's.

Finally, the group milling around the representatives broke up. Christopher disengaged himself from his table companions and quickly approached Doctor Solomon Tylor.

Though not one of the men selected to attend the meeting in Frederick, Doctor Tylor was a local political activist who appealed to the middling sort. Unlike the aristocrats, whose primary concern was ensuring continued control by their own kind, Doctor Tylor was anti-elitist and a democrat, because only mass political involvement would expand leadership roles to include a larger number of the increasingly assertive middle class, of which Solomon Tylor was a member by default. Because of his democratical approach to politics, Doctor Tylor appealed to Christopher's sense of fairness, even if some of his opinions struck Christopher as a bit extreme.

"Solomon!"

Tylor looked at him, his self-absorbed look turning to one of recognition. "Ah, Christopher...how are you?"

"Oh fine, Solomon. Let's share a drink and you can tell us simple farmers what's going on." As he said this, other concerned neighbors crowded around the two of them, interested to hear what Doctor Tylor had to say.

Christopher caught Sally's attention and ordered a bowl of punch, which she quickly brought, thrusting it at Doctor Tylor with a bright smile before disappearing in the palpitating throng. "Thank you, Sally," Christopher said to Sally's disappearing back.

Then turning to Doctor Tylor, he quipped, "Now that we're plying you with drink, Solomon, let's hear your rendition of what was decided up there at Frederick."

"My pleasure, gents, and thankee for the drink." Doctor Tylor took a deep pull and passed the bowl to Christopher.

"Ah, but that's fine." Happily knowing that such a big bowl would come back to him again, Solomon quipped, "Mary serves a bowl large enough to have swimm'd half a dozen young geese." They all laughed as the bowl made its round.

Keeping an eye on the punch bowl, Solomon offered his interpretation of the Frederick meeting. "Well, I'll tell you as accurately as I can. The county Committee of Observation, carrying the resolves of the Continental Congress and the Provincial Convention, has called for the mutual defense and protection of all of the colonies 'in opposition,' and I quote, 'to the settled plan of the British administration to *enslave* America.'

Our representatives also agreed to the Committee of Observations's request that the lower county raise the sum of $1,333 as our share for the purchase of arms and ammunition."

There were a few breathless whistles at the amount of money mentioned, then silence as the men around Doctor Tylor thought about so much money to be spent for arms and ammunition. The last time such spending was necessary was during the Great War for the Empire.

Catching their breath, someone finally uttered, "Doctor Tylor, what does all this mean?"

"What does it mean?" asked Doctor Tylor rhetorically, building the tension as he accepted the bowl to begin another round. "Why, sir, it means that we Americans are finally setting out on the road to independence!"

Tylor noticed the blank looks. "Oh, you don't have to believe me, gentlemen. Go ahead and talk peace with Doctor Wootton or Captain Griffith—or, better yet, go pray for peace with the Reverend Crabbe. But—mark my words—we'll be at war with the British oppressors within the year!"

As he said this, Doctor Tylor sounded very righteous, and looked a little smug as he passed the bowl to Christopher.

The talk ebbed and flowed, as men went off to hear the opinions of others, while still others came over to hear Doctor Tylor's opinion. And the talk went on, as men discussed, argued, agreed, disagreed, all in an effort to fathom the current turn of events.

Despite Doctor Tylor and a few other hotheads, the thought of independence was not taken seriously by *reasonable* men—although more and more people accepted the fact that it was now a debatable matter. At the very least, the corrosive word *resistance* was now being commonly used when describing the colonies' relationship with the British government. This alone was enough for a good many people to worry that matters were starting to get out of hand.

Grown tired of all the disturbing talk, Christopher took a last sip of punch and with a wag of his head indicated to Jeremy that he was leaving. Jeremy, quickly downing the remainder of his cider, disentangled himself from his crowded bench and joined Christopher.

Together they left the tavern, stepping out into the bright freshness of this December afternoon. Picking up their muskets and rucksacks, which they had placed on the porch before entering the tavern, they set out for home.

3

SALT OF THE EARTH

Middle Potomac Hundred,
Lower Frederick County
Mid-December 1774

AT THIS CRUCIAL TIME American history, Christopher Sims and Jeremy Heynon were both twenty years of age, old enough to have assumed both the prejudices and the responsibilities caused by the social and political passions of preceding generations. After all, the colonials were discarded malcontents or the progeny of such people, the jetsam of the Old World washed up on the shores of the New World.

Christopher and Jeremy were different in appearance, but not remarkably so. Jeremy was five feet eight inches in height, which was about average among men at the time, and of medium build, while Christopher was an inch or two taller but a little on the thin side. Both had blond hair and blue eyes, although Christopher's hair was turning brown and would eventually be dark like his father's, while Jeremy would always be fair-haired. The farmer's life had seasoned their skin to the texture of soft leather and created a permanent squint in their eyes. But they were both healthy and stood straight, and the work in the fields had made them sinewy and tough.

In dress, the two men looked almost identical, as did most working farmers in these parts: leather breeches worn to a shine; a rough linen shirt, in this case buttoned to the neck; a long wool vest; stockings of gray wool; and sturdy shoes with inexpensive iron buckles. Each wore a hat with a floppy brim and low crown, which, unlike the popular tricorn hat of the day, offered good protection from the sun and rain. All of their articles of clothing were drab in color—country colors of browns and naturals; these were work clothes, worn everyday, and they showed it.

As they walked home from drill and stopped to relieve themselves of some of the Griffith's cider and to rest a few minutes, Christopher and Jeremy did not talk about great issues, but about things that affected their everyday lives, things such as the farming life and marriage and, of course, the local gossip.

"It's for sure that Sally is looking seriously for a suitable husband and it's just a question of time before she claims one."

"Sally *has* become a handsome woman," Christopher noted with a hint of surprise. "Have I been inattentive to her coming of age or is she using breast enhancers?"

"Oh my, no, Chris. The gropers—and I am not among them, mind you—are singing the praises of Sally's little apples, which they aver from the feel of 'em are crisp and ripe for the tastin'. Tempted?"

"Nay," laughed Christopher, "I'll not play the salivating Adam to Sally's Eve. Even I know to avoid forbidden fruits." This referred not to God's ire, but that of the tavernkeep's wife, Mary Hungerford. "Besides, though I like Sally and hope the best for her, I'll love only Hannah."

"Well, at your age, Chris Sims, you ought to be at least practicing the art of love in preparation for marriage—and you know you won't be able to do that with the parson's bound girl," Jeremy noted as he used a twig to scrape mud from the soles and welts of his shoes.

"That's enough, Jeremy," Christopher interrupted.

Jeremy had married his Constance back in June and here in December they were already parents of a four-month old boy. This wasn't unusual, a good many young women were with child on their wedding day—but, then, their men did not have to deal with the Reverend and Missus Crabbe in showing affection to the women they loved.

Jeremy grinned at Christopher, but then became serious.

"Ye know, Chris, it's obvious to everyone, including the Reverend Crabbe, that Hannah is a woman now. How much longer do you think he'll allow you to come mooning around his house claimin' you're there to do your neighborly chores?"

"Hannah said she'll be allowed suitors when she is eighteen. That's less than a year away."

"Oh sure, Chris, and the Reverend Crabbe will make sure the suitors are proper gentlemen. Why don't you just run off with the woman?"

"And as hunted criminals, I could become a highwayman and Hannah could be—what? No, we'll be patient, Jeremy, and if we have only a moment to steal here and there for the next couple of years, so be it."

"Then there's the Reverend Crabbe's unswerving loyalty to the Crown, which is beginning to irritate folks. Your 'devotion' to him might be misunderstood—if you know what I mean, Chris...."

"Aye, I do. 'Pears I'm not in an enviable position to woo Missus Hannah Williams, am I?"

The men soon resumed their journey, picking up their pace a bit, for they were now hungry and it was another two miles to home. The road cut through land known as Middle Potomac Hundred. A hundred—there were eleven of them in the lower county—was officially a tax district; but for its inhabitants, each hundred also represented their corporeal world.

This was tobacco country, poor looking with tired land cleaved by the Great Road, which was a "rolling road" built to move the large hogsheads packed with tobacco from farm to the port town of George Town. Dotting the numerous clearings were a variety of structures: dwellings, outbuildings, a mill house here and there, mean slave quarters, and awkward-looking tobacco sheds. Occasionally a fine manor house of fieldstone or English brick could be seen; but generally, the buildings in this region were rude, ramshackle affairs built of logs or, at best, roughly riven boards.

As Jeremy turned off to walk down the path to his family's little cabin, the two men parted with a wave, expecting to see each other again at the Jones' annual rant.

A little later, Christopher arrived at the family homestead, located just off the road in a clearing marked by the staggering course of a drunken-man fence. The dwelling itself was nondescript. It began as a one-room log cabin, built by Christopher's grandfather in 1739. A more elegant frame section with a second story was added years later. Each of the two sections had a door and a glazed window. Most recently, Christopher and his older brother, George, put up the shed-roofed porch which provided cover over both doors. The improvised construction and unpainted, weathered wood siding gave the house a homely, even dilapidated appearance, when actually it was a substantial dwelling.

Entering into the hall, a room which served the Sims family as a common room, kitchen, and bedroom, Christopher saw his sister-in-law at the hearth preparing the afternoon dinner.

"Hullo, Susan." He walked over to the fireplace and rested his musket in the corner and hung his bag on a nearby peg.

Susan looked up and smiled. "Hello, Chris. Will ye hand me those beans?"

She then barraged him with questions. How went drill? What was discussed concerning the growing troubles? Was the Convention doing the right thing? They had discussed all the rumors that morning at breakfast and now she wanted to know the facts. Susan had worried about this all day.

Christopher explained as best he understood.

His rather casual explanation did not satisfy her. *Resisting the Crown government. Calling out the militia for twice a week drill...talk of independence...burning ships...threatening government officials...*This, she thought, was not right.

"Men playing at boys' games," his sister-in-law said disgustedly. She took the pot of beans Christopher handed her and gave him a glare—not directed at him, but at men in general, always strutting around like bantam roosters. She had little tolerance for all their weaknesses.

"Oh, never mind, Chris," Susan said, dismissing the possibility that men could ever be reasonable. Her mind now on dinner, she called to Christopher's sister, Mary, to come help with preparing the meal. At this command, a swirl of petticoats and skirts descended the ladder from the loft.

"Whew, I hetcheled near forty pounds of flax," Mary proudly informed her sister-in-law. "Can ye imagine!" Like most farm families, the Simses depended upon their sheep for warm woolens and their small field of flax, with its lovely, drooping blue flowers, for linen.

"Forty pounds! My, that's more than I ever did at one sitting," Susan exclaimed in true admiration at Mary's production for the day. "Now, would you fix the bake-kettle and put the bread on. Chris, I sent your brother out to fetch some water a long time ago; would you please see what's become of him."

As the two women busied themselves about the hearth and table, Christopher slipped out of the house and went in search of his younger brother.

"Hullo, Runt. Whatcha doin'?" Christopher found his younger brother, John Paul, tossing pebbles in the brook which ran under the springhouse, the bucket sitting empty and forgotten off to the side.

"Nothin'," John Paul mumbled sullenly.

"What's the trouble, John Paul?" Christopher knew a mood when he saw it.

His brother, just waiting for the right moment, blurted out, "All I do is women's work—hetcheling or luggin' water and such. 'Tain't fair."

Christopher understood. John Paul was upset that he was not allowed to go to militia drill. So of course he was left with the womenfolk doing chores around the house which offended his burgeoning sense of manliness. At twelve years old, John Paul was at an age when females had little to offer: he was too old to delight in being coddled by them and too young to be interested in fondling them. An awkward age, Christopher thought with a smile.

"Look here, John Paul, you'll be going with us to attend Militia Day. That's not too far off. In the meantime, you're not left here to do women's work, but to be here to protect 'em. Dontcha know that?"

"But I don't got a gun, Chris."

"I'm not thinking ye have to defend the home from savages, John Paul—but y'know, from wild beasts, or snakes, or...well, wasps. That sort of defending," Christopher replied lamely.

"Oh, sure, I see," said John Paul, not seeing it at all. But he had got his point across and was tired of pouting. Tossing the rest of the pebbles in the water, he said, "I have to get the water to Susan now." They picked up the bucket, filled it with water from the brook and, both holding the handle, started back to the house.

When Christopher and John Paul entered the house they found that George was there. Christopher joined him and they became deeply immersed in conversation at the table while the women were completing preparations for the meal.

With the addition of Christopher and John Paul, the small hall became crowded. As head of the family following the death of their father, Christopher's older brother, George, sat in his ladderback chair, the only chair in the room, at the head of the trestle table. More and more, thought Christopher, George is becoming to act—and look, for that matter—more like their father every day, as if the burdens of running the farm and caring for the family required a certain visage.

Christopher and the other family members seated themselves on two benches. The table was placed near the fireplace both for illumination and for warmth.

Beside the table and a standing bed, there was not much in the way of additional furniture in this room: a sideboard, a cupboard, two small tables, and several trunks used for storage. There was a looking glass and a rack for eating utensils on the wall and a gingham curtain was tacked over the window. Smoked hams, peppers, and ears of corn hung from the rafters. Along the back wall were sacks of cornmeal and flour, and pots of herbs and spices. Small, dim, and chilly as it was, this was a cheery, lived-in room, made comfortable for socializing, eating, and sleeping.

All of the food having been placed on the table, the women and John Paul took their seats. George offered a quick but reverential thanks to the Lord for their bounty, and the group set to their meal.

Following dinner, the women cleared the table and scraped leftovers into the slop pail, which John Paul took out to dump into the garbage pit out back. While this was taking place, George, rum bottle in hand, and Christopher went into the parlor. This room was used for more formal entertaining, or for private conversations, and had several comfortable chairs and a table in finished oak, a rag rug, and a fireplace with a carved mantle; it also served as the master bedroom and had a canopied great bed with an elegant set of hangings in a floral motif. A narrow staircase led up to the second floor, which was a bedroom for Mary and overnight guests.

With a fire now burning and a candle on the table, the men made themselves comfortable. They lit their long-stemmed clay pipes and poured themselves each a large rum.

They discussed chores and such—the daily life of a farmer—and because George had been excused from drill that day, Christopher summarized for him what was discussed at Hungerford's.

George Sims was not an argumentative man and he simply could not fathom the anger between Maryland's proprietary and popular parties.

"The Atlantic Ocean seems to cleave Englishmen into two decidedly different geographical camps," he said with sadness. "And for no reason I can see."

On the other hand, Christopher saw more than a geographical separation: "George, the difference is that we are *Americans* and *not* Englishmen."

They discussed politics for a while longer, but Christopher, realizing that George did not accept nor understand the growing chasm between Englishmen and those who would rather call themselves Americans, changed the subject to a discussion of the chores that needed to be done tomorrow.

Returning to the hall, the two men found the rest of the family involved in the usual evening activities. Mary was carding wool, while Susan was busy spinning the rolls into yarn on the great-wheel, doing her graceful dance to make the wheel sing and the spindle flash. John Paul was busy worrying the mice who, by the telltale holes and meal scattered on the floor, had been burrowing in the sacks. Christopher picked up his musket and began cleaning it, while George wrote a letter to his factor concerning this year's tobacco crop.

And so it went until it was time for bed. While the women made a final trip to the necessary house out back, the men took a piss off the side of the porch, their streams steaming in the cold evening air. After these ablutions, all of them were in bed by half past nine o'clock.

Here among the isolated fields and woods of western Maryland, in the simple life of farmers and hunters, a world away from kings and governors, it was hard to understand the coming revolution....

...And harder still to understand that they had started this revolution a long time ago.

4

THAT ORNERY PLANT

Leeke Forest,
Middle Potomac Hundred
Mid-December 1774

THE SIMSES WERE TENANT FARMERS, as was their father, and his father before him. This didn't sound like much of a success story, but if old Samuel Sims could see from beyond the grave, the results of his efforts would have pleased him no end.

Christopher's grandfather came to the New World as a miserable bondsman. Exactly what brought him here in such a condition was suppressed in the dark recesses of family history. Christopher remembered his mother once commenting to his father (with a hint of malice) that apparently the Sims' family tree had a number of wayward branches that had needed pruning.

Once in America, however, Samuel overcame this miserable start to his adult life, made a modest but honest living as a roper, married, raised a family, and took advantage of the proprietary government's offer of rewards for those who would work the land grants west of Prince George's County, in Maryland. He rented a few acres of workable land from an absentee landlord on what was known as Leeke Forest and set to work to make something of nothing.

Although Samuel Sims never owned any land, he prospered as a farmer and became a respected member of the primitive community of lower Frederick County. His four daughters married well and his only son, William, and then William's first son, George, continued to work the Leeke Forest land and they, too, prospered.

Christopher was William's second son. As a second son his prospects were less certain. William, before his death, and George purchased some land from Charles Jones, who was selling parcels of his wife's vast holdings along Rock Creek, called Clean Drinking Water. This purchase was made with the idea that Christopher and later John Paul would have land of their own to work. It was admittedly tired land but, given time, would eventually provide for the Sims family and their posterity. Trouble was the land needed to lay fallow another ten years.

Christopher's mother, Ruth, had another idea. Her second son was her favorite, mainly because he reminded her so much of her adventurous sister, Jane, who had escaped the backcountry and gone to Baltimore Town, something Ruth herself would have done had she her sister's courage.

Ruth knew in her bones that Christopher was not meant for the life of a tobacco farmer. So she argued until the day she died that Christopher should be sent to the Nottingham Academy, perched prettily above the Susquehanna River over in Cecil County, to prepare him for studying the law in Baltimore or Annapolis.

The problem was the Sims family did not have the ready money necessary to do this. After the deaths of William and Ruth, George, as head of the family, worried this problem to death. He finally had to accept the fact that he did not have the money to fulfill his mother's dream for Christopher and likely never would.

But while the Nottingham Academy appeared to be out of the question, another possibility perhaps existed. Their Aunt Jane had once written to her sister Ruth that Christopher could come and live with her in Baltimore and she was certain she could help him find a trade to his liking there.

As for Christopher himself, he was, indeed, his mother's son. He had shown absolutely no proclivity for the farmer's life, which, in his mind, characterized the dumbing effect of routine, the day in, day out sleepiness of certain boredom.

At one point in his life, he thought he wanted to be a surveyor of the frontier, which in his mind was not only an honorable profession, but one which promised the adventure of an uncertain future. He had never said this to his mother, because he knew it would crush her, but going to an academy and then studying the law never appealed to him. He associated the law with the tedious accusations and counter-accusations he had witnessed during the circuit court sessions held at Hungerford's.

The idea of obtaining a trade and living in Baltimore appealed to Christopher. He talked about this with Hannah in those stolen moments he cherished. Hannah had spent her first eleven years in Annapolis before being bound out and had fond memories of town life. So it seemed it could be a dream come true for both of them. But that was years away and in the meantime Christopher was a sot-weed farmer and Hannah a bound servant living in the Maryland backcountry.

The cash crop in the lower county was tobacco. In fact, tobacco was legal tender in Maryland—worth a penny a pound—even while the province's paper currency was not. Almost all the farmers in the lower county grew the weed, from the lowest tenant farmer to the great planter.

In these parts people would be hard-pressed to imagine life without that ornery plant. Just yesterday, Christopher was prizing cured leaves into a hogshead in the tobacco shed, with its sickly-sweetness painted in the air and a cold wind rummaging through the chinks in the logs; while Susan was ankle deep in dung, strewing seeds in the quarter-acre plant bed.

The weary cycle had begun all over again. The toil over the sot-weed never ended. Fifteen months from seedbed to hogshead … and the continuing anxiety over last year's crop had already overlapped with the growing anxiety over this year's crop. They all referred to it as the tyranny of the weed.

The Sims farm had about four acres planted in tobacco, good Orinoco, which provided the family an income of forty-five to fifty pounds per annum, depending on the London market. This, and the money earned by the women who sold their finer linen cloth to a merchant in George Town, provided them with sufficient cash to purchase the few manufactured goods they needed, and such other things as spices, liquors, some schooling for the children, and certain items of clothing for special occasions. Then there were the subsistence crops and some livestock.

Hard as it was, the simple life of farming and nature's bounty from forest and stream provided the Sims family with a good life over the years. More importantly, their circumstances gave them independence and freedom.

This feeling of freedom and independence was felt by most of the people in this part of Maryland. Being a tenant farmer didn't diminish the feeling. Being a bonded servant didn't diminish the feeling. It was this sense of freedom and independence amongst the population in general which made them argumentative.

The freedom and independence these so-called Americans had achieved provided them with the opportunity needed to improve their lot in life, to create surpluses which could be used to build a modest security unknown to the average Englishman across the sea, and to ensure that their children would have a better life. Posterity—the idea of providing for future generations—was a consuming moral imperative for these people. Not unreasonably, the colonials concluded that the more independent and free they were, the greater the opportunities for bettering oneself. As one wag put it, "America was the best poor man's country in the world."

"But right now," many Americans openly complained, "we stand to lose everything we have unless we resist the Crown's plan to draw us all into bondage."

5

CELEBRATING THE SEASON
WITH PIETY AND LITTLE LIBERTIES

Middle Potomac Hundred
Christmas, 1774

"JOYFUL CHRISTMAS!" Gunfire broke the early morning quiet as young and old celebrated the birth of Christ by firing fowler and rifle.

"Joyful Christmas!" The guns thundered again.

"Joyful Christmas!" Another volley.

"Now, that's enough, John Paul. The next shot ought to be intended to put food on the table—hear?"

"Yes, sir."

For Anglicans, and especially Anglicans in the southern provinces, December 25 began a festive season which lasted until Twelfth Day on January 6. Susan Sims loved the midwinter holidays because they clothed the bleakest time of the year in wreaths and sprays of greenery, a surfeit of candlelight, special foods, and with what she referred to as "fine entertainments" shared with neighbors. The Sims house was decorated as early as the fifteenth, with sprigs of evergreen and holly filling vases and tucked in the muntins of the windowpanes, and, of course, a huge cluster of mistletoe on the trestle table in the hall.

Christmas Day itself may or may not be a day of celebration, depending upon what day in the week it fell. There were six days of toil and only the seventh day–Sunday–was a day of rest. So it was this Christmas season.

The Sunday following Christmas, the Sims family went to church, traveling the six miles to Rock Creek Chapel, which was nothing more than a small wooden structure with a number of rough benches and a high table which served as a pulpit. The interior had been prettily decorated with holly and strung ivy, and pungent herbs had been scattered about.

The attendance was unusually small. Many of the congregation disagreed with the Reverend Crabbe's Crown sentiments and showed it by not attending his services. But this did not appear to discourage him as he preached lively from Isaiah 9:6 and even led those attending in a metrical hymn which he had composed himself.

"Assist me, Muse divine! To sing the Morn
    On which the Savior of Mankind was born
    But oh! What numbers to the Theme can Rise?
    Unless Kind Angels aid me from the skies?"

Even those who did not like the Reverend's politics liked his poetry.

It didn't matter to Christopher how many people attended the service because he knew Hannah would be there. He saw her as soon as he entered the church, sitting on one of the front benches with Missus Crabbe and the two children. As Hannah greeted the new arrivals, she saw Christopher and her smile took on a little more radiance...but it was in her eyes, briefly sparkling with a passion no one knew she had, which acknowledged her special fondness for him. In the company of others, that was the most emotion she allowed herself to show.

Following the service, the Sims family was invited to dinner at the home of Thomas Mills, whose family had donated the two acres of land above Rock Creek upon which now stood Rock Creek Chapel and its little rectory. The Reverend Crabbe and his family were also invited and this allowed Christopher to offer his and John Paul's services in providing transport for the Crabbe children on the Sims family's two ancient but dependable horses.

"Joyful Christmas, Christopher Sims."

"And joyful Christmas to you, Missus Williams."

He helped her mount the horse, tingling at the light touch of her hand on his shoulder as she steadied herself on the mounting block. She would ride the one horse with the youngest child, with Christopher leading, while John Paul would ride the other with the oldest, showing off his equine skills, of course, because he was now a young man.

Seeing Hannah this way, astride the horse like a man, the canted skirts, the display of stockings, reminded him of their day trip–that incredible day trip two years ago this coming June–to Little Falls, an outing which had changed his life forever.

It was the day he blurted out that he was in love with the bound girl Hannah Williams....

...She and Jeremy's Constance pulled the hems of their skirts between their legs and stuffed them in their waistbands, creating a sort of pantaloon which allowed them to sit comfortably astride a horse. Once the girls were mounted, each in tandem with one of the Crabbe children, the party set off on a picnic at the Little Falls on the Potomac River, whose serrated course formed the western boundary of Frederick County, all the way from its navigable head at George Town to its historic beginning at Fairfax Stone deep in the Alleghenies.

They took an old Seneca Indian trace deep into the woods which wound its way around rock outcroppings, huge old trees, and small ravines, eventually coming out on a broad flat rock just before the terrain began a dramatic descent to the very edge of the river.

This rock was called "Indian Rock" because of a curious device chiseled on its surface: concentric diamonds surrounding a fish-like symbol, which according to tradition marked an ancient Indian fishing area; indeed, the slow moving eddies below the rock abounded in fish of all kinds–giant sturgeon, shad, rockfish, shellfish, and the ugly but tasty catfish.

Here the river was known as the "Wild Goose Stream," as it shot southward, frothing and tumbling, forcefully carving out its course in a series of plunges which had started at the Great Falls cataract and would continue until it reached the calming influence of the coastal plain.

From Indian Rock, one could view this scenic river, until here hidden by thick woods, as it careened between its canyon walls. Adding further to its enchantment, the rock was shaded from the sun by several old sycamores, whose high open branches and translucent leaves cast a memorable pale golden light over its surface.

In the ravines and among the rocky crevices of the palisades grew colorful spring flowers: Solomon's seal with its ruby red fruit, golden moss and Dutchman's breeches whose little white "pantaloons" would forever remind Christopher of Hannah's rare display of ankles and stockinged legs, which, in turn, would forever remind him of the first time he had ever told a woman that he loved her and then held his breath waiting for her reply.

She looked at him curiously, as if she couldn't fathom any man having such a passion for her—even though she prayed to Saint Jude that Christopher Sims would. She had always been a tall, gangly girl whom boys stayed away from because she was often taller than them. At fifteen, she was still too tall, but now she was a girl-woman and more slender than gangly.

"No one has ever said they love me, Chris...." It was the first time she referred to him using the diminutive of his name.

"Well, I do," he said emphatically, "and...well ... there it is, Hannah," he added defiantly.

"Does that mean you want to kiss me, Chris," she asked quizzically, "like Constance and Jeremy kiss? I think I would like that."

Christopher had kissed women before, even passionately, but that was the most wondrous kiss he could ever imagine....

...An older Hannah knew what Christopher was thinking and enjoyed being desired.

"Mister Sims, pray tell me why you are looking at me in such a bold way."

Christopher grinned. "I'm imagining the kiss you'll permit me in celebration of the New Year."

"Aye, I'll permit you that…at least," she added provocatively. "As soon as little Peter falls asleep."

"Mess it Forth"

The horses clopped along the narrow path leading from the chapel to the Mills house, set prettily on a high hill above Rock Creek. It had not snowed yet, which disappointed the children, and the winter, thus far, was mild; but this Sunday turned out to be a cold wintry day, blustery and dark, and all of them welcomed the sight of the Mills house where there would be a warm fire and good food.

The Mills house was one of those southern Maryland manor houses whose construction could not be called grand like the one or two Georgian-style houses built for the county's truly rich families. For the backcountry, though, it was still a marvel of architecture. Like many comfortable dwellings hereabouts, it was originally built of logs and nogged with brick. The first floor was divided into two large rooms and a second floor contained a number of small bedrooms. However, it also had a broad central hall with doors front and rear which caught the slightest of breezes during the hot, muggy summer months.

For today's celebration, a trestle table and benches were set up in the hall for the children. The adults would eat in the dining room which had a large dining table and sideboard brought from England. The table was set, with a little provincial imagination, according to the "grand table" illustrated in Missus Mills' well-worn copy of *English Housewifery* and the sideboard was full of decanters of wine, brandy, rum and gin.

Because the day was cold with a windy wetness to it, the fireplace was blazing with eight-foot logs, enveloping the room in warmth. Even the hall was comfortable. The roaring fire, candles and decorations made the house lively as new arrivals greeted those already there, all now a part of the hustle and bustle of this special holiday gathering.

The Mills women were running back and forth between the dining room and the kitchen, which was an out-building, seeing to the preparation of the food.

A line had formed in front of a kettle set upon a trivet in the fireplace from which a slave was ladling hot wassail into the flared glasses thrust at her. Christopher had his glass filled after standing in line with Lloyd Beall and Bill Deakins, both prosperous county farmers and George Town merchants, who talked about the increasing difficulties with England and how this might affect trade. In fact, almost everyone was talking about The Troubles.

It was talked about over dinner, a magnificent feast featuring many decorative foods, and meats boiled to a healthy ghostly white, though a little cool to the palate after their journey from the outside kitchen to the dining room.

And it was talked about even over dessert, including the serving of the plum pudding–the symbolic Christmas favorite throughout English-speaking Christendom. Christopher had never liked plum pudding and found the reason after hearing Doctor Wootton's description of it: "...a detestable compound of moldy brown bread, suet, withered plums, salt and pepper, all made into a paste, liquefied with mutton broth and boiled in a pail of water." Lit with alcohol before being served, the blue flame represented the fires of hell, which, as the flame dies down proves that goodness triumphs over evil. "Unfortunately," continued Doctor Wootton, "the fires of hell consumed some delectable brandy before goodness triumphed."

And, of course, the political discussions continued over rum, brandy and the Mills' frothy syllabubs.

Almost all of the discussions concerned the question of non-importation and non-exportation. And everyone was agreed that non-exportation of tobacco would go into effect only if Virginia and North Carolina also agreed. One could be principled and still be a concerned businessman.

Most of the guests considered themselves good subjects even though they took issue with any number of the Crown's policies towards its children. Being of a middling temperament, most people in the lower county had not yet reached the stage of political animosity where they divided themselves into patriots and loyalists. There were a few exceptions though. Most of the local extremists were patriots, like Doctors Wootton and Tylor and the Griffith brothers, and others. But a very few of them were devout loyalists, and the Reverend Crabbe was one of them.

The economic arguments did not interest the Reverend Crabbe. What disturbed him was the growing idea that people are equal.

"'Tis ill-founded and false, sir, both in its premises and its conclusions. Government requires some degree of inferiority and superiority. Government requires governing people, and governing people requires that people accept this as every man's duty. This is enjoined by the positive commands of God."

No one here was interested in arguing with Reverend Crabbe over this ill-defined concept of equality. For them, the issue was *enslavement* and the Crown's use of economic sanctions which they believed were calculated to deprive them of their hard-earned liberties.

Reverend Crabbe did not contribute to this conversation. He remained quiet, his lips pursed and his face growing more red at each slight to Crown authority. And it was not until the issue of armed resistance was raised that he was forced to cry out in outrage.

Livid, he spoke with a passion he usually saved for the worst of sins. "The call for collecting arms and ammunition bespeaks treason, sir! I will instruct the people to continue their allegiance to the British government and to God Almighty! These blasphemies must end."

"Reverend," spoke up Bill Deakins, "All this is merely posturing, I assure you. But the Crown must take our sometimes childish cries for fair and equitable treatment seriously. If this is granted us by the government, all will be put right." Others, but not all, tended to agree.

****

What finally put an end to all the political wrangling was the singing of the Christmas carols, a tradition at the Mills Christmas party, which all present sang with gusto and love for fully an hour.

All of them, including the slaves, loved singing the hymns of Isaac Watts, their favorite being "Joy to the World." The Reverend Crabbe had a lovely voice, a full and rich tenor, and sang several carols to the delight of all. Missus Crabbe had once had a beautiful voice, which, in tandem with her husband, would spellbind all listeners; but unfortunately, she now suffered from the cough.

During all this time Hannah was with the children in the hall. Now she had joined the adults in the dining room, accompanying the children there to join in the caroling.

Christopher discreetly worked his way over to Hannah, who quickly squeezed his fingers and just as quickly let go. Together, they joined in the singing of "Here We Come A-Wassailing," mouthing "Love and joy come to *us*" as the rest sang the stanza "Love and joy come to you," and then heartily concluded the carol with

> *"And God bless you, and send you*
> *A Happy New Year*
> *And God send you a Happy New Year."*

Because this was to be the year that Hannah and Christopher could declare their love.

As the celebration went on and on toward the early morning hours, many of the guests departed for home; but not a few, finding themselves either too drunk or too tired for a long trip home, sought out a bed in one of the Mills' little bedrooms. The Sims family decided to stay the night and Christopher ended up sharing a bed with John Paul and two local farmers who had already fallen into a stuporous sleep.

He and John Paul quickly crawled into bed and under the covers to escape the cold, drafty room. As he settled in bed, the dried cornhusk mattress crackling, Christopher was consumed with the "torments of carnal lust," of which the Reverend Crabbe regularly warned all would-be fornicators at Sunday service. Knowing once again on this festive day how pleasurable it was to feel a woman, Christopher was tormented for sure—in a fashion not intended by the good Reverend.

6

CHRISTOPHER AND HANNAH'S DILEMMA

Middle Potomac Hundred
Mid January 1775

THE COMING OF THE NEW YEAR held great promise for Christopher and Hannah. In September, Hannah would turn eighteen, finally reaching the age when the Reverend and Missus Crabbe would allow her to entertain suitors. She would still have another two years to serve out her bond, but youth is optimistic and Hannah had learned to be patient. As it would turn out, however, the year 1775, a year of anticipation and hope, did not start out as auspiciously as either Hannah or Christopher had imagined.

Christopher looked forward to the traditional celebration of Twelfth Day at the home of Charles and Liza Jones, who owned the patent "Clean Drinking Manor," a mill, and a toll bridge across Rock Creek, all of which represented a sizable chunk of Middle Potomac Hundred.

Liza Jones was an affable and good-hearted woman, who simply liked people. Thanks to her dowery and a compliant husband, the Joneses saw to the welfare of their neighbors and opened their house to them. Unlike the fancy "assemblies" held by the neighborhood's upper class, the Joneses were plain folks who enjoyed barnyard parties, the kind of gatherings fondly referred to as "rants."

The Jones rant was one of those rare opportunities for Christopher and Hannah to truly enjoy each other's company and actually share a dance or two. As the older people danced to sedate minuets inside, the younger people gathered outside, drinking cider and beer, and dancing to country music and Negro jigs.

The afternoon turned to dusk, the bonfire burned brighter, the music became more compelling. One of their favorites was "Soldier's Joy," played by a Negro fiddler and banjo player, who more or less knew the tune. This would be a signal for serious dancing, as well as an even more serious mating ritual. With sweat-glistened faces and heaving breasts, young women, not unconsciously, would arouse young men, who would be all too eager to respond.

When blood warms, matches are made,
Thus on goes love's jolly trade,
Oh! Such were the joys of our dancing days.
Oh! Such were the joys of our dancing days.

The Jones party would also be an opportunity for stolen intimacies, provided by the sunken garden with its maze of huge boxwoods and a high lilac hedge. The garden's intricate design made for wonderful hideouts for children playing *I Spy,* as well as for young couples seeking a secluded niche.

It was here at the Joneses' Twelfth Night celebration last year that Christopher and Hannah tentatively, then passionately explored their feelings for each other.

But this year would be different, and the long awaited reprise of those past joys was not to be. The Crabbes did not come to this year's celebration as a protest against Charles Jones' patriot views–views which the Reverend Crabbe considered seditious and was speaking out against in an increasingly strident voice.

The growing crisis with Great Britain notwithstanding, both Christopher and Hannah had ordinary lives to live–difficult under any circumstance, but made even more difficult because simple civility was becoming colored by one's political agenda.

Christopher and Hannah were in love and intended to marry, but their relationship was yet to be tested.

****

Hannah Williams was something of an enigma to most local people. She had always been quiet and to those who did not know her well she might have appeared meek. However, she proved to be full of surprises for those who came to know her as more than the Crabbes' bound girl.

Not too long after her arrival, she approached one of the Carroll daughters, of a prominent Catholic family, and boldly announced that she was Catholic when it was not acceptable to be Catholic. She told the woman that she desperately needed to know the proper words for a "Prayer to the Guardian Angel."

"Dear girl, there are no *proper* words for such a prayer! It comes from the heart. And to whom do you wish to pray?"

"To Saint Jude, ma'am."

"The Saint of Lost Causes? Are you lost, child?"

"I am until I can talk to him…"

To a special few, Hannah was variously endearing, maddening, headstrong, self-deprecating, and sweet. All of which defined Hannah as a special girl, and later as a special woman.

Hannah Williams was originally from Annapolis, from a poor Catholic family whose mother had died in childbirth and whose father was a laborer and a drunkard. When Hannah was eleven, the father was murdered by an unsavory and vicious leader of a dock gang during a dispute over a debt. Without parents, she and her brothers and sisters were (fortunately) ordered by the court to be sold to the churchwardens for use of the parish until they reached the age of majority. As it turned out, the Prelate assigned Hannah to a young rector and his fragile wife who were off to serve God and King on the Maryland frontier. Of her siblings, Hannah could only recollect that her older sister, Anne, whom she adored, was sent to Charleston, in the province of South Carolina.

Now approaching eighteen, Hannah was an attractive young woman despite the awkwardness of being tall (she had to force herself to walk with a ramrod straight back and to slow her pace). She had soft brown hair, a pleasant face, beautiful brown eyes under perfectly arched eyebrows—eyes which were always large and round as if she was constantly amazed by the world around her. Her one flaw was a tight smile which she hoped hid a gap between her two front teeth. She wore hand-me-down clothes but these were often donated by well-to-do parishioners and could be quite fashionable.

Hannah also had a good mind. She had learned to read and write, though still haltingly. She also had a knack for reducing things to their essentials and she could reason better than most people.

All in all, a desirable woman.

And a woman who was bent on marrying Christopher Sims. She decided this at the age of fourteen as she watched Christopher one day doing his chores for the Reverend Crabbe.

He was seventeen then and taller than she.

"Christopher," she asked, "Do you think I'm too..." she hesitated, looking for the right word, "...too awkward to be attractive?"

She remembered how Christopher stopped stacking the wood and looked at her—like he hadn't really seen her before. After a bit, he said, "I think if you stood proud and stopped stoopin' like an old woman, Hannah, and wore that look you're now wearing, you'd be about the most beautiful girl in the entire province."

"Then you'd consider dancing with me at the Cooke's frolic?"

"*No*, I would not, Hannah Williams—you're not too tall to be pretty, but you're too young to be dancin' with grown men."

She considered this. "Well, *Mister* Sims, have it your way—*but* ...someday you're going to dance with me...and after that, you'll never need to dance with another woman." And with her tight smile and a swish of her skirts, she walked off.

It never occurred to Christopher on that day that he would ever fall in love with Hannah Williams, but, in fact, he *had not* really seen her before. From then on, though, whenever she looked at him it was as if she were asking, "Well, Christopher, am I old enough to dance with yet?"

It wasn't until Hannah was almost sixteen that Christopher actually danced with her, but the seed had been planted on that day when she practically dared him to think about it.

It was at one of the barnyard dances when young men and women lined up facing each other, jockeying for position to be paired with a preferred partner for a favorite line dance, that Christopher found himself opposite Hannah.

She had learned the basic steps and protocol from girlfriends. Though not yet adept–and she was sure she never would be–she was fairly confident that she would not embarrass Christopher Sims or herself.

Having planned this out carefully with Constance, Hannah wore one of the more fashionable dresses handed down to her, with a bodice which was modest but also, Constance had assured her, just a tad revealing.

There wasn't much Christopher could do as he faced Hannah, who had a pleading look on her pretty face, but smile and gracefully accept her as his partner.

"Missus Williams, may I have the pleasure…"

"You may, Mister Sims."

And they danced all night. They danced jigs and country dances and the "Sir Roger de Coverley" to scratchy negro music that seemed to ring clear and crisp in the cold night air, the notes brilliant and popping like embers from the bonfire. Their favorite was "Rural Felicity," a violently active tune, simply because of the physical excitement it caused.

Christopher and Hannah worked their way down the longway set, in a swaying rhythm of hooked elbows as they reeled down the line, from dancer to dancer, ever faster, the music growing more forceful. He felt a pang of jealousy as he watched Hannah hook arms with other men, wisps of her soft brown hair now streaming out of her mob cap.

Christopher was amazed at Hannah's transformation, from a quiet, almost meek young woman to a woman with a knowing laugh as she looked at Christopher's face, which had taken on an intense look, as if this had become more than just a dance.

Hannah's own face was shining with sweat, her nostrils flaring—moreover, her chest was heaving prettily, her palms in Christopher's hands were as warm and moist as a dog's tongue, and her unadorned scent was appealingly provocative.

Feeling the small of her back and the swell of her buttocks during the ladies' chain, Christopher finally abandoned himself to the inevitable....

He wasn't sure exactly when he decided that he loved Hannah Williams, but once he saw her as a woman and not as a young girl, he concluded that he was the luckiest man in the world.

And later, on Indian Rock above the Potomac, when she told him that she would like to kiss him the way Constance and Jeremy kissed each other, Christopher discovered that love for a woman was passion sweetened with fondness....

He would always remember that first kiss, because as first kisses went, it was as good as a perfect dream: memorable, the kind of kiss which a man remembered all his life; a kiss, an embrace...the always memorable experience for any man of a woman's assertive breasts and soft stomach pressed against him. He was enfolded in her rammish smell—a heady mixture of female muskiness and sour sweat, with a hint of evergreen in her hair. She tasted of pears and her lips—those tight lips—were as soft as custard.

It did not take him long to give up his boyish dreams of becoming a frontier surveyor and put all his thought into what he needed to do to keep this woman's love.

Rock Creek Chapel
Late February 1775

As usual, Christopher was doing his neighborly chores for the Crabbes. It also continued to be his thinly disguised excuse for visiting with Hannah. This time of year, it was chopping and stacking firewood, a job he looked forward to because the wood was stacked in the lean-to attached to the back of the house, near the springhouse and garbage pit, all of which found Hannah in close proximity as she did her own daily chores.

Later in the day, Hannah brought him a hot toddy and a slice of warm apple pie, because the day was cold with a wind-driven rain which struck their faces like little spears. Particularly on a cruel day like today, the Reverend and Missus Crabbe were always kind to parishioners who contributed their labor to the upkeep of their little church.

They huddled in the woodshed, the drink and the pie and their breaths together making thick white clouds of vapor which made the space look as cold as it felt in their threadbare woolens.

This pause from their work allowed Christopher and Hannah to continue their discussion started earlier.

"—people still like and respect Reverend Crabbe, Hannah, but he has clearly sided with the Crown against his neighbors and that is causing resentment."

"Chris, ye must not blame Reverend Crabbe for this. 'Tis not his fault. He is a hard man, but principled. We are, after all, Englishmen and women and subjects of our monarch. That's all he's sayin', Chris."

Hannah and Christopher never discussed politics. The only statement Hannah had ever made in the least suggestive of a position regarding the growing political crisis was that she was *not* free and sympathized with those who wanted to remain free—an allusion to the colonial charges that the mother country intended to enslave them.

"That is not all he is saying, Hannah. The Reverend Crabbe opposes any idea that people have a right to a freer life. *That* means, young lady, that you were born to be a bound woman and I was born to be a sot-weed farmer and that, in his mind, is the way it should be. We have no freedom to *choose*, for chrissake."

"Chris, please don't swear—"

Chastised, Christopher's rising tone softened. "The Reverend Crabbe stands for the powerful, in this case people who have dominion over other people and have been corrupted by it. That is the Crown government, Hannah."

"Reverend Crabbe has been a good master, Chris."

"You're still a slave, Hannah, just like the black laborers you see in the fields." Christopher said this almost casually, without the anger he felt. If slavery meant being obliged to act, or *not* to act because of the arbitrary will of another, then he too was a slave because he could not marry the woman he loved.

"No one has the right to have power over another person without their consent. We talk about what we're going to do when you gain your freedom in two years. Yet, the people who rule us do not have to cede us real control over our own lives even then."

The inactivity made them cold and they both began to shiver at the same time. Laughing, they huddled against each other, with Christopher wrapping his arms around Hannah's shoulders, while she bent her arms and hunched herself against his chest. He buried his face in Hannah's warm, slick hair, smelling its natural oils and the smoke from numerous fires. The cold quickly went away.

After a bit, without letting go of him, she leaned back to look at his face. "So, what do you propose, Chris? That we run away and disappear into the depths of the dark forests, to live like savages and forsake our dreams? That is not the life I choose."

This caught him short. "Oh, Hannah, of course I'm not suggesting that. For God's—" He caught himself just in time, and controlled now, said carefully, "But you and I should have the freedom to do as we please, Hannah, and not have our lives depend upon any man's whimsy, be he king...or preacher."

7

THE REVEREND CRABBE'S DILEMMA

Rock Creek Chapel,
Lower Frederick County
Late February 1775

BECAUSE THE FAR REACHES of many backcountry parishes often went without a preacher, the Church of England selected worthy young provincials to be educated in London to the calling, then assigned them as assistant rectors to the more inaccessible—meaning undesirable—regions in the North American provinces. This is how the Reverend Crabbe came to be the preacher for a little, out of the way chapel-of-ease.

Roger Crabbe was assigned as rector of Rock Creek Chapel in 1768. As primitive as this was, he welcomed the assignment. His young wife Anne was frail and suffering from consumption and her physician had strongly recommended country air. It was this which encouraged Roger Crabbe to request assignment to western Maryland where the air, dancing across fresh-water creeks and blowing through fragrant forests, was infinitely kinder to the lungs than the noxious air along the coastline.

The Crabbes had two children at the time. Molly was three and Peter was two. Anne was pregnant with a third child and this put her very life at risk. Roger Crabbe was desperate to find a soothing climate for Anne and trusted to God and the Anglican Church that he had found it in the far reaches of Maryland.

As healthful as the air of western Maryland might be, the Prelate knew the hardships awaiting the Reverend Crabbe and his sickly wife. He assigned to them a young bound girl whom he had to have beaten because she insisted she was Catholic. Despite her display of intemperate behavior, the Prelate liked the girl and believed that she would be a good servant for Missus Crabbe in helping that poor woman care for little children and a household on the frontier.

The rector of Prince George's Parish traveled with the Crabbe family to their little chapel off the Baltimore Road near Hungerford's Tavern. This was a good day's ride from the Parish church, located on the Piney Branch not too far from George Town.

While the fine stone rectory of Rock Creek Church was comfortably English, the rectory of Rock Creek Chapel was a rustic log cabin with a few simple furnishings. But it and the even less imposing "chapel" were set on a hill surrounded by fruit trees, with fresh breezes and the creek below. It was a lovely location which, despite the primitive accommodations, reminded Roger Crabbe of the Bible's description of Eden. "I just pray that we are better tenants than Adam and Eve," he said only half-jokingly.

The Crabbes immediately fell in love with their new home. In addition, neighbors came by to welcome their new curate and his family, and brought enough food and drink to sustain the Crabbes (and half the neighborhood) for a week. They also offered their help in fixing up the little church and cabin to the Crabbes' liking, as well as planting gardens for kitchen and herbs.

Roger Crabbe and family settled in and quickly became valued members of the local society. Anne Crabbe, it appeared, was responding well to her new environment, the children were happy, and Roger Crabbe gloried in his role as leader of a Christian flock.

Among the additional, voluntary duties that Reverend Crabbe wanted to take on as minister was the establishment of a school for the youngsters. For a trifling tuition, he began to teach Bible reading, a little writing, and even cyphering to both boys and girls. The fact that most of his students attended his classes irregularly didn't bother him a bit. Some of them, like the Bayley boys and perhaps Christopher Sims, though the Reverend thought him intellectually lazy, would go on to take Latin, natural philosophy, and mathematics in preparation for attending an academy, before going on to the law or medicine.

Unfortunately, some months later Anne Crabbe suffered a still-birth. Despite this tragedy, the Crabbe family gave thanks to the Lord for their good fortune. The years went by and these were good years. By 1774, the Reverend Crabbe was a leader in the community and well-esteemed throughout the lower county. Satisfied with his two living children, hopeful for his wife's health, his opinions listened to by men of importance, he enjoyed his station in life.

All the while, Anne Crabbe became more and more frail and more and more dependent upon the bound girl Hannah Williams to do the daily chores involved in caring for the children, the chapel, and the house. She did, however, keep up appearances. She was always animated when mingling with the Reverend's congregation after Sunday services and at social events, and she spent hours instructing Hannah in the preparation of the family meals, which she insisted on serving even when there were no guests.

****

Most of the inhabitants of the lower county were nominal Anglicans. Many people from outside the province thought of Maryland as being papist, but this wasn't so. While founded as a refuge for Catholics, the province eventually surrendered that claim in fact if not in reputation. Even the proprietary family, the Calverts, eventually saw the wisdom of forsaking such an un-English faith.

Christopher's grandfather was once a papist, but converted to the Church of England, with the comment "If Lord Baltimore himself saw fit to disavow the True Church for the Established Church, then who am I to stubbornly maintain there is any such thing but the latter?"

Still, Samuel Sims resented the fact that he was forced to compromise with his God to please his sovereign, or suffer disadvantage to his family.

A good many Maryland Catholics and dissenters, all disenfranchised simply because of their religious beliefs, were similarly angered by the pervasive influence of the Anglican Church in their lives.

Then there was the malevolent Society for the Propagation of the Gospel in Foreign Parts, a part of the ecclesiastical conspiracy against American liberties, which served as political arm and tax authority for both Church and State. It was this society, people claimed, which paid the Reverend Crabbe's salary and claimed his true loyalty.

Yet preachers like the Reverend Crabbe came to the primitive backcountry not only to interpret God's word for a motley group of inhabitants, but also to bring them learning, and perhaps to awaken in some of them the suggestive power of the arts and literature. More often than not, these men of the cloth were great contributors to the communities they served. They were also frequently fanatic in their vows to Church and Crown and brought with them both strong convictions and strong prejudices.

As the crisis between mother country and her colonies became more and more vitriolic, many Anglican ministers used their pulpits and a captive audience to defend the Crown and speak out against the rabble-rousers.

Reverend Crabbe was a deeply spiritual man and a provincial, who took both God and the natural rights of man seriously. Torn between his sworn loyalty to his king and his country roots, he had decided upon an ill-starred attempt to reconcile the two.

It was in this context that he penned his most important sermon, the drafting of which had taken him several agonizing weeks; and on a fair Sunday in February he stood before his dwindling congregation, at the high desk which served as his pulpit, nervous but steadfast in the righteousness of his belief.

"Parishioners, Neighbors and Dear Friends, today's Sermon is from Romans, Chapter Thirteen, Verses One through Five:

> Let every Soul be subject unto the
> higher Powers: For there is no Power
> but of GOD; the Powers that be are
> ordained of GOD: Whosoever therefore
> resisteth the Power, resisteth the
> Ordinance of GOD.

"As Christians, we must listen attentively to the Word and make it truly a part of our lives, no matter how great the cause appears to do otherwise.

"So, I have chosen today's quotation because it appears to confront us with a conundrum in these sad and tumultuous times.

"That is: as aggrieved as we may feel over certain policies of our government, which some will wrongly claim have deprived us of our constituted rights as Englishmen, do we have the right to challenge authority?

"Many misguided men will say yes; but I will say to you, no!—no, we do not."

As he spoke, the Reverend Crabbe looked out over the congregation and was discouraged. Hardly into his sermon, he realized that his listeners were openly hostile to what he was saying. He did not presume to think that he could easily talk away the anger these people felt; but perhaps he could redirect them from the wayward path they were now being led by pernicious men calling themselves patriots toward a more balanced and eventually, one might hope, harmonious relationship with the mother country. With this in mind, he continued.

"...Some of a petty, ungenerous mind may think that by this statement—and some other expressions I have made lately—that I aim to speak out in favor of oppression. But this is not the case, I assure ye. Rather, it is my purpose to put our legitimate grievances and disappointments with our government in the context of God's Will.

"The very idea of consent and equality is too fantastic and can only lead to confusion and futility. The true liberty of man is to know and obey God. The quotation just given is to remind all of us that submission to government is an eternal Rule of God.

"...Some will question how it came to be that we are subject—not to the British Crown, because that is ordained by God Himself, but to the authority of the British Parliament, at whose whims we British Americans have suffered unfair treatment from time to time."

There was a murmur of agreement among the congregation. The Reverend Crabbe thought he saw in the now focused light of his listeners' eyes that he was on the right track. He could feel this commonality of interest soothing raw emotions as he got into the crux of his sermon. These, after all, were good Christians....

"...My answer to this question is that it is by the same binding compact which entitles us to enjoy all the benefits of the English Constitution and common laws; and that we as provincials derive advantages even from our subordination, onerous as it may be from time to time, because without this higher authority we would have no fair arbiter, and we would be thirteen independent states, which would bring anarchy and confusion amongst us.

"Now, I ask you, if left to our own separate devices, how would these thirteen entities coexist with each other? Let us seek the opinion of our Provincial Convention, members of which are amongst us today, whose enlightened labors for the commonweal, as well as dedication to the rights of all the people in our province, are without parallel. Even as others speak treason during the so-called Continental Congress"—he spate out the words in contempt—"our Convention remains staunchly loyal to our legitimate government.

"Why? Because the Convention acknowledges that the 'mildness and equity of the English Constitution...provides a State of felicity not exceeded by any People,' even while recognizing that the unbridled ambitions of other colonies would give them power for interference and oppression far greater than that of England."

Somewhere during this discourse, the Reverend Crabbe again lost his audience. He recognized this, even while failing to understand that the congregation had raced ahead of the Convention in its desire to resolve the crisis to its liking, something Doctor Wootton could have told him from experience, had he taken the time to ask. In short, the Convention was acting in the same misguided fashion as was Reverend Crabbe, both laboring under the illusion that all of this was due solely to the other side's misjudgment, or perhaps mismanagement, of this sorry affair.

At this point, the Reverend Crabbe could finally defend his personal position. With a shortness of breath and rush of words which gave away his anxiety, he forced himself to look squarely at the most uncompromising among his listeners:

"As many of you know, I have refused to sign the Association. It is not because I disagree with the rightness of our legitimate grievances against the government. As all of you know, I spoke out strongly from this very pulpit last June in support of the Hungerford Resolution which took a bold position in support of Boston and the securing of our rights.

"No, it is not from a want of love for our English freedoms that I refuse to sign the Association, but because of the extremes to which certain irresponsible elements would lead us; that is, away from righteous disagreement and toward anarchy and perdition...."

Feeling more like a defendant giving his testimony than a minister delivering a divine message, Reverend Crabbe finally ended his sermon with a few additional words about the compact between ruler and ruled and the obligations on both the contracting parties.

Following the service, Reverend Crabbe stood at the door as was his usual custom to greet his congregation and exchange pleasantries. Today was different, though; people appeared almost embarrassed as they passed him. Doctor Wootton and the Griffiths spoke to him not unkindly, but too many others, like William Bayley and Solomon Tylor, strode past him with tight mouths and curt nods. Most of the departing congregation was clearly upset with him.

Well, at least I've got them to thinkin', the Reverend Crabbe tried to assure himself. *That in itself should act as a purgative for festering wounds, and with that will come healing.*

As the congregation departed the chapel, Hannah came up and squeezed Christopher's arm. He looked at her and offered a dramatic wince to indicate his disappointment with the Reverend Crabbe's sermon. Hannah, understanding, simply shrugged, as if to say *sadly, all this seems to be inevitable.*

Instead of strolling on the grounds of the church conversing with friends and neighbors as they usually did, many people hurried off. Those who stayed a while tended to be those who were disappointed rather than angry with the Reverend Crabbe.

By this time, people on both sides of the issue had come to terms with their God on the question of His Will regarding capitulation or resistance, and they were now focused on more secular considerations.

For a radical such as Solomon Tylor, it was a simple matter: "if England will not give us the rights and liberties due all Englishmen, then we must cease to be English—or, more accurately English colonials; and become what in fact we are—Americans...but in the political, not just the geographical sense."

And a growing number of people were now inclined to agree with him.

8

LOCAL POLITICS

Hungerford's Tavern
Early March 1775

INDEED, POSITIONS WERE HARDENING. People who were once "friends of government" but still thought of as sincere patriots were now being called "tories" or "loyalists," new political descriptions which made it clear that being a loyal subject of the Crown would henceforth be considered an act of hostility, no matter what else a man thought.

Doctor Thomas Sprigg Wootton was deep in pessimistic thought. "Where are we going with this?" he asked rhetorically.

He and Doctor Tylor were having a discussion following a raucous committee meeting which had tried, unsuccessfully, to grapple with the question of neutrality in this growing conflict.

The two men were now alone at their favorite table–the one nearest the window and furthest from the fire. In addition to the rough trestle tables and benches, Hungerford's long room contained two card tables with real armchairs for the comfort and ease of those gentlemen who, like Doctors Wootton and Tylor, enjoyed a contemplative pipe and a measure of good liquor or the tavern's "ordinary"—the fixed meal—while leisurely reading the latest news from outside, or discussing the latest political happenings.

"...And what pitfalls await us along the way?" Wootton continued, and then quoted from Milton,

> *They baul for freedom in their senseless moods,*
> *And still revolt when truth would set them free;*
> *License they mean, when they cry liberty.*

Solomon Tylor misunderstood. "'Tis not unreasonable to fine those who are unwilling to sign the Association or otherwise contribute to the cause," he maintained.

"So it is, Solomon. But rebelling against your king is a dangerous undertaking, even for British subjects." Wootton stated this without his characteristic condescension, evidence enough that he earnestly wanted to persuade people on this serious issue. "So it might behoove us to be discriminating in the enemies we go and make."

"But they're already enemies, Thomas," argued Solomon, lumping together those who were loyalists with those who were neutral or noncommittal. "Not siding with the cause is the same as siding against it because a man's *got to* choose a side, and those who are not with us are against us. I don't trust people who go around professing their neutrality. How the hell can you be *neutral*, for Christ's sake?"

"Let's not get ourselves involved in a diversion against the Quakers," intoned Wootton. "Some of 'em, and I point to the Brookes as an example, are true patriots. Most of the others take God at His word that it's sinful to kill your fellow man. The Quakers do not pose a threat to 'God's Great Design,' as some describe our situation, just an embarrassing moral dilemma. Let's not alienate these people for no advantage."

Disagree as they might, both did agree that Americans, as many colonials were now calling themselves, were obsessed with the idea of there being a great conspiracy directed against them by their own government. How this would play out, neither could guess. But Doctor Wootton probably came close when he sighed and said wearily, "We seem so bent on dissolving all of society. I wonder if we as a people will ever *like* government again?"

At a loss for words following this pessimistic reflection by Wootton, both men sat quietly, drinking their flip. Their silence continued until Christopher entered the long room, waved hello to Mary Hungerford, and walked directly over to their table.

Unlike the two doctors, Christopher was dressed in his usual farming garb, the style and neutral colors repeating themselves year after year, as if Christopher himself were repeating the seasons year after year without noticeable change. But this was an unusual call on these two distinguished gentlemen because their answer could change his life forever.

"Doctor Wootton, Doctor Tylor. Beggin' your pardon, sirs, I would like a word with the two of you, if I might."

"Sit down and have a drink with us, Christopher."

Nodding his thanks, he asked Sally for a cup of rambooze which she brought him. Saucy as she was diminutive, the serving girl bent over to place his drink on the table in an exaggerated manner to proudly display her budding breasts, pushed up and almost out of her new, artfully laced bodice.

The two doctors looked with amusement at Christopher as Sally swished off.

Christopher grimaced. "No, gentlemen, I'm *not* in the market," and laughingly told them about his exchange with Jeremy Heynon not too long ago.

"Oh, to be young again and devilishly attractive to women," Doctor Wootton said. Turning to Christopher, "Now, how may we help you, Christopher?"

Christopher became serious. "Well, I have a problem. There are rumors that the committee intends to drive the Reverend Crabbe out of the lower county. Is that true?"

Tylor looked solemnly at Christopher. "Has it occurred to you, Christopher, that the Reverend Crabbe is an agent of the Crown who is involved in a conspiracy to deprive us of our rights?" He leaned forward, eyebrows raised. "Why, ye look surprised. But 'tis true—the good reverend is a hireling of the government in its efforts to impose civil and ecclesiastical oppression over all of us."

The Church of England did in fact serve a quasi-governmental function in Maryland which affected the lives of nonmembers as well as members. In fact, through the Society for the Propagation of the Gospel in Foreign Parts—referred to as the "S.P.G"—the Anglican Church extended the weak but grasping hand of royal authority into regions of America which would nevertheless have dealt successfully with God, nature, and society without the benefit of either of these overly ambitious institutions.

Christopher thought about this. "I think you are overstating the facts here, Solomon, but—"

"The Reverend Crabbe's discourse runs to priestcraft," Tylor interrupted, his animated gestures showing his passion on this subject. "He spends his time subverting the Committee's every intent—and perhaps acting the government spy. Be careful who ye stand up for, Christopher."

"I didn't come here to argue in defense of the Reverend Crabbe, Solomon." Looking at Doctor Wootton, who had remained quiet throughout this diatribe, "Doctor Wootton, I don't agree with the Reverend Crabbe's politics, but I have ... well ... a personal interest in whether he stays or leaves."

Doctor Wootton looked puzzled, then bemused as it dawned on him. "Ah, and might that be a young woman named Hannah Williams?"

"It would be, sir; so, you'll understand my concern. She has more than two years to go on her indenture—which is bad enough...but you can imagine if she was taken away—"

Having listened to this, Solomon also now understood the situation. Waving airily in the direction of the western frontier, he suggested, "If that's the case, why don't ye just run off with the woman, Christopher?"

Christopher sighed. "Because we would be criminals. We want to go to Baltimore or maybe Annapolis. As runaways, we wouldn't have a chance for a normal life in those places."

"True," said Doctor Wootton, looking reprovingly at Tylor. "And I agree you should not go off half-cocked, despite what Solomon so casually suggests." He hesitated, then added, "Christopher, the committee does not want to drive the

Reverend Crabbe from Rock Creek Chapel, it just wants to make sure that he is not doing harm to the cause."

"I'm relieved to hear that, Doctor Wootton."

9

A VIOLENT INCIDENT

Rock Creek Chapel
March 12, 1775

TODAY, BOTH CHRISTOPHER AND JEREMY were working at the Crabbes'. Last year, neighbors had set fire to trees and brush which had been growing wild since time immemorial and had to be cleared for a new planting field. The charred remains were allowed to rot for a year or so to give nourishment to the soil. Now, it was time for the trunks and stumps to be cut and hauled off, which was what Christopher and Jeremy were doing. Nothing smelled worse than burnt wood which had been decaying and water-soaked in the woods for a year or more.

The cool, but dry, weather made the chopping and hacking and hauling less exhausting; and Christopher had brought the family ox to pull the heavier trunks and limbs to the edges of the woods, which made that task easier. Still, it would be a solid day's work to finish what they had promised the Reverend Crabbe, who was intent on planting this spring.

It was hard work, and Hannah frequently brought them cool water. Periodically, Christopher and Jeremy would recline on a burnt tree trunk, backs against a branch not yet cut, their legs stretched out, just to rest a spell. Admiring their work, Jeremy suggested that they reward themselves with a good pull from the bottle of rum sitting inside the springhouse. Christopher was tempted but discouraged the idea with the observation that they'd no doubt wake up the next morning entangled in branches with all this work still to do. So, they soon set to work again, both now thinking about some good rum and an end to work.

During lunch, which consisted of cold chicken, bread and cheese, and beer, Christopher and Hannah had a quick chance to talk to each other.

"...The truth is, Hannah, the Reverend Crabbe has offended just about everyone in the lower county and some are even talking about driving him out." Christopher cut her off as she was about to speak. "–*Hannah,* listen to me, please. This is not about the Reverend Crabbe, but about us. It's about what we must do *if* he does leave."

Drumming up his courage, he finally asked, "Would you come with me if that happens?" Christopher waited nervously for her reply, his whole future depending on one word.

Christopher knew that Hannah was not one to make hasty decisions. She looked directly at him with those great round eyes of hers, not blinking, not averting her gaze, as if she were staring at her future.

Finally, she closed her eyes, then opened them and nodded her head.

"Aye, Christopher."

Whenever Christopher and Jeremy finished their work, the Reverend Crabbe would come out to thank them for their help, then stay to chat a while. This afternoon was no different; but there was a sad banality in the conversation between the two men and their former teacher which reflected the growing chasm between the Old World and the New.

By now, the sun had disappeared behind the horizon and the sky was awash in deepening colors of gray and purple. Dusk was setting in, and brought with it a welcome excuse to end the awkward conversation. Christopher and Jeremy excused themselves, stowed the tools in the shed, and retrieved their haversacks and muskets. The two young men said a few final words to the Reverend, who had an especially sad look in his eyes as he thanked the men. Saddened too by their rift with the Reverend Crabbe, Christopher and Jeremy set out in a somber mood for home.

They had gone only a short distance when they saw a small group of men with a cart coming down the Baltimore Road. The men could be on practically any business between the backcountry and Baltimore Town, so Christopher and Jeremy gave a neighborly greeting to them as they passed, and received the same in return.

Jeremy mused that it was an odd hour for strangers to be on the road. "Why, they'll be on the road long after nightfall before they come to the next public house."

This caught Christopher's attention. Nowadays you had to be careful about highwaymen since the road had become so well traveled. These men seemed harmless enough, but, then, they were strangers and one had to be wary of strangers.

"Say, you have a point, Jeremy. They aren't wagoners...might be itinerants plying their wares or trade, but they have the look of townsmen, don't they?"

Looking back down the road, they watched as the group of men stopped on the road by the chapel and the Crabbes' cabin. They appeared to be talking to each other, then as a group they climbed the small hill up toward the cabin. Even while this was happening, two of the men broke from the others and headed for the chapel.

As Christopher and Jeremy watched curiously, it suddenly dawned on Christopher that the group of men might be intent on some mischief as a result of the Reverend Crabbe's Crown loyalties.

Concerned now that this might well be the case, Christopher turned to Jeremy.

"We better see what this is all about, dontcha think?"

"But Chris, what'll we do if they be ribalds bent on trouble?"

Christopher hesitated. "I don't know, Jeremy. Best load our muskets."

Jeremy stared at his friend. "We're *not* goin' to shoot anyone," he said with conviction.

"No," Christopher assured him, clearing his throat to get the words out—the possibility of an altercation made him nervous. "No, just talk to 'em reasonable-like and, if they intend to trouble the Reverend, hope our showing up makes them change their minds. You with me, Jeremy?"

"Aye."

After loading their muskets, the two retraced their steps back down the road to where the cart was stopped. Jeremy peered into the cart. "Booze bottles and little else," he noted. Men who are pot-valiant could be trouble.

Even as they approached the cabin, they could hear strident voices from within. They stood outside and listened. They heard the Reverend Crabbe lash out as if damning sinners from the pulpit.

"By whose authority do ye make these demands? Tell me!"

"The Committee of Observation, that's who. And by God you'll hand 'em over to us or we'll just get 'em ourselves."

"The Committee of Observation, you say? Now, I was just talkin' to Doctor Wootton yesterday and he didn't say anything about *his* committee, which I'm assured is *the* committee of observation in these parts, wantin' to look over my sermons or any other so-called seditious papers of mine." He spate out the word "seditious" as if he had just tasted a piece of tainted meat.

The speaker of the group seemed to be taken aback by this statement and looked at his comrades. One of the others shook his head angrily and stepped forward.

"Preacher, the order was made in secret so ye wouldn't go and destroy the papers the committee seeks. We know such papers exist and we demand to have 'em now."

The Reverend Crabbe stared at the group of men, the silence thickening, before stating calmly and steadily, "I will not submit to such a travesty of civil law."

"All right, Reverend, you've had your say. Now you'll do as we say."

Then Christopher and Jeremy heard a woman's voice–Hannah's voice–yell "don't you dare touch me," then scuffling, and they immediately entered the cabin.

Once inside they saw the frightened children, a helpless Missus Crabbe trying to calm them, the Reverend Crabbe dropping papers to go to the assistance of his wife...and two men intent on groping Hannah...

They also saw that the Crabbe's sparse but neat little home was being savaged, a chair was kicked over and bounced against the wall, pages of paper were swirling in the air, a china dish was tossed on the wood floor, and even the coverlet of the large standing bed had been pulled off and lay messily on the floor, trampled upon and dangerously near the fire.

"What's this all about?"

Christopher's question came from behind and took all by surprise. The strangers spun around to face the questioner, their postures those of instinctual self-defense, to see two stern men with an angry determination and armed with muskets.

Turning his musket on the two men hovering around Hannah, Christopher ordered "You two, move away from the woman."

"I'll ask you again, gents: what's this all about?"

The man who had taken over the talking wore filthy clothes and was ill-kempt. He licked his lips, looking the two men up and down, noticing the threatening way they held their muskets—but only at half-cock. He assessed the situation and made his decision.

"This be committee business, men. If you're good patriots, you'll leave us to our business. Understood?" The other men nodded in a friendly manner, assuming these men would agree. Their point made, they went to return to the business at hand. Laughing, one of the men went for Hannah, "And I'll take care of this Tory bitch."

Christopher pulled the hammer back to full-cock and leveled his musket at the man reaching for Hannah. "If you take another step, mister, I'll put a ball in your head." The man froze.

"You say the lower county committee authorized you to pillage the Reverend Crabbe's home and *our* chapel?" Jeremy asked this question politely but pointedly.

The strangers, unexpectedly frustrated, began to show their anger as they once again had to confront these meddlers.

"May I see the order." Christopher prayed that he sounded strong and confident as he made this demand. He certainly felt neither.

"Now just a minute, mister, ye don't go talkin' like that to men in authority. Hear?" The scruffy man's disposition had changed from patronizing to malevolent. He was tired of this distraction. They were just farmers, for chrissake. With arm raised across his body as if he intended to cuff a misbehaving boy, the man took a step toward Christopher.

Christopher hadn't been taught in militia practice how to parry a bayonet thrust, but it made sense to him to quickly raise his musket across his body to protect himself from the arc of the man's intended blow.

The man's wrist struck the musket lock. "Ahh, goddammit to hell!" He twirled around in pain, holding his injured wrist against his chest, grimacing and puffing.

The blow against his musket had driven Christopher back. He stumbled, caught himself, and, having recovered, quickly brought himself to the make-ready position. Breathing hard, he placed his right foot to the rear, ready now to take aim. Jeremy nervously followed suit.

"No, no," yelled the Reverend Crabbe. "This has gone too far! Put down your firelocks, Christopher and Jeremy!" Turning to the stranger who had first confronted him, the Reverend addressed him with open condescension. "You may have all my papers…then be gone, and leave us and these men be."

The man with the hurt wrist was looking at his wound—a nasty red scrape and darkening bruises. His pain quickly turned to rage.

He made an angry motion which caused a trembling Christopher to flinch, his nerves shuddering.

Then his musket went off.

All the world seemed soundless and motionless as the primer ignited with a sizzle, followed an instant later by the sharp report and jets of smoke of the discharge.

The stillness resumed as surprised men, Christopher included, tried to make sense of what had just happened. Looking around, they all breathed a sigh of relief. No one had been struck—the ball had smacked harmlessly into the clapboard ceiling of the chapel.

Anything could have happened at that point. The group of strangers, with a wary eye on Jeremy and his poised musket, were fighting mad now, but uncertain what to do; while Christopher and Jeremy braced for the worst.

It never came. The strangers had not bargained for a serious fight. Hectoring a preacher was one thing; dodging wayward shots by nervous men was another. They had the papers, so they would get their shilling and some more gin. They were not foolish men. And they'd see to these damn'd men later.

With angry words and glares, and some posturing, the strangers departed with the papers they wanted, leaving the Reverend Crabbe, Christopher, and Jeremy wondering if they had been lucky to escape with their lives—or had they been too easily cowed by a few raffs?

A sobbing Missus Crabbe and Hannah comforted the children, while Christopher loaded his musket just in case, the powder horn tapping too nervously on the rim as he tried to coax a charge of powder down the barrel without spilling precious grains.

The Reverend Crabbe went outside and watched intently as the group of men disappeared up the road, then turned to look sternly at the two men, who had also come outside.

"Tell me now, Christopher Sims and Jeremy Heynon, when have the British authorities *ever* committed such an atrocity as this against any inhabitant of this region? Tell me that!"

Shaking his head, the Reverend turned disgustedly toward the door of his home. Suddenly, he stopped and turned to face Christopher and Jeremy. The anger in his face had faded; now with a pained expression and tears in his eyes, he said in a quiet voice, "I do appreciate you comin' to the aid of a neighbor. I do, indeed...God bless the both of you."

With head bowed and shoulders hunched, he slowly walked into his house and shut the door.

Christopher had no chance to say a word to Hannah....

****

"Malicious discharge of a firearm? By damn, ye will not make me out to be the culprit in this!" Christopher was so mad he could hardly speak, sputtering and searching for some scathing words to describe the absurdity of such an accusation.

It was several days later when Christopher heard this outrageous charge against him being bandied about. Furious about what had happened to the Reverend Crabbe, his family, and Hannah, he had sought out the lower county's leadership in their lair—pursued them into their lair, was the way Jeremy put it, the lair being, of course, Hungerford's Tavern. Mary Hungerford saw the clenched fists and fire in Christopher Sims' eyes as he stormed into the room; and young Sally, with no thought of puffing out her bosom on this occasion, was unusually meek in bringing Christopher his usual drink. Even Doctor Wootton was put on the defensive.

"Calm down, Christopher," Doctor Wootton intoned. "I didn't say you would be charged—only that some folks are suggestin' that's what should happen. Discharging a firelock at people is serious business."

This did not mollify Christopher's outrage. "People are actually talking such nonsense?—when they should be calling for the sheriff to round up those damn'd George Town rakehells who attacked the Reverend Crabbe *and*, mind you, insulted our women. If the sheriff can't do it, why, then, let's call out the militia. It's outrageous, Thomas, that such wanton acts can be gotten away with just by using the name of the Committee of Observation."

There was a pregnant pause before Doctor Wootton, looking embarrassed, replied. "Ah, actually, Christopher, those men acted with the authority of the committee...more or less," he added lamely.

"More or less? What on earth are ye saying, Doctor Wootton ...that you people sponsored an attack by hirelings on a neighbor? That's contemptible."

"Perhaps it was ill thought out, Christopher, but it was not an 'attack.' The men were unarmed. They were instructed to seize papers which the committee believed were incriminating. We've been advised by the George Town and upper Frederick committees that intercepted letters prove there is a loyalist network actively engaged in seditious activities. We must ferret out its members."

"My God, now the committee's intercepting letters and stealing a minister's papers! So, what did the Reverend Crabbe's papers reveal, Thomas?"

"Nothing proving espionage, I admit, but his letters to the Church authorities prove that he is conciliatory to a fault."

"Conciliatory to a fault? Sounds like our Provincial Convention to me—What's becoming of us, Thomas?"

****

While the idea of charging Christopher with malicious discharge of a firearm soon faded away, he was not in the clear by any means.

"Christopher," his brother George said, "you'll need to accept the fact that there is a price to pay when you go against the current. Now, I'm not sayin' you were wrong, just that what you did is not taken kindly by some of the people around here. Remember the talk we had about the hotheads, and how they always seem to think the worst of a person? Well, this is a case in point. It doesn't matter that the committee acted wrongly in this matter—people will only remember that you joined sides with an enemy to the cause."

And George was absolutely right....

"Sims, you've shown your true colors. You're in league with that Anglican spy and have shown your willingness to injure good patriots."

James Bailey was from a somewhat wealthy family in the lower county and did not hesitate to use that to his advantage. Since they were youngsters, he and Christopher had always been competitive—over games, and shooting skills, and finally girls . . . and here they were at Hungerford's continuing their feud.

"For a man who won't even show up for militia drill, Bailey, you are hardly one to describe good patriots."

"Gentlemen do not serve as common soldiers, Sims."

"James, you're an asshead."

"Why, you can't talk to me like that!" James Bailey was sputtering. "Such an insult demands satisfaction. Dammit, *sir*, I challenge you to a duel!"

"A duel?" Christopher stepped back in mock amazement. "Why, James, duels are between gentlemen. And neither of us is a gentleman. But here's what I propose: bare fists, right now—you little pissant!" and Christopher placed a looping right fist smack against the side of James Bailey's head and down he went like a felled tree.

Jared Mitchell, who was neither here nor there in the local social hierarchy, watching this, said, "While I applaud what you jus' did, Chris Sims, I think you might someday regret irking the upper class...."

Hungerford's Tavern
March 24, 1775

The Reverend Crabbe was brought before the local Committee of Observation for his criticisms of that august body and for the draft of a pamphlet, found among the papers seized two weeks ago, which condemned "the teaching and inculcation of principles subversive of all good government."

Before the committee, the Reverend Crabbe freely admitted that he intended to have this pamphlet published. He also staunchly defended his opposition to the calls for collecting arms and ammunition by asking the people to continue their allegiance to the British government.

"I am a loyal subject of the Crown, and, at the very least, I expect my congregation to speak no treason. That, sir, is my explanation—I need no defense."

The committee disagreed and demanded that he sign a paper recanting every criticism he made against the committee and the cause.

Indignant, the Reverend Crabbe refused, declaring, "I would suffer my right arm to be cut off before I would ever sign such a filthy document, *and* I would wish if I ever recanted my beliefs due to duress that my tongue might cling to the roof of my mouth and never come loose."

The committee could do little else but condemn the Reverend Crabbe and fine him a sum which he refused to pay.

The situation was growing intolerable.

10

A SIGNAL FOR HOSTILITIES

Middle Potomac Hundred
Late April 1775

NEWS OF THE FIGHTING at Lexington and Concord in Massachusetts arrived at Hungerford's Tavern within days of the event. It took a few days longer for word to spread throughout the lower county, to all the other local taverns and to all the isolated farms.

There was pride at the heroism of those Massachusetts farmers, who had so valiantly defended their homes and way of life.

And there was anger over the husbands, and sons, and brothers who were killed and wounded by soldiers of their own government.

That April morning told patriotic Americans all they needed to know.

Not surprisingly, emotions were running high in the weeks following the fighting at Lexington and Concord. Patriots declared war on loyalists. The Reverend Crabbe was high on the list of tories to be silenced. The Reverend again ended up in front of the lower county committee to answer for his defense of the British army's actions around Boston.

The Reverend took this opportunity to tell the committee that it and the Continental Congress were depriving the people of the North American colonies of their freedom.

"*Yes,* it's true," he yelled. "There is more freedom in Turkey than there is here in this province!"

Again, the committee could not find in itself the outrage to actually punish the Reverend and proved itself helpless in not only disciplining him, but controlling him.

Doctor Wootton made it a point to seek out Christopher.

"Christopher, since you told me your situation, I suggest you immediately speak to Hannah and agree on a course of action. I'm afraid the Reverend Crabbe has sealed his fate and will be 'encouraged' to leave the neighborhood."

Doctor Wootton looked at Christopher. "Young man, I won't presume to tell you what to do. *But,* if you and Hannah can possibly avoid it, don't resort to running away. Now, that's just my advice."

"And I appreciate it, Doctor Wootton."

After his conversation with Doctor Wootton, Christopher hurried over to Rock Creek Chapel to speak with Hannah.

He decided against directly approaching the Reverend Crabbe and risk a possible confrontation; instead, he hid like a footpad until she came out on one of her chores, hoping he would not scare her to death.

"Hannah," he whispered as she approached the trash pit. She started, then recognized him as he peeked through some leafy branches.

"What on earth…is that you, Chris?"

He came out from under the dogwood shrubs and underbrush where he had hidden himself, feeling like a child discovered during a game of hide and seek.

"Hannah, quickly—there is serious talk of driving the Reverend off. We have to have a plan—"

Hannah became very composed. "Chris, I know all this. One of his parishioners warned him."

She hesitated, trying to collect her thoughts in all the confusion. She was a deliberate person and needed an anchor—something to keep her from being swept 'round 'n' 'round like a flower in a creek eddy.

"*Must* you go, Hannah?" Christopher said this with passion. He touched her cheek and felt moisture.

Hannah responded to his touch by nuzzling his palm. She considered his question, began to stammer in reply, and had to collect herself before replying.

"I'm prepared to come with you right now, if we have no other choice. But I pray that is not the case, Chris." She looked so sorrowful. "We've talked about this and are agreed that we do not run off if it can be avoided. Is that not so, Chris?"

"Aye, Hannah, it is." He looked to her for some sort of further explanation.

"Well, the Reverend Crabbe is talking about going to Baltimore Town if worse comes to worst. 'Pears he has a mentor who is priest of the town's parish. Have we not talked about goin' to Baltimore? If that be true, can we not work around that?"

She looked so hopefully at him. Their eyes met, both welling with tears just thinking the worst.

Christopher considered this, looking intently at Hannah. He knew how good she was at following orders—it was just the way she was—"Hannah, I'll never ask ye to do something that bothers your conscience...remember this: Jane Everett who has a house on Lovely Lane. She's my aunt and knows me. If you go to Baltimore Town, contact my Aunt Jane. I swear I will come to Baltimore as soon as I can and will be found at my Aunt Jane's."

Hannah smiled, this time showing the gap between her two front teeth. "Chris, I'll place a note...here." She pointed to an old hollow log. "The children and I hide secrets here all the time. It'll let ye know everything I know," and she shrugged, tears now running down her cheeks. It was the best she could do.

"Hannah, I want you to have this," and Christopher showed her a Spanish milled dollar. It was a large silver coin, now tarnished with age, pierced and hanging on a leather thong.

"This belonged to my mother, who was given it by her father with the admonition that she save it for the worst of times."

Hannah held the old coin in the palm of her hand, hefting it. The surfaces had been buffed almost smooth by years of usage, the original designs–two pillars on one side and on the obverse a faint profile of some long dead Spanish king–now reduced to soft lines and curves and unshapened letters. She looked curiously at Christopher.

Christopher took the coin with its leather tie from her hand and looped it around her neck.

Never in her life had Hannah been in possession of so much money. Now, a Spanish dollar was worth maybe a pound sterling anywhere in the colonies and would usually suffice to buy a body out of nearly any predicament imaginable, except for the burying hole.

Tucking the coin in the pit of her bosom, Christopher repeated what his mother had been told: "Save it for the worst of times." Christopher took her face in his hands and gently kissed her on her forehead. "Hannah, I love you. And I promise you this–and never, *ever* doubt it–I will follow you to the ends of the earth...."

****

The Sunday following his censure, a defiant Reverend Crabbe stood before his congregation. Filled with righteous anger, he read the homily of obedience.

This time he did not beseech, but instead lectured those who sat before him. His message was simple: obey the Crown government or be punished by the Lord. He knew this would outrage his audience, who would indignantly spread the word to a community which had already irreparably hurt him.

"Let those who have chosen to dance with Satan burn in Hell," he had earlier confided to his wife.

Within days, the Lower County Committee of Observation advised Reverend Crabbe in writing to "consult his safety" and consider a departure from the county.

Before the next Sabbath, the Reverend and his wife, without a further word, abandoned their comfortable cabin and the little chapel; and, leaving a lifetime of memories behind, set out on the road to Baltimore, turning their backs on Lower Frederick County and all its inhabitants.

And just like that, the bound woman Hannah Williams was gone.

The Hollow Log
May 9, 1775

It had rained and the writing was hard to read. Fortunately, Hannah had written the note in lead and not ink, so Christopher could make out much of it, written laboriously in a girlish roundhand.

> *My Dear Christopher*
>
> *I rite this in hast and hope you wil red it soon so you wil know my warabouts. We are going to Balimer town any day now and wil stay at the Rev. Johnston at Ste. Pauls church in town but I do not know the street. Perhaps your aunt wil know. I wil send a message and hope*

Here the writing became unintelligible as moisture had permeated through a fold of the paper. Enough was preserved, though, and Christopher knew what he had to do.

11

SHE'S GONE . . .

Leeke Forest
June 1775

CHRISTOPHER'S FIRST INSTINCT had been to grab his fowler, saddle the ancient mare, and strike out on the Baltimore Road to race down the Reverend Crabbe and his entourage.

But cooler heads had prevailed.

"What would you've done then, Chris?" asked Jeremy.

Christopher was at a loss to explain exactly *what* he would have done. He gave a frustrated shrug. "I've got to go to her."

"Of course ye do, Chris," said Constance, adding, "but goin' to Baltimer as you and Hannah had agreed is the better plan."

"'Tis true," seconded Jeremy. "Get situated with your aunt there, find work, and the time will come for you and Hannah sooner than you think."

"Aye, you're right—both of you." Christopher smiled sourly.

Later, his brother George advised him: "Chris, make your plans, take care of your affairs here, and then, and only then, get goin'."

It wasn't easy being patient, though.

Once after drill, he even visited the little chapel and cabin, stark now in its emptiness. Entering the cabin where Hannah had once lived, he lit a candle to lighten the murky gray interior and looked around. With a feeling of great loss, he climbed the ladder to the loft where Hannah and the children had slept. He sat down on a small chair, imagining Hannah sitting in the same chair, perhaps watching over a sick child.

There was a country-made chest of drawers near the cornhusk mattress. Furtively, as if he were secretly inspecting Hannah's most private world, he opened the top drawer of the chest. What, he wondered, would she have kept in here?

A little of that question was answered when he discovered, tucked in the rear corner of the drawer, a light green garter, perhaps overlooked as she hastily packed to leave.

He fondled the length of ribbon, rubbing the creases of the knot marking where it was gartered above her knee, associating this bit of cloth with one intimate moment....

...*Which seemed so long ago,* he thought wistfully.

****

Among the things Christopher had to take care of before he left was to help George get the tobacco to George Town.

George, Christopher, and young John Paul had done well in getting their cured tobacco to Rolling House, the pretty brick inspection house located on Rock Creek at the edge of George Town. It was brutal work rolling a one-thousand-pound hogshead nine miles down the rutted, narrow road, often so sloppy the ox that did the hauling practically had to be carried on a rail by the three of them. Fortunately, it was all downhill, and only another two trips had been needed to finish the task.

On the day when they off-loaded the last of their tobacco at Rolling House, where it would be graded and credited to the family account, George requested the equivalent of two pounds in money. This was advanced him in paper bills of credit, real coin being scarce. So, with seven provincial dollars in their pockets, the three of them went to town.

A Time for Celebration?
George Town, June 26, 1775

In 1775, George Town was a small but bustling port situated on the Potomac River just below the falls. As the Great Road crested a high hill above the town, one was offered a fine prospect of this little settlement sitting on the waving hills below, with a wide river and Mason's Island in the background, and usually the spectacle of one or two sloops tied up at the public wharf at the end of Water Street.

Not an elegant town as was Alexandria, Virginia, which could be seen a few miles downriver, George Town consisted of perhaps a dozen buildings. While a twenty-year-old plan of the town showed the entire tract parceled into neat lots, narrow and deep, along straight streets, most lots remained empty, dotted here and there with a few solid brick or stone houses, one or two clusters of row houses along Bridge Street near the market house, and a number of single-story wooden houses, all scattered along unpaved streets. There were two churches, three taverns and a number of tippling houses.

Small as it was, George Town was a considerable town for country people who only went there for the fairs which were held twice a year for their benefit. The Sims family was among those who went to town on these occasions to sell their produce and linen and buy a few manufactured goods or special items. The stores offered a wide variety of domestic and imported goods, and it was during one of the fairs a number of years ago that William Sims bought the beautiful rifle made by John Yost, George Town's only gunsmith, whose work rivaled that of any artisan in Frederick or even in Lancaster.

Most of all, the Sims family came to enjoy the excitement of mixing with the crowds and looking at all the merchandise and latest fashions from London in the various shops and under the many canvas tents set up in the open lots for this occasion. There were also sporting events, gambling, imported foods, plenty of spirits, and the most recent outside news.

Though it was not fair time, the town still offered the Sims men a huge variety of attractions.

As the three walked through town, or visited a shop, or stopped for a drink, all the talk was about the fighting outside Boston, up there in Massachusetts, and what this might mean. Everybody had an opinion, including George and Christopher (John Paul, at twelve, couldn't care less), though the bottom line was nobody knew for sure. They all admitted this; but nodding sagely, all also agreed that King George would now surely see the folly of Parliament's reckless policies and redress the wrongs which had brought on this crisis. There was still that hope....

Despite the special occasion, the Sims men were far too frugal to spend their hard-earned money at a place like Travers Tavern, which catered to the planters; but they did treat themselves to a proper town meal and good drink at a reputable public establishment on Bridge Street.

For a first course, they had pea soup and ham, followed by a second course of boiled turkey with oyster sauce, then, in rapid order, they were served a fricassee of veal sweetmeats, salad greens with pork, a variety of cakes and cookies, cheeses and a dessert of fruits, all washed down with Rhenish wine and coffee.

Throughout this long meal, with the debris mounting after each course, and the table becoming strewn with greasy bones, bread crumbs, stray peas, and dollops of various dishes, the Sims men engaged in the postulated talk of men left to their own company.

With a final noisy suck on a joint, George punctuated his last point by flipping the bone in the direction of a plate. He missed and the bone fell with a crack on the plank floor.

"That's 'sactly my point, Chris." George's speech was becoming ever so slightly slurred by the drink. "Radicals like Bayley and Tylor don't speak for the rest o' us. They're takin' ar' grievances with the Crown and creatin' a rebellion, when most people would settle for a lot less."

"George, I'm not sure that's the case anymore," Christopher said carefully. "Now, I'm not sayin' the extremists are right, mind you, only that they're maybe right in sayin' that the Crown shows no inclination to see any merit in our side of the argument. Sendin' armies to wage war on loyal subjects isn't meant to soothe ruffled feathers, much less appeal to any existin' loyalty."

George winced. Extremes bothered him, and he saw in this conflict the potential for too many extremes.

"Well, I truly feel more comfortable with the thinking of men like Mister Griffith and Doctor Wootton than I do with the likes of Mister Bayley or Doctor Tylor, who appear all too ready to invite death and destruction just to say 'I told you so!'"

While he had considerable respect for Doctor Wootton and liked his sharp way with words, which cut through debate like a razor's edge, Christopher actually favored the heated statements of Doctor Tylor and–though he was loath to admit it–James Bayley's father.

"It seems to me, George, the British government has shown itself to be opposed to everything we colonials hold dear. If that be the case, then we have to resist…with arms as well as words. If separation is our only recourse, then so be it. In the end, we'll either win or we'll lose…if we give in to 'em, we lose for sure–simple as that."

"So ye be an unrepentant rebel, Christopher Sims!" George exclaimed with a touch of reproof.

"I be no rebel, George," Christopher shot back emphatically. "I'm a *patriot*."

While few of them realized it at the time, this careful distinction would make them and many other Americans, revolutionaries and not rebels.

Finished with their midday meal, the three of them went down to the wharf to enjoy some cockfighting and other bawdy entertainment available around the docks.

Like any port, George Town's waterfront was a rough area and contrasted sharply with the more genteel atmosphere found on the upper streets. The local watermen were not as rowdy as the seafarers of the larger ports, but they enjoyed their time on land, endeavoring mightily to do everything to excess, whether it be drinking, catting, gambling, or fighting. After a huge meal, the frenetic activity of the "Keys" was just the place for the Sims men to work off their sluggishness.

All three enjoyed the cockfights even though they almost always lost a shilling or two betting on the birds. Tonight, however, they were lucky and won twenty shillings in hard coin– a whole pound sterling–which encouraged them to go on a binge. Feeling flush, they went off to spend most of it on gin, a few games for John Paul, and, a little later, a modest supper. After a walk along the wharf so John Paul could get a closer look at the ships tied up there, they headed for Suter's Tavern where they knew they could obtain a relatively clean bed for the night, one which didn't have too many fleas.

The next morning, a little worse for the wear but otherwise feeling pretty good about themselves, the Sims men prepared for their return journey home. They were careful to purchase gifts for the women–pinchbeck necklaces with paste gems–and a wooden sword for John Paul, who, after all, was still a boy.

Then, laughing and slapping each other on the back, they set off for home—almost forgetting to retrieve the ox at Rolling House.

12

MAKING IT A WAR FOR THE CONTINENT

Hungerford's Tavern
Mid July 1775

WORD OF NEW FIGHTING between the New Englanders and the regulars was reported. This time the ferocity of the fighting was even more violent than that of Lexington and Concord. People simply could not believe the reports.

"The newspaper accounts say more than 1,500 were killed or wounded in a matter of a few hours."

People were silent as they tried to fathom that number of men littering a few acres of ground, lying still, their bodies smashed and bloodied, or writhing in pain, not yet dead from their wounds.

Shocked, most Americans did not see any sense to the battle for Bunker's Hill...or Breed's Hill, accounts being somewhat confused as to the exact hill upon which the battle was fought. "Name don't make any difference," many concluded, only that this battle was "unnecessary and discredible."

"It does show, though, that the regulars are no match for the patriotic fervor of free men."

"While the militia don't possess the discipline or experience of the regulars, our brothers from Massachusetts have proven we don't need it."

This overly confident and rather cavalier attitude toward waging war against the Crown was not subscribed to by every one. Including Doctor Wootton.

"…There is a vast difference between protest and rebellion, Solomon–let's think seriously about that. The Crown may vacillate toward the former, but I fear it will react savagely toward the latter. With no clear goal in mind, we have a war to fight and be won against the most powerful army in the world. And with what–*that?*" Wootton pointed a finger dismissively in the direction of the militia company drilling outside.

"Their brethren in New England have already demonstrated our military superiority," retorted Doctor Tylor.

"Oh, I know there are enough trees and fences and mounds of earth for all our men to hide behind," Wootton noted, "but I'm not all that sure that there are enough British generals stupid enough to follow that scenario time and again to certain defeat."

Exasperated at this point, Solomon Tylor could only respond, "The militia will do, Thomas. They'll have to… they're the only army we've got."

It *was* difficult to see the "glorious will of God's favoring the American cause" while watching the painful practice of the Middle Potomac Hundred militia company.

This company was one of forty minuteman companies authorized by the Maryland Convention for the defense of the province against the threat from British regulars.

Today was the now weekly drill session—a terrible burden for farmers—but one necessary to maintain a well-regulated militia in these tumultuous times.

Upon being dismissed, the men would usually hurry off to the tavern to have a mug of cider and talk about the latest news from Boston. Since the most recent fighting at a place called Bunker's Hil—some said Breed's Hill, but never mind—talk of war and how it should be waged in the fields and forests of North America went on from dawn to dusk.

"...Henry, the British can't shoot straight, probably because of those damn'd manuals of yours," George Winston pointed out patiently to the company's acting lieutenant. "That's why they depend on the bayonet. Now, most of us are middlin' good with a musket or rifle and can get off a couple of fine shots in the time it takes a man to cover a hundred paces. But I'll give the regulars use of the bayonet, which is exactly why we shouldn't take 'em on at that, even if we had the damn'd things."

"Right you are, George," piped in George Purdy. "We ought to use the means that the Frenchies and injuns used, which always worked against the regulars–concealment and aimed fire, and run like the devil if they had to. We ought not to be foolin' 'round with fightin' parade-style."

There were urgent military preparations throughout the thirteen colonies for the coming war, which most Americans now accepted as inevitable. The Continental Congress called for a true continental army to gather around Boston and was not subtle in selecting the Virginian George Washington as its commander-in-chief. The Congress also called upon other provinces to go to the aid of the current New England army besieging Boston. Maryland answered this call by recruiting two rifle companies for service before Boston.

Christopher was at Hungerford's the day Dugan Fife, a lower county boy who had gone west to become a backwoodsman, stopped by the tavern on his way to Frederick Town, and regaled the patrons on how Maryland riflemen were making the journey way up north just to show the regulars *and* those Eastern farmers how real fighters finish off their enemies.

"Yep, goin' to join Cresap and git me a bunch of redcoat scalps, I am." Fife assured his audience. "Always envied the Frenchies gettin' all those chances to shoot regulars–men dumb enough to stand in line waitin' to be kilt, with pockets filled with hard round coins fer the takin'—no have-bits nor paper money, no siree. And those farmers up there couldn't kill but have of 'em...no offense intended, neighbors; it ain't *farmers* I'm critercisin', but *Yankee* farmers, ye realize.

"Shit," Dugan Fife expelled the word just before he sucked in a great gulp of rum, compliments of his enthralled audience. Smacking his lips, he shook his head so that his lanky locks whipped around, looking like the snaky hair of Medusa.

Fife wondered aloud just how bad Yankee marksmanship could be. "I mean, ye're given a hill to stand on and fire down on a line of waddlin' ducks, fer God's sake. How kin ye *not* fail to kill every damn one of 'em? I ask ya! But nooo, them fellas caint kill thorough-like, but enough of 'em are left to drive our boys from a hill which they shouldn've been able to climb in the first place!

"There it is—plain as truth. Now, its sartin we Marylanders are needed up there to put an end to this business. An' we'll do it in no time. Why, even the Virginie riflemen goin' up there to help us out will do fine…yes, sar!"

Dugan Fife made quite an impression on these backwoods farmers. Though his leather hunting shirt and leggings were filthy and poorly patched, with much of the fringe torn off and the once finely rendered bead and quill embroidery reduced to bits and pieces, Dugan was still an imposing figure. While his apparel was considerably worse for wear, he carried himself with an easy grace, and cradled in his sensitive hands was a beautiful longrifle, which stirred a man's blood same as a woman and seemed a perfect harmony of beauty and deadliness.

"With bold men like Dugan Fife," they all assured each other, "how can we be defeated by men who fight only for the King's dirty shilling?"

****

Farming and war…Christopher hated his toil, hated the farming and militia drill and the preparations he must make before he left for Baltimore. All conspired to prevent him from going after Hannah. The weeks became a month, and still he had responsibilities to meet before he could leave.

"Each day brings with it a new pang," he said one day, feeling a particular sense of urgency.

"Don't despair, Christopher." His sister-in-law Susan said this in her usual gentle and understanding way. "The Good Book says God 'has appointed a time for every matter, and for every work.' And that includes a time to seek and a time to love. Ye do believe that don't you, Christopher?"

"Aye, Susan, I do," he sighed. "Each in its own good time, was the way mother used to put it."

"Your mother was right and would approve your patience, Chris."

His mother also used to say patience is the only cure for impatience.

There is a time for every matter under heaven, which is an excuse for being patient, he concluded. You have to believe that at a time like this or go mad, Christopher supposed, because impatience can rack the soul like the mad dog disease can rack the body.

There is a time to plant, and a time to pluck up what is planted: didn't he know that as a sot-weed farmer.

There is a time for war, and a time for peace: this country has never known peace.

There is a time to embrace, and—

—Two weeks later, finally a time for Christopher to seek a new life with Hannah....

13

THE ADVENTURE OF AN UNCERTAIN FUTURE

On the Baltimore Road
July 31-August 1, 1775

THE THREE TEAMSTERS who had tippled themselves into a stupor the evening before—and ended up sleeping in front of the fire in the great room—were long gone as the Sims party arrived at Hungerford's. Here Christopher would hitch a ride with Doctor Wootton, who was that same day traveling to Baltimore on committee business.

John Paul remained outside, hand on hip and wooden sword pointing forward leading an imaginary charge just as Lieutenant Tune did the other day at militia practice. George and Christopher entered the long room. They saw Doctor Wootton as he sat in comfortable solitude breakfasting, while Sally scoured the floor with wet sand and stone. Mary Hungerford, not yet recovered from the teamsters' merrimake, threw them a tired greeting from behind the slatted enclosure of the little barroom tucked in the rear corner.

"Thank you for your kindness in allowing me to accompany you, Doctor Wootton," said Christopher, as he seated himself in a chair at the Doctor's table. Thomas Wootton was just finishing breakfast and offered George and Christopher a noggin before they set out, which they gladly accepted.

"Kindness?" Doctor Wootton laughed. "Kindness has nothin' to do with it, Christopher. I need a strapping young man with me in case the damn'd chaise gets stuck in one of the fords." Wootton had little confidence in the province's backcountry roads.

Finishing their rum, and with a farewell for Christopher from Mary Hungerford and Sally, they started on their way. Christopher's belongings were tied onto the rack behind the seat along with Doctor Wootton's portmanteau.

And just like that the time for parting had come. With smiles that looked like grimaces, the Sims men said goodbye, and Christopher set off with Doctor Wootton on the road to Baltimore.

Unfamiliar with the art of sitting on a chaise, Christopher shifted his weight abruptly, almost tilting over the two-wheeled vehicle. "For heaven's sake, man, don't rustle about like that! It's delicately balanced, if you see what I mean." Christopher now realized that this cart would be as easy to overturn as a canoe. He inwardly cringed at the idea of swaying in tandem with Doctor Wootton for two days.

"Should I assume that you don't know how to manage one of these?" asked Doctor Wootton. "Of course you don't. Well, you'll learn, startin' now. Here, take the reins an' hold them like this. Keep 'em loose on flat stretches and the horse will set its own pace. See?"

They soon passed Rock Creek Chapel and the small cabin which served as the parish, now empty and forlorn, their current abandonment a symbol of the community's political and social distress.

As they passed the chapel, Doctor Wootton looked at Christopher. "So, you're going to claim your young woman, Christopher?"

"I am, Doctor Wootton."

"Well, good for you. Every other young man in the hundred seems hell-bent on going off to war with that miscreant Dugan Fife. Good to know there are a few sensible men hereabouts.

Never understood why young men would leave young women to go off to war."

Christopher laughed. "Well, I'll tell you, Doctor Wootton, *if* it wasn't for a certain young woman, *this* young man would very likely be tempted to go off to war with our riflemen. Trouble is, I'm not very good with a rifle and I'm certainly not good at skulkin' around woods with no obvious path, talents which I gather Price and Cresap are lookin' for in the men wanting to join their companies."

Soon the narrow, rutted road twisted and inclined sharply downhill toward Rock Creek and both Christopher and Doctor Wootton stopped talking to concentrate on maneuvering the chaise as it sped downward.

"Now pull up on the reigns, Christopher, so the horse will slow its pace a bit—we don't want to go barrelin' down the hill. And push down on the brake to slow the wheel… like this."

Christopher quickly got the hang of it. They descended the hill at a comfortable speed and forded the creek, the wheels sliding precariously on the uneven, mossy rocks.

Despite the generally fast roads over which they careened, the journey to Baltimore took them into the next day, which allowed Doctor Wootton to discuss, advise, and lecture Christopher on a mind-boggling range of topics, most of which the latter hadn't known existed.

For the better part of the first day, Christopher was entertained by Doctor Wootton's conversation and by the excitment of finally realizing his dream of adventure and the anticipation of seeing Hannah again; but by the end of the day he was mentally exhausted from Doctor Wootton's questioning, and physically exhausted from being buffeted about as the chaise jumped and slipped over rocky and rutted roads. He couldn't wait for the journey to end.

His flagging enthusiasm was temporarily renewed when they stopped that evening at the Sandy Spring home of Richard Brooke, a Quaker and the wealthiest man in the county. As Christopher turned the horse into the driveway leading up to "Brooke Grove," he saw a large ungainly house, actually two houses connected together, one of logs and plaster with a hip roof, the other of stone with a sharp-pitched roof, the two forming a mongrel house so typical of this part of Maryland.

The conversation was cash crops, the state of the province's finances (not good), and, of course, the polemics between Great Britain and its colonies, the latter causing much concern for Richard Brooke, who did not want to see the Friends unfairly punished for their humane beliefs.

Doctor Wootton glanced at Christopher. "You'll have to forgive us, Christopher, such mundane things occasionally interfere with the rousing business of waging war," Doctor Wootton stated with mock solemnity.

What did fascinate Christopher was the house, the largest he had ever seen, even larger than Doctor Wootton's or the Griffiths' houses. It was full of polished wood, wall paper hangings of trees and flowers in bright colors, crystal chandeliers and colorful Turkey carpets with wonderful designs. This must be a palace, he decided. He even had his own bedroom for the night, with a commode chair set near the scotch-coal fire.

Dinner took place in a spacious room softly illuminated by dozens of imported candles: set in a glass chandelier, wall sconces, and strategically placed candlesticks, the small flames reflecting off cut-glass crystals or through faceted glass vessels to bathe the room in a pale yellow light, the flames sparkling and dancing over red walls. *Spell-binding*, Christopher thought, even as hot wax from the candles above dripped on the tablecloth and his sleeve. He also had his first taste of cognac, a heady drink made more memorable by Wootton's remark that he imagined Aphrodite's breast milk might taste like this.

A pleasant interlude, indeed, but early the next morning, they were back on the road again. For Christopher, it had already become tiresome as the chaise clattered in concert to the staccato thumps of the horse's stride, carrying an increasingly anxious young man further and further from home and closer and closer to his love.

They had left behind Frederick County long ago, passed through Anne Arundel County, then into Baltimore County, crossing two rivers in the doing. They waited two hours to cross the Patapsco at a ferry whose grubby public house lay in a weed-grown clearing full of trash and broken bottles, its interior consisting of a few crude table boards and benches, serving greasy stew and rot gut. The ferry itself was little more than a flat-bottomed scow, coming apart at its seams, which by means of a cable and pulley was heaved forward by the man in the bow, to hopefully reach the other side.

Late on the second day, they finally crested a rise and Christopher had a panoramic view of Baltimore. What he saw did not impress him after everything he had heard about this town.

Oh, it was large enough, all right—Doctor Wootton had told him that Baltimore had more than five hundred houses and near seven thousand inhabitants—but it was disordered in appearance and not pleasing to the eye. Located in a small stream valley and hemmed in by clay hills covered with trees, with muddy marshes and water on three sides, the town originally comprised sixty acres and was laid out in the shape of an arrowhead with its head pointing westward like a providential sign, its notches formed by a looping stream called Jones Falls and the harbor basin.

By 1775, Baltimore had expanded by half, or perhaps a little more; but more than forty years after its founding it still gave the appearance of being half-finished and slow to develop, as if its future was still in doubt. It was a fact that Baltimore was not well-situated as a port for the tobacco trade and farmers of corn, wheat, and hay avoided the stream valleys of Baltimore County in favor of the open lands of the Piedmont.

As a result, the town struggled to find a purpose until people realized that its rapidly descending streams could drive powerful mills. So precipitous was their flow in and around town that streams were not referred to as such but were called "falls," and they gave Baltimore not only its unique character but unexpected commercial power. As the tobacco lands wore out and farmers came to depend on wheat as their new cash crop, ten flour mills sprang up on Jones Falls alone and Baltimore came to dominate the flour trade. Even Pennsylvanians brought their grain down here instead of shipping it to Philadelphia or to the port of Wilmington in Delaware.

Commenting on this same prospect, Doctor Wootton said, "It's a dirty, presumptuous town of no great character. But believe it or not, Christopher, it *is* one of the largest cities in British North America. Indeed, New York, Philadelphia, Boston, and, as I recollect, only one other city are larger. Oh, those cities are far more magnificent and are populated by tens of thousands of people—and even Annapolis, which is smaller than Baltimore, is much more elegant. Still, Baltimore is becoming one of the most important ports in the colonies."

As they descended, Christopher began to make out the town's general plan and distinguish a number of significant landmarks and buildings. "It appears to have a great many crooked little streets lined with crooked rows of little houses, and only a few large buildings. And I don't see any large vessels, either," he said with obvious disappointment.

"Most of the ships drop anchor lower down at Fell's Point, which ye can't see from here. The town isn't directly on the Chesapeake Bay, y'know. That small harbor is the 'Basin,' then you have the 'Harbor' where Fell's Point is located, then the Northwest Branch of the Patapsco River, and finally the Bay itself."

As they entered Baltimore proper, it began to have the feel of a real city. The hodgepodge of buildings seen from a distance now appeared as shops with painted signs advertising a variety of fascinating goods and services; more people than Christopher had ever seen in one place walked the narrow, unpaved streets; and rows of small wooden houses, a great number of them only one story, painted white and blue and yellow, if painted at all. Many of the structures were in odd relation to each other and the street, "like our militia company trying to line up properly," Christopher said with a laugh.

After soliciting directions to the house of Christopher's aunt on Lovely Lane, they finally drew up before a two-story wooden house painted blue, and the two men separated, with a parting word from Doctor Wootton.

"Well, Christopher, here ye are! Now, find your young woman and don't ever let her go." Doctor Wootton had a faraway look in his eyes as he gave this advice, apparently remembering something deep in his past.

"I certainly will do that, sir," was all Christopher could come up with in response.

"Well, fare thee well, Christopher Sims."

"And you, Doctor Wootton."

Christopher untied his belongings and walked away from the chaise. As he stood near the door of his aunt's house, he watched intently as Doctor Wootton disappeared down the street.

Christopher knocked on the door.

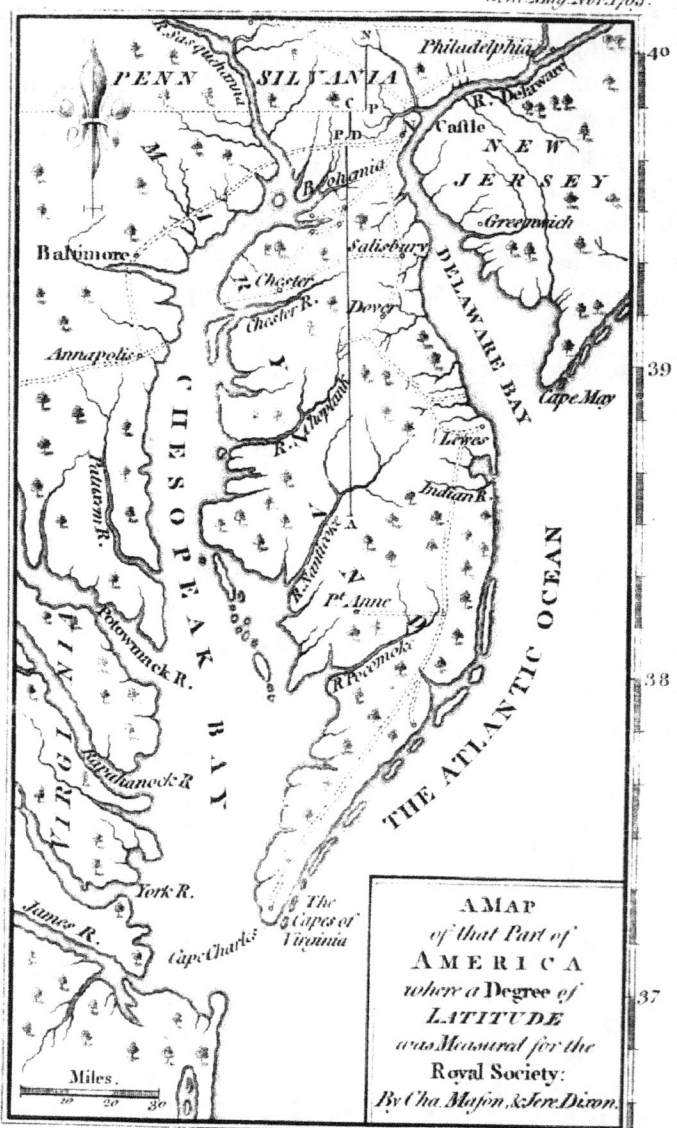

The Eastern Shore of Maryland in 1775

Courtesy of the Maryland State Archives SPECIAL COLLECTIONS (Huntingfield Collection) Charles Mason and Jeremiah Dixon, *A Map of that part of America where a Degree of Latitude was Measured for the Royal Society*, 1769. MSA SC 1399-1-227.

Part Two

The Perfect Crisis

... tell me, whether you can hereafter
love, honor, and faithfully serve the
power that hath carried fire and sword
into your land?

Common Sense, Anonymous, 1776

14

HIS MOTHER'S SON

Lovely Lane
Baltimore Town
Mid August 1775

AFTER WATCHING Doctor Wootton disappear down Lovely Lane, and after a befuddled look at the strange new world in which he found himself, Christopher's knock on the door led to it being opened by his aunt, who half expected him but was pleasantly surprised anyway.

Jane Everett was Ruth Sims' younger sister, and she turned out to be a delightful person, whose enthusiasm and warmth overwhelmed Christopher. Far from feeling nostalgic, he felt perfectly at home, almost as if his mother had not passed away all those years ago. At thirty-seven, his Aunt Jane was growing old gracefully. She still retained her figure, although it had never made much of an impression on men even when she was in her prime. While her dark brown hair was graying, it retained the fullness and luster of youth; and her large, round eyes were blue and sharp with intelligence. It was her nose, however, an exact duplicate of his mother's nose, a grand Romanesque ornament, which made Christopher feel he was in the presence of family.

After sitting him down in one of her arm chairs in the parlor, she fetched him a rum, and then proceeded to drill him on the family.

A little later, staring at him, she said, "Well, Christopher, I can't say you look like your mother's side of the family." Aunt Jane tapped her nose, "Fortunately I should add. Heavens, I haven't seen you since...well, your mother's funeral." She waved her arm in a dismissive fashion. "What I want to say is that you're a man now."

"Twenty years of age, Aunt Jane."

"Well, it is certainly good to see you again after all these years. Now, Christopher, tell me your plans. After reading George's letter, I was convinced that if and when you showed up, you'd have a young bride with you."

"I wish that were the case, Aunt Jane," He then told her the story...

"...and that's what brought me here."

"So, your young lady is bound to this Reverend Crabbe, who is staying with the Reverend Johnson at St. Paul's here in town. Well, my advice to you, Christopher, is that you don't dash off to see Hannah, because you don't want to confront the Reverend Crabbe."

"I guess I have to agree with that."

"Good. Let me make a discreet inquiry or two. I know several ladies who are active at St. Paul's and I should think I can obtain accurate information on Hannah's situation without raising any eyebrows. How's that?"

"Thank you for offering to do this, Aunt Jane."

"Oh, I couldn't do otherwise. This reminds me of the time I was a country girl and met Francis—my dearly missed husband—and ran off with him to live in a real town full of people and excitement. I can't imagine spending a lifetime, as your mother did, in the backcountry tending those demanding little tobacco plants." She glanced sheepishly at her pipe lying on the table as she said this. Aunt Jane, thought Christopher, was not like the serious widows and aunts he knew back home.

The next day, while his aunt tended to her commerce—she owned a successful variety and trimmings business—Christopher spent most of the day wandering around Baltimore, curious to experience the multitudinous and seemingly frenetic activities of town life.

Though Baltimore was a raw provincial town not to be compared to Philadelphia or New York, its population was quite cosmopolitan and its economy thriving; at the same time, it was also a quaint little place which even had a "town wall" to the north, erected as protection not against attack by human enemies but rather from wandering cows!

As Doctor Wootton had pointed out, Baltimore Town was unprepossessing, mostly small frame houses seemingly arranged at random, and only a handful of larger public buildings—two imposing inns, the assembly hall, and the county courthouse. Dirt streets were variously dust or soup, depending on the weather, with rivulets of foul water from slop and ordure buckets eroding the surface; between the wagon ruts, the wagons themselves, horses, and people, Christopher found it difficult (if not hazardous) navigating the streets.

To a farmer who grew up in the fresh, pristine lands of western Maryland, the odors of Baltimore were so powerful that they seemed to physically strike him, as if he spent all day in the outhouse on a hot, summer day; but this vied with other, more attractive smells, too, like fresh paint, or perfumed women, or the smell of cooking foods, all wafting pleasantly in the light breeze.

Christopher soon changed his first impression of Baltimore, admitting that it *was* indeed a fascinating place.

He strolled along Market Street looking at window displays and shop signs, then up Calvert Street to the courthouse, with its tapered roof ending in a lookout and tall spire topped by a wonderful weathercock. In back, he stood on the promontory overlooking the Ravine, with Jones Falls below and Jones Town across the way. "Now, Jones Town is a den of iniquity, Christopher Sims," Aunt Jane had pointed out the night before, as she enthusiastically described Baltimore's expanding

commercial and entertainment districts, "which I'm certain you'll
come to know all too well before you leave this town."

He carefully avoided St. Paul's Lane, knowing that the
temptation to seek out Hannah would be too great and might
lead to disaster. He did not come all the way to Baltimore to lose
her again just because of his impatience.

A Night Out On The Town

A couple of days later, Aunt Jane took Christopher to her
favorite tavern for a memorable meal of Bay seafood and good
drink. Almost too consumed with his crab cakes to talk, he did
manage to describe his adventures and impressions of Baltimore.

They also discussed politics, a subject upon which Aunt Jane
proved well-informed—at least to a twenty-year old rural man.

"Doesn't surprise me at all," said Aunt Jane. They had been
talking about his brother George's lukewarm embrace of the
cause. Nonchalantly removing a piece of shell from the food she
was chewing and placing it carefully on her plate, she continued.
"Knowing how much George is like your father, Christopher, I
know he is too practical to be a rebel, and too realistic to be a
revolutionary."

Christopher looked at her quizzically, but said nothing.

"Oh, I know your brother well, young man! He's perfectly
happy with the liberties we've secured under the colonial
government and the British Constitution. What does 'taxation
without representation' and such mean to backcountry
inhabitants? On the other hand, 'liberty' means makeshift
governments—no government at all, actually, which is what we
have now—and that means *abridgment* of rights. He can't see
beyond that, 'cause he needs set boundaries to his life. George is
jus' like your father. Now, you're more like your mother...."

Christopher laughed. "Aunt Jane, mother used to tell me,
particularly when she was angry with me, that I was the spittin'
image of *you.*"

Jane laughed. "So, you're your aunt's son, are you!"

"And you, Aunt Jane. What persuasion are you?"

Jane Everett hesitated, wanting to give this question the dignity of a well considered answer.

"Christopher, I'm not at all sure that there is a right or a wrong involved in this dispute…But, I do believe we Americans need to be unshackled to realize our true potential. Now, those are just my thoughts on the matter."

He mulled this over as both of them concentrated on their meal. The crab cakes were delicious, the delicate flavor of the meat enhanced by the mayonnaise and seasonings. He had seen these blue crabs alive and scrappy at the fishmongers' stalls down around the inner harbor; monstrous creatures, some a foot across, out of their element and scratching around in their splint oak baskets, their claws hoisted in self-defense.

When they were ready to resume their conversation, he prompted her away from talk of politics by asking about Baltimore's streetlights, a fascinating thing he had heard about from Doctor Wootton.

"Streetlights? Why, there are some around the Fountain Inn, but that's about it. Baltimore *should* have streetlights, just like it should have paved streets like any other proper city…embarrassing it doesn't. But sure, you ought to see 'em."

In the failing light, they began to retrace their steps in the direction of Aunt Jane's house. As night set in, the town disappeared in darkness; to see their way, pedestrians had to rely upon the dim light cast by candles in windows or carry tin lanterns, the light beaming through perforated holes, which give the streets an eerie, trembling glow.

She took Christopher round to the Fountain Inn, where Doctor Wootton stayed while in town, to see these streetlights— oil lamps hung from posts higher than a man—which bathed the cobbled sidewalk and planted trees in front of the Inn in a comforting light. "Now, this isn't anything compared to Philadelphia, where every street in the city is illuminated at night, if you can imagine that. But it gives you the idea, doesn't it?"

As they continued on their way, they saw a commotion further up on Market Street, near South Lane, and stopped to investigate. At first Aunt Jane thought it might be a fire, which was a common occurrence in this town of crowded wooden structures. "If that's the case, you'll soon see the Mechanical Company trot out its new 'fire engine' which spews water from a cannon. Simply amazing."

However, what they had first taken as a destructive fire turned out to be firebrands carried by a small but raucous crowd which was gathered in front of a three-story brick building. They then heard the sound of breaking glass as objects were hurled at windows.

"Uh oh," said Aunt Jane. "It looks like they're goin' after Mary Katherine again."

"What?—who…?" Christopher began to ask.

"Mary Katherine—Missus Goddard. She owns the *Maryland Journal* newspaper."

"Oh, sure. Hungerford's Tavern often has the *Maryland Journal* for readin'. What's this all about?"

"Christopher, let's go see if we can help, and I'll explain later." The two of them hurried toward the crowd, arriving just in time to see it being dispersed by the watch.

"Move along, move along, gents. We don't go 'round breaking windows and acting un-neighborly, now do we? Move along, move along." The two watchmen were not armed and therefore the use of force was their choice of last resort, particularly in the case of civil disobedience, a relatively new phenomenon; instead, they used their now waning authority as law enforcement officers and cajolery to persuade this small crowd to move on.

As a stone or clod bounced off the building and just missed a window, one of the watchmen confronted the culprit. "Tom Skerrit, you scum, I know you. Tomorrow we could be talking to your master and ye might be applying your wages to fix broken windows instead of towards that cheap gin you swig all day long. Ye, too, MacGregor—if the two of you don't move away from here now!"

The two young men, both mechanics out for an inexpensive evening of mischief, saw no reason to push their luck and, after yelling a few final epithets at the building, quickly departed the scene. Now leaderless, those remaining quickly followed.

Christopher and his aunt had to step quickly out of the way as the frustrated men walked past them down the street, at least temporarily discouraged from causing more trouble. That was the best the watch could do in these times—break up groups of mischief makers and hope that their timely presence would discourage such ill behavior. Not that such people could be easily discouraged.

It was obvious to Christopher that the group, as it aggressively elbowed its way past him, was looking for a fight, particularly one fellow, a small, misshapen man, with a forehead which protruded over sunken eyes, and a large beak for a nose hiding a little mouth. *What a strange looking person,* Christopher thought, *with—what—the look of a scavenger?*

"Well, that solves that problem," Aunt Jane concluded. "Now, let's see if Mary Katherine is in need of some assistance." Nodding to the watchmen, who were about to resume their rounds, Aunt Jane pulled Christopher through the door.

Inside, he saw a woman and an elderly man bustling about cleaning up broken glass. As they entered, the woman looked up worriedly as she heard feet crushing glass.

With a relieved look and a wan smile, Missus Goddard exclaimed, "Well, if it isn't Jane Everett—and I was fearful the savages might be inside the blockhouse. How are you, dear?" As she was saying this with apparent good humor, Missus Goddard was bending over to sweep some shards onto some paper.

"Well, I'm doin' fine, indeed, Mary Katherine." Not forgetting her manners, Jane Everett properly introduced Christopher.

"How do ye do, Mister Sims," the woman said in obvious distraction, but with a warm smile.

"What was that all about, Mary Katherine?" Jane asked.

Mary Katherine Goddard was a tall, angular woman with a large nose and thin lips, which were always curved in a gentle smile as she spoke—no matter how pointedly. She wore a simple dress and bodice, with an unnecessary modesty piece, all well-stained by printer's ink, and her head was covered by a lace cap which more or less contained riotous strands of dark hair. She had a strident voice and blazing brown eyes which seemed to aim her words toward their target.

A headstrong woman, Mary Katherine Goddard had assumed sole responsibility for publishing *The Maryland Journal and Baltimore Advertiser* in 1775 when she and her brother became estranged, and he had gone off to Annapolis to run another newspaper. Radicals by a different standard, Mary Katherine and William felt compelled to editorialize on every unworthy absolute uttered by king or loyalist or patriot, thus irritating a good cross section of her readers.

"Oh, who knows," Mary Katherine shrugged. "I might have irritated our local Committee...then again, maybe I've just become the neighborhood whipping boy."

"Well, Mary Katherine, it's often hard to tell whose side you're on, you know. Ye might want to set 'em straight." Jane Everett said this as she grabbed the broom from Missus Goddard's helper and began to sweep energetically; and at the same time, she instructed Christopher to help the old man pick up the small pieces of metal type which had dropped from the latter's nervous hands when the first object struck a window.

"Of course I'm a patriot, on the assumption that we Americans can foul up civil society just as good as the British, and we can do it without all the pomp and circumstance...*and* at half the cost in taxes and patronage. And I've said that in no uncertain terms, so I doubt its outraged patriotism that motivates these shallow-brained huffs."

"See, *that's* exactly what I mean, Mary Katherine. What do you expect when you go on like that?"

"Intelligent discourse," the other woman said simply.

In short order, the print shop was back to normal and Missus Goddard was anxious to return to her composition. Thanking both, she promised to have supper on next Friday with Jane and sent Christopher off with a copy of *The Maryland Journal* and an invitation for him to visit so that she could thank him properly for his help.

By the time they returned to the house, it was late evening. "Christopher, I think you and I could use a bit of whiskey, eh?" Aunt Jane poured two generous cups and gave one to Christopher; as she did, she asked, "Well, young man, what do you think of town life?" Christopher shook his head in amazement, matching her wry chuckle with a like smile.

As he took a deep draft of his drink he heard a feminine voice say, "Good heavens, the two of you have certainly made a night of it." Looking up he saw a woman descending the stairs.

Aunt Jane quickly made introductions. "Ah, Christopher, this is Missus Jones who is presently boarding here. Missus Jones, this is Mister Christopher Sims, my nephew from Frederick County, who'll be staying with us for a time."

The three exchanged pleasantries, after which Aunt Jane described their day's adventures, detailing their brush with the uncivil gang in front of Missus Goddard's print shop. "The rats had waddled out of the garbage pits tonight!"

The latter event caused Missus Jones considerable discomfort. "Imagine the watch simply *asking* them to leave. What have we come to if we allow such lawlessness? Even I and other solitary women have been accosted just walking down the street. Makes you wonder about our ability to govern ourselves, doesn't it?"

"Now, Rachel—"

"Well, *really*, Jane. These gangs call themselves 'the Sons of Liberty' or other such patriotic labels, but are nothin' more than bullies and common rakehells."

Christopher's initial impression of Rachel Jones, reinforced as he glanced at her from time to time, was that she was *somehow* attractive. She was an older woman, perhaps in her late twenties, and everything about her was unusually colorless, like a vague but pleasant memory: fair skin; light blue eyes, with faint webs of lines which age was spinning around the corners; and ashen blond hair. Her face was pleasing to look upon but too full to be comely, and she had a strange nose—a little too spread with an odd little crease at the very tip.

In contrast to her indifferent physical appearance, however, Rachel Jones had direct, intelligent eyes which displayed a keen interest in their subject; a soft, kindly smile; and a way of speaking, a lilting hesitancy, as if her thoughts distracted her speech, which was unusually sensual. Christopher was also very much aware of her hands, which moved as she spoke, as if she were using them to shape her words.

After Aunt Jane and Rachel vented their distress over the growing lack of order in Baltimore, the three engaged in small talk for a short while before the day's activities finally took their toll on Aunt Jane and Christopher's interest in social chatter. Realizing this, Rachel said that she must retire, and, together, all three climbed to the second floor, where goodnights were exchanged; and with that, Rachel and Aunt Jane went to their rooms, while Christopher climbed one more flight to his little room in the attic.

Making sure the small window was open to allow a draught, Christopher undressed to his long, loose shirt. Making himself comfortable on the small straw mattress, he fluffed his pillow, wrapped himself in a blanket, and lay on his back, thinking about his experiences since leaving home just a couple of days ago.

He then reached for his rucksack and rummaging in it drew out Hannah's note. Reaching out, he pulled the candle closer to his face, and, bending toward the light, opened the folded paper. By now, the creases, being folded and unfolded so many times, had torn and the single page was now in two halves, and would soon be in quarters. Ever so carefully he opened the letter and read her writing again. The note was her physical presence and never ceased to excite him, which was why he read it only at night, just before he drifted off to sleep.

Finally he folded the paper and carefully put it back in his rucksack. He then turned on his stomach and fell off to sleep, imagining that in a day or two he would be reunited with Hannah.

15

A SECRET PLOT

The Rectory, Saint Paul's Church
Baltimore Town
July 25, 1775

THE RECTORY HAD BEEN BUILT of heavy, gray fieldstone which, with the leaded windows so loved in Anglican church architecture, made the prelate's office damp and cool and hinting of moss. It was so very English. It gave the visiting official from the Society for the Propagation of the Gospel in Foreign Parts the happy feeling that he was home in England.

He was dressed in a black suit—in fact, his extensive wardrobe consisted only of black suits. The shoulders of this black suit were sprinkled with white powder from his hair.

"You say this man's name is 'The Vulture?'" The S.P.G official asked the prelate. "What, pray tell, shall we read into the character of a man with such a name?"

The Society official was a gray eminence even to those who knew and respected him. He was from a wealthy London family who felt a need for the discipline of the Established Church, and found his true calling in the Society for the Propagation of the Gospel in Foreign Parts; which combined the dignity of the

Anglican religion, the absolutism of the Crown government, and, best of all, political conspiracy, all in one delicious guise.

The prelate was self-assured in his response. "As you know, Your Excellency, we English have proven ourselves quite adept at the art of espionage. *I* suspect it's because we have learned how to use riffraff in the service of the Crown rather than simply exterminate them for their petty crimes."

"So, Reverend, you intend to use this"—he searched for a suitable noun—"this *creature* to carry sensitive information between the two of us?" The S.P.G. official was incredulous. "Is the Crown so desperate that we must depend upon such demi-men?"

"Now, now, Your Excellency," said the prelate soothingly, "It is, after all, the mission of the Church to save the sinner. This 'Vulture,' as he is called, has been tested as a courier and will suffice until he is called upon by God to pay for his sins. In the meantime, let him earn a little forgiveness by serving his king. And actually, he's not so bad; but you can judge for yourself since he is waiting in the anteroom for our orders."

The other man thought about this, finally deciding, "I'll accept your assurances, Jonathan. But I do not want him or any like him coming here again."

"Fair enough. I will use a cut-out. Perhaps under the sanction of a petticoat. I have one or two young women in mind. Let me think on that."

"Good. Now, What think you of the Reverend Crabbe?"

"Roger? A good man. A provincial who is absolutely loyal to the Crown."

"Yes, but a very angry man. Can we trust that his emotions will not get the better of him and risk our grand plan? The mission we have in mind for him requires...well, a carefully calculating mind."

"He'll do fine, Your Excellency."

The S.P.G. official smiled, wanting now to end this discussion on a positive note. "Jonathan, you're doing great service to our government and to England." He grasped the other man's arm affectionately. "Now, let's talk to this 'Vulture', shall we?"

16

A TERRIBLE BLOW

Lovely Lane
Baltimore Town
August 23, 1775

WITHIN DAYS Aunt Jane obtained news of Hannah and it was, when Christopher learned of it, the worst news he could imagine. He just returned from the bakers with the evening meat dish and found his Aunt Jane and Rachel in the parlor. With his entrance, the two women fell silent, and stared at him, as if looking at a deathly ill loved one.

With a crestfallen look, and nervously clasping hers hands, which was not like her at all, Aunt Jane suddenly grasped Christopher's hand, and clutching it tightly, said, "Christopher, I have disappointing news for you." Looking at Rachel, she almost pleaded, "Rachel, dear, would you please get us all a whiskey."

Taking a deep breath, Aunt Jane informed Christopher that Hannah and the Crabbe family had departed Baltimore over a week ago…"and according to my sources, Christopher, there is no definite word on their destination. I don't know what to say."

Christopher was stunned. Not only was Hannah not in Baltimore but he had no idea where to begin to look for her.

He slumped in one of the chairs, as Rachel handed him a glass of whiskey, "Good lord," was all he could muster.

"I'm so very sorry, Christopher," said Rachel. "But perhaps there will be news soon."

Christopher dismissed this with an irritated wave of his hand. "I will go and speak to the Reverend Johnson."

Aunt Jane looked alarmed. "Oh, my, Christopher, you mustn't do that! We have no idea why the Reverend Crabbe and family departed Baltimore so…precipitously, I guess is the right word."

"And I would add that disappearing with no word of their destination is suspicious, to say the least," Rachel added forcefully.

Christopher was up and pacing the small sitting room now. "Well, I've got to start somewhere—perhaps Annapolis. That is where Hannah is originally from…and, well, maybe a patriotic court there can help."

"A fool's errand, Christopher," said Rachel, with no effort at being placating. "What if the Reverend Crabbe doesn't want people to know where they are going? Or perhaps his superiors don't want anyone to know—there is much talk of an S.P.G conspiracy. What would it mean if you or anyone else started asking questions about their whereabouts?"

Rachel looked intently at Christopher, expecting him to see the sense in this. "Besides," she went on, "the one place Hannah knows you will be is here in Baltimore, and that's where you ought to be when she comes looking for you. But I've said enough," she said in finality. "Do what you think best."

****

A fool's errand. Would any attempt he made to recover Hannah be a fool's errand? He was reminded of the child's game "blind man's bluff," where the target moved in unseen ways and the blinded player lurched furtively here and there to no avail.

Fortunately, he listened to his aunt and to Rachel. He realized later that their advice was in his and, just as importantly, Hannah's best interests. It was hard to show his appreciation when their advice seemed so unhelpful, but at least Aunt Jane and Rachel appeared to understand this.

Still, the need to do *something* was overwhelming. Christopher sought desperately for information on Hannah's whereabouts. As the winds of rebellion increased and the surging tides of anger began to crash destructively upon the very foundations of society, Christopher considered the possibility of recruiting a gang to confront and bully the Reverend Johnson. He was a known loyalist and could no doubt be coerced into giving news of the Crabbe family's whereabouts if threatened with a drenching of tar.

Ah, but that would be a fool's errand. He remembered Rachel Jones's expression as she said this in response to his first fit of pique. In a later conversation, Rachel had been a little more measured in counseling caution: "You must make a life for yourself *and* for Hannah."

So be it. In the meantime, Christopher needed to find an outlet for his pent-up energy.

There was his developing friendship with Rachel Jones, which was beginning to impress upon him the importance of patience. But it also worried him a little bit, because when he was with Rachel or, now, even when he thought about her, he had the impression that he might be showing more patience than he ought to be.

Then, as both Aunt Jane and Rachel pointed out, he needed to set out making a life for himself, so that he could offer one to Hannah....

Visits to Missus Goddard's

"We do more than publish the *Journal and Advertiser*, Christopher," Missus Goddard said as she showed him around the first floor, filled with light from large windows, some of which still had empty panes from the breakage caused by the most recent demonstration.

Christopher had taken her up on her offer following that incident and occasionally visited her establishment to learn more about the printing and publishing trade, becoming more and more fascinated each time.

Here on the first floor, she pointed out, was the stationery and bookselling counter, a shelf of books for sale, and her counting "room," a corner of the room which included a desk piled high with sheets of paper, some written in her crabby hand which contained news of recent happenings, while others were advertisements, or letters to the editor, most of which would go into the next edition of the newspaper. Much of the news revolved around the issue of independence, pro and con, a matter which was causing increased consternation and tension around town.

While her newspaper was her first love, Missus Goddard was also a practical businesswoman.

"A printer couldn't stay in business if he just published newspapers or notices," she advised. "Most of my business comes from being the public printer for the town and county— you know, government forms and announcements, which are now ordered by the Committees of Observation." Missus Goddard stated this without enthusiasm. "Despite our occasional differences, they do business with me, and I with them. In truth, 'tis better business than most, which comes from people who can only offer country pay because there's a lack of ready money.

"In addition, the shop sells stationery, a few books, and pamphlets by subscription, and serves as a post office. Quite a diversity, isn't it? I know printers who even sell knick knacks or hire out to mow hay. A printer will do most anything to earn a shilling or two. But a printer's true passion ought to be the broadcastin' of information."

Missus Goddard said this with passion, and it struck Christopher that this was a noble vocation...*the broadcasting of information*, he thought, now that's a life's work.

She continued this train of thought. "Now, the trouble with publishing newspapers and pamphlets is you're caught in the middle of some pretty intense differences. You're damn'd if you do, damn'd if you don't. Patriots and kinsmen alike want their say at the expense of the other." She sighed contentedly, which apparently indicated both her disgust at men's inability to differ with each other in a civil manner *and* her relish for the resulting contentiousness.

Taking him down a rickety set of stairs, Missus Goddard showed Christopher the press and composing rooms in the basement. Her two presses occupied the center of the room, set on footings on a brick floor which was heavily spotted with droplets and smears of black ink. The smell of wet paper, moistened to take impressions, and the oily stink of ink permeated the air. Iron sconces on the walls supplemented the poor natural light provided by the half-windows.

The presses were quiet, but the sounds of metal scraping on wood and the clickety-clacking of metal against metal was heard as the old man set type in a composing stick. Christopher and Missus Goddard watched quietly as his hands rapidly roamed over the four partitioned trays, capital letters in the upper case, small letters in the lower case, selecting the appropriate sort to assemble the type in his stick.

"Henry is changing the galley for the next edition of the paper to accommodate new intelligence we just received from London concerning a speech by Mister Fox in Parliament." Missus Goddard added that Fox was pro-American in his outlook and opposed harsh measures against the North American colonies. "Anyway, Henry is in a rush and doesn't have the time to chatter with us. Next time you come, he'll have more time to show you how he goes about his work."

Missus Goddard came to treat Christopher like a favorite nephew. And after every visit, she would send him off with the latest edition of *The Maryland Journal,* or loan him one of the new pamphlets she had just printed.

Christopher looked forward to these visits to Missus Goddard's shop. Missus Goddard, herself, referred to her work as a "calling." Despite his riling at the class system, Christopher had always grudgingly believed that one was, unfortunately, born to his work. Now, for the first time in his life, Christopher began to *believe* that a man's lifework might actually be decided by choice, or even chance, but not necessarily by birth.

17

COUNTRYMAN TO TOWNSMAN

Baltimore Town
September 1775

AUNT JANE rarely spent afternoons at home. She would, however, make it a point to enjoy a late afternoon dinner with Christopher and Rachel. By the time Aunt Jane was finished with her shop work, dinner would be ready and waiting on the table. The meal and attendant conversation was enjoyed by all three, with Aunt Jane always taking the lead, pouring drinks and insisting that life had never been as enjoyable as it was now because she shared their company.

Like most of Baltimore's small townhouses, Aunt Jane's house did not have an adequate hearth for cooking. A sign of prosperity—and Aunt Jane's dream—was to add a kitchen ell onto the rear of the house; in the meantime, she and Rachel would go daily to the bread shop up the street and take meat and pies to the bakery there to be cooked. Other foodstuffs were bought as needed from the peddlers who came by, or on twice-weekly visits to the market house.

Christopher and Rachel now enjoyed doing these errands together, walking along Lovely Lane, past the single-story wooden boxlike houses with their single door and front window, past the equally small Methodist Church on the corner, dodging puddles and garbage. Frequently, they would stop to chat with the shopkeepers, vendors, and neighbors who had come out of their dark houses to enjoy the sun as they did their daily chores.

The more he got to know Rachel, the more fascinating he found this woman. This budding infatuation took him by surprise, and he thought it might be a sign of loneliness—because he truly missed Hannah, but he felt guilty nonetheless.

He hardly considered Rachel to be a handsome woman, and he did not dwell on the shape of her body. Rachel referred to herself as "stout," which was decidedly an exaggeration; but men who hadn't spent any time with her would hardly have given her a second look.

Yet her soft face, the purling sound of her voice, and her dancing hands all combined in an inexplicable way to dazzle him. Following some of his encounters with her, Christopher would go to sleep that night with a strange, tingling sensation . . . the echo of her pleasing voice and memories of her occasional touch creating a physical sensation on his skin, as if caressed by the pads of some invisible fingers.

One day Rachel had asked Christopher to carry a small trunk up to her room. It was a small cubicle filled with a bed, washstand, and a dainty chest above which was hung a mirror marred where the silver had worn off, her clothing hung on door and window lintels. Christopher had never been in such a concentrated female space. It had the overwhelming smell of a woman, an unnerving mingling of pleasant, fresh toilet waters and the medley of feminine odors which always lurked beneath those staid veneers. It was an intimate moment—a secret moment?—that reminded him of the day he found Hannah's garter in the abandoned chest in the loft of the rectory at Rock Creek. It was...a disturbing moment.

They would spend hours talking, mostly about themselves. Christopher learned that Rachel was from Annapolis and was a spinster by choice. She had just recently come to Baltimore with plans to open a girls' finishing school—Rachel was unusually well-educated for a woman. She told him she had a small inheritance, the source of which she did not expound upon, which she intended to use to rent a modest house in town and begin to advertise for pupils. In the meantime, she was boarding with Aunt Jane, whom she thoroughly enjoyed.

"Why haven't you married, Rachel?"

Rachel looked with amusement at Christopher, remembering what she thought about people ten years older than her when she was twenty years old. "Why, I haven't decided that I won't marry. At thirty, I'm not yet a dried-out old prune, am I, *sir*?"

"Rachel, I didn't mean it that way...."

"I know you didn't, Christopher," and she gave him a peck on the cheek to show she wasn't upset with him.

Actually Rachel was not married because she was not convinced that she would find happiness as some man's chattel. Once married, she realized, a woman can't change masters, even though the meanest servant may. *'Wife and servant are the same/But only differ in the name,'* she would sometimes quote Lady Chudleigh.

She tried to explain this to Christopher. "To acquire the status of *feme covert* with all the restrictions is asking too much of this body. Oh, that's a legal term which describes a woman's plight as a married person. Coverture means that a woman's identity is submerged in that of her husband's. Goes against my idea of 'American Liberty.' " Christopher understood the irony.

In fact, Rachel had spent most of her life as a man's mistress. She found that this particular arrangement (she thought of it as a "little marriage") suited her need for the spiritual growth and self-fulfillment which matrimony would no doubt deny her, while still allowing her to enjoy the pleasures of being with a man *and*, she admitted, an acceptable degree of financial freedom.

Rachel sensed Christopher's interest in her *and* his guilt at having that interest. One day out of the blue she said, "You know, my experience tells me that marital fidelity is hard enough to accept in the flesh, much less in the mind. We view natural emotion—dare I say lust—as base, and claim respect and friendship—but oddly not emotion—are reasonable basis for a man and woman to marry, even tho' copulation is the purpose of the institution. 'Tis a silly way of thinking—isn't it, Christopher?."

Rachel would make other inflammatory comments which disconcerted him, often when she appeared at her most prim and proper.

"Do ye know the punishment for fornication in Maryland, Christopher?" Trying to look terrified, she whispered, "'Tis death—indeed, it is!

"Well, actually," she conceded, "they won't put you to death anymore—seeing how we're living in such an enlightened age: nowadays, they just fine the man and…only *whip the woman on her naked back*." She emphasized the latter by clutching him as a frightened woman might do. Christopher's horrified look brought a delighted laugh from Rachel.

And Christopher would talk to Rachel about his and Hannah's dreams of a life together.

Rachel thoroughly enjoyed these conversations. They went on and on, but essentially, came down to practicalities.

"So, Christopher, you and Hannah planned on coming to town all the while?"

"We did. Hannah was from Annapolis and had fond memories of it, and, as you know, I had Aunt Jane here in Baltimore. Seemed like a good idea. Neither of us wanted to be sot-weed farmers."

Rachel laughed along with Christopher. "Well, I can appreciate that, but what did you—or, do you—have in mind as work here or in Annapolis?"

"Well, I'm developing a respect for the printing business. I spend a lot of time at Missus Goddard's shop and she might have need of some help for old Henry.

"She might indeed! And that's what you want to do?"

"I think so, Rachel. The idea of spreading information and ideas is exciting. When I was young, I wanted to be a surveyor of the wilderness. Thinking about it, the two aren't really that different, are they? After all, both deal with describin' the unknown, or that which is little understood."

Rachel hadn't thought of it that way, and said so.

Christopher also talked about the journey which brought him and Hannah to this point in their lives. Christopher's rendition of it reminded Rachel of one of those romance novels, *The History of Tom Jones*, which she had read to forget an elderly lover.

And so she said excitedly, "Ye put the coin in this hollow log and"—

—"No, no, Rachel, I just gave the coin to her and it was *Hanna who put a message in the log....*

"But this coin, which was your mother's—right?—had magical properties?"

"So she thought," Christopher said, perhaps not really believing it. He described the coin, giving its date, and the fact it had a hole bored through it so it could be worn around the neck.

Rachel turned serious. "I don't put much credence in talismans; but sometimes objects seem to take on the spirit of the giver...if you know what I mean. In such cases, they seem to work a peculiar form of magic."

Christopher shrugged. Either it was true or it wasn't true. "In any event, it was to be saved 'til it was really needed—'save it for the worst of times, Chris Sims,' was the way mother put it. And that's why I gave it to Hannah...so she would have a means to run away if she had to."

"Well, if used judiciously, Christopher, that Spanish milled dollar can bring her back to you. That's the important thing."

Fumbling With the Type
Missus Goddard's Shop,
On Market Street

In return for a payment of one shilling per diem, Christopher worked long hours at Missus Goddard's shop, trying to learn the printer's trade.

It was not rewarding work for a former farmer—not like erecting a fence or hunting turkeys. He began his new trade by returning each character from the imposing stone to its rightful compartment in wooden trays, learning the difference between

Roman and italic type. Laboring through this tedious business, Christopher realized it would be some time before he would be allowed to set a page, to actually create information that wasn't there before. He also practiced many of the other less skillful, but nonetheless necessary, tasks required to print a single page.

To break up the boredom, Missus Goddard would occasionally send Christopher out to drum up advertising which was very important to the success of a newspaper. So, Christopher would distribute handbills around town to solicit the business of those who wanted to buy or sell houses, land, goods or cattle, apprehend runaways, or whatever else a person wished to bring to public notice.

In truth, having done various petty tasks now for some weeks, Christopher wondered if he had the patience to become a master printer. However, every time he saw a finished newspaper, or pamphlet, or even a government form he realized with more and more certainty that this was what he wanted to do.

And so it went as Christopher learned a trade and immersed himself in plain old hard work which numbed his mind to the fact that Hannah had gone missing.

****

It was while laboring at Missus Goddard's that Christopher met Terrance Simon.

Terrence Simon was a regular customer and one day Missus Goddard decided to introduce Christopher to him.

"Mister Simon, I would like to introduce you to Jane Everett's nephew, Christopher Sims of Frederick County, way over there in western Maryland.

"Good grief, a frontiersman? I've never met one!" Terrence Simon said this in seeming awe, as he pumped Christopher's hand.

Christopher was not sure how sincere this young man was about meeting a frontiersman, and said, "Pleased to meet you, Mister Simon, but, in fact, I'm just a sot-weed farmer from that part of the country. Always wanted to be a frontiersman, but I was told I was not skilled enough at skulking around dark forests, nor was I a particularly good marksman!"

"What a pity. We could have written a wildly adventurous story about you on Missus Goddard's press here, and never minded what a pack of lies it was, but I do admire an honest man!"

The two chatted for a while and found that they rather liked each other despite their obvious differences.

At twenty-one, Terrence Simon was a bright man from a comfortable family. This would have made him much like his peers: privileged, coddled, groomed for leadership roles in the province of Maryland—except that Terry came from a Catholic family.

Terry was raised to be successful in business, or law, or medicine. But as a papist, whose family attended illicit Romish services stealthily held at the homes of prominent Baltimore Catholics, Terry understood that he could never aspire to be a political leader in the very province founded by Catholics for Catholics. So, it wasn't surprising that Terry became a political radical.

It didn't take long for Christopher to see Terry Simon's radical bent. After their initial meeting, the two men began to spend an occasional afternoon together at one of Terry's favorite coffee houses, to drink away the afternoons and engage in discussions which were always political and always emotional.

"...you see, Christopher"—they were quickly on a first name basis—"in *our* country, indentured servitude will be illegal. Even now, for crissake, the convention should empower the courts to declare null and void such legal agreements involving loyalists. In fact, the convention should go further and ban slavery of any kind. And I'm speaking here of black slavery, too. In fact," Terrance was on a roll now, "we should do away with the whole caste system perpetuated by the British upper class."

Such a radical idea was more than Christopher could fully absorb, but the idea of banning indentures would mean that

Hannah could be free now—and not almost two years from now. That was a radical idea he could support whole-heartedly.

In his former life, Christopher would have looked upon Terry Simon as being a gentleman. He was from a good Baltimore family, well-educated, and thoughtful in a droll sort of way. He was also a great reader and was introducing Christopher to the remarkable world of literature. But mostly the two men talked about politics and war with the mother country.

Terry Simon was a dyed-in-the-wool revolutionary. Men like Doctor Tylor and Mister Bayley back home might be strong independence men, but their vision was limited: Doctor Tylor, Christopher knew, disliked the upper class, while James Bayley's father craved a preeminent role as a member of that class. But Terry, Christopher soon realized, imagined a marvelous country: "Our country, Christopher, yours and mine, in which all citizens will experience the benefits of a perfect national creed: we Americans will not be subjects, we will have full individual rights, under a political system which avoids every past mistake. As citizens of this nation, we will be filled with the ideal of service to our fellow man and to our God, we will experience an ever-expanding intellectual enlightenment, and all will enjoy the great wealth of this bountiful land of North America. How's that sound?"

One day Terry Simon walked into Missus Goddard's shop in an elegant uniform—a regimental coat of red turned up in buff, white smallclothes, two pistols in his belt and a brass-hilted hanger carried in an elegant belt-frog covered in velvet and embroidered tape.

Missus Goddard and Christopher looked up from their work as Terrance entered, and the latter exclaimed, "My god, Terrance Simon, did you drink too much last evening with some loyalist pot companions who convinced you to join the British Army?"

"Why, I'm a member of the Baltimore Independent Cadets," he said proudly in response to Christopher's quip. "The company is under the command of Captain Gist. It was formed at the direction of the Convention in 1774.

"Captain Gist is Mordecai Gist in civilian life," Missus Goddard added, "and is a successful merchant and one of our most prominent citizens."

"It's a truly handsome uniform, Terrance," said Christopher appreciatively, before averting his admiring look to his own ink-stained linen shirt and country breeches, noting that even his shoes were spotted with ink.

"You'll be interested to know that I was a member of the 'Potomac Associators' under the command of Captain Henry Griffith, also formed at the direction of the Convention. How's that, general? Tho' I have to admit that our only uniform belonged to Lieutenant Tune and that consisted of an old British Army coat and buff belt-frog to hold his hunting sword!"

Terry laughed, adding, "Well, perhaps you would want to join the Cadets. 'Tis wonderful fun."

"Can't afford a good gun, much less your finery," Christopher confessed.

This sobered Terry. "Which reminds me this *is* serious business." Looking at both Christopher and Missus Goddard, "The Congress has established a Middle Department of the Continental Army and has requested that Maryland contribute regular troops—to include, if necessary, service outside the province. Captain Gist has formally volunteered the Independent Cadets. Should our company be so designated," challenging Christopher with a devilish grin, "the province will pay for your equipment, Christopher, should you want to join."

Missus Goddard showed her displeasure at Terrance's offer. "Terrance Simon, Christopher has better things to do than gallivant about with you young 'gentlemen of leisure'—and I use that term loosely."

18

A DISTURBING STORY

Lovely Lane,
Baltimore Town
October 10, 1775

THE YOUNG WOMAN sat uncomfortably on the edge of one of Aunt Jane's occasional chairs in the parlor, looking out of place in her old calico gown, aged linen apron, and coarse country-made shoes. Rachel was talking softly to her as Christopher entered the room.

"Ah, Christopher, this is Alma Lynch. She's the daughter of the caretaker at Saint Paul's Church. She has news of Hannah, and"—Rachel suddenly had a worried expression—"and a disturbing...well, story you need to hear."

The young woman perked up, now looking a little more like she had a purpose for being there. "You're Hannah's Christopher, then?" she asked anxiously.

"Aye, I'm Christopher Sims, and your servant, ma'am. You have news of Hannah? You know her whereabouts? I—"

"—Nay, sir," she interrupted nervously, "I don't...I'm sorry for that—but I do have information which may lead to her...I think...I really don't know...." She looked helplessly at Christopher and then at Rachel. "I want to help," she pleaded.

Rachel saw her rising distress and tried to calm her. "Alma, we know you want to help and we appreciate it. Let me get you some lemonade."

"Mister Christopher," Alma said, still sniffling but now composed, "Hannah Williams would have been my older sister and my best friend had she stayed. I don't know exactly why she had to leave, but I'm sure it had something to do with plans afoot to harm the patriot cause. I heard the Reverend Johnson say to the Reverend Crabbe, 'We must subvert this immoral rebellion before *it* subverts the king's authority.' That's exactly what he said, sir, and it sounded like a threat to me, and Hannah thought so to when I told it to her."

Rachel returned with lemonade for Alma, who took a deep gulp, before continuing.

"Thankee, ma'am...then, much later—after Hannah and the Crabbes had gone—the Reverend Johnson called me in to his office and talked to me about an important task he would give me. Then he commenced to tell me that I was duty bound to obey my King and the Church. I agreed that this was required of me as a loyal subject—even tho' I'm Irish," she added seriously. "Finally, I had to swear to follow his orders without fail.

"Then, he gave me a letter addressed to a Reverend John Scott in Annapolis and said, 'Alma, you are to deliver this letter to Tom Skerrit who lives in Dog Town and he'll see that it gets to Annapolis.' He reminded me that I had met Tom Skerrit the other day and ask't me if I remembered."

Alma shuddered, as if suddenly cold. "Indeed, I remembered this Tom Skerrit fellow and the first time he laid eyes on me he tried to...well, you know..." and Alma's voice drifted away.

"The Reverend Johnson told me to tell Tom Skerrit who the letter was from and he would know exactly what to do with it."

Christopher looked at Rachel, plainly mystified. "Very strange. Why on earth would church correspondence be sent in such a roundabout fashion, unless there is a sinister reason...."

Both Christopher and Rachel now realized why Alma might be suspicious and scared.

With a sigh of relief, she saw that they understood.

"I don't want to do anything wrong. Here's the letter. I'm asking you, Mister Christopher, for help in gettin' the letter to Tom Skerrit and maybe he'll know something about Hannah's whereabouts..." She left it at that, hoping it would be enough to get him to help her.

Christopher looked at the letter, which was a sheet or two of paper, folded and sealed with a wafer of red wax and pressed with arabesque letters.

"When's this letter supposed to be delivered, Missus Lynch?

"I got the impression I was supposed to get it to Tom Skerrit as soon as I could. After that, I don't know."

Christopher mulled this over. "Missus Lynch, leave the letter with me and I'll figure out a way to get it to this Skerrit fellow. Should the Reverend Johnson ask about the letter, tell him that you delivered it to Skerrit. If he learns different, then admit that you had asked a friend to deliver the letter for you. Say it was because this Tom Skerrit had mistreated you—which would be the truth. Now, how can I contact you in the next few days?"

Following Alma Lynch's departure, Christopher and Rachel discussed her visit and what it might mean. How it might help find Hannah was far more important to them than the strangeness surrounding delivery of some letter.

Shaking his head, as if the incident offered false hope at best, Christopher said, "I don't see the connection between Crabbe and the Reverend Scott. But perhaps I should go to Annapolis anyway and see—"

"No, Christopher. I have friends in Annapolis who can determine whether or not your Hannah is there, and they can do it without the risk of asking wrong questions."

Once again, Christopher's desire to take some action, any action, to find Hannah was frustrated by the good intentions of a friend. And once again, he saw the good sense in following a friend's advice.

Sighing, "So what do we do about this letter?" He held it up impatiently.

Rachel was obviously tired of the matter. "Oh, it could be important. I don't know. The Church of England and many of its officials are actively working against 'the rebellion' as they call it. Perhaps we should bring it to the attention of the authorities."

Rachel then thought about this, and added, "On the other hand, I don't want to cause that poor young woman any unnecessary trouble."

"Fair enough," agreed Christopher. "I believe Terry Simon has a relative on the county Committee of Observation. I'll mention it to him when I see him next."

For the time being, the incident was left at that.

****

It was several days before Christopher got around to mentioning the interview with Alma Lynch to Terrance Simon.

"So, what do ye think, Terry?" Both men were now using the diminutive of each other's name. "Rachel and I wonder if it might be some sort of loyalist plot."

Terry lazily dismissed any mystery surrounding the letter. Fingering the seal, he said, "Easy enough to determine, we'll just read the letter. Watch this." With that, Terry held a table knife to the candle flame and then simply slid the heated blade under the seal without damaging its impression, and the letter was open.

He grinned. "Wax seals make letters pretty, but not necessarily secure."

He unfolded the letter, which turned out to be two pages, and began to read. "Well, well...."

"Terry, for crissake, *what* does it say?"

"Don't know, Chris, it's in cipher." He handed the sheets of paper to his friend.

Christopher looked at the first, then the second sheet of paper and saw line after line of letters, long strings of letters with no end, no spaces, no punctuation, and the whole appearing nonsensical.

"What language is this?"

"English," was Terry's reply. When he saw Christopher's blank look, he explained with a smile. "My backcountry friend, what you see is writing transposed into cipher which makes no sense unless the reader possesses the same key as the writer."

Christopher glared at his friend. "Mister Simon, I can understand the Bible, why can't I understand you?"

'It's called secret writing, Chris. You take the plain text—I LOVE YOU," he said as he wrote the phrase on a piece of paper. "Now, you substitute this text using a predetermined 'key'—this key can be nothing more than writing the alphabet backwards," and he wrote,

A B C D E F G H
Equals Z Y X W V U T S

"In this case," he continued, "the letter I is substituted by the letter R, L by O, O by L, V by E and so on...' After a few minutes of scribbling, Terry completed the substitution.

"There, now you have a ciphered text which reads—" and he wrote out,

R OLEV BLF

Terry underlined the enciphered text with a flourish.

Fascinated, Christopher studied what Terry had written down. "This secret writing...doesn't this prove that the Reverends Johnson and Scott are involved in a plot against the people?"

"Not necessarily, Chris. You see, ciphers are used all the time in correspondence. Our company uses it routinely in correspondence to protect price quotes, ship manifests, sailing dates—for all sorts of things. On the other hand, *this* letter is suspicious, if for no other reason than the correspondents are loyalists."

Terry looked at the letter, shaking his head in perplexity. "The girl said this Skerrit lives in Dog Town? That's a pretty rough area of town. The only gentlemen I know who have commerce in Dog Town lead shady lives themselves. Now why would an Anglican priest employ such a low life? Does make you wonder."

"So tell me. What should we do?"

Terry thought about this for a moment. "I have a friend at the Literary Club who enjoys solving conundrums. I'll wager he can break this code in no time. Let's let him have a go at it."

19

AN INDEPENDENT SPIRIT

Chester Town,
On The Eastern Shore of Maryland
Mid October 1775

THE CHILDREN LOVED THE PUBLIC DOCK and every day Hannah would take them there for their afternoon walk. Peter, all of nine years old, would run off to scamper around one of the tied-up ships, preferably a sloop armed with swivel guns bow and stern; while Molly, older by a year but more sedate like her mother, would walk quietly, hand-in-hand, with Hannah.

Today, there was a cutting breeze from the bay charging over the near perfect flatness of the Kent County peninsula, to whip skirts and muss hair and threaten to send hats and bonnets skittering into the white-capped waters of the Chester River. In fact, it was chilly and windy enough for Hannah and Molly to flee for shelter, calling to Peter to come along. They hurried up High Street with the boy complaining loudly until Hannah suggested they stop at the tavern up the street for a hot chocolate.

Out of the windy cold, they sat near the fire, and the children were still for once as they sipped on their hot drinks and nibbled on ginger cookies. Hannah sniffed at her drink, took a sip, and savoring the smell and taste of chocolate, looked out the window with its central view of the town.

It was a pretty town, with substantial houses and public buildings of brick, many of them, like the tavern, of Flemish bond and glazed headers. The tavern was on the corner of High and Cross Streets, bordering a huge common area around which were situated the courthouse (with a small jail behind it), Emmanuel Church with its beautiful Palladian window looking out over the High Street side, and all around a growing number of fine merchant's houses, attesting to the town's importance as a royal port of entry.

It could be a good life for a young woman, Hannah had to admit, but only until she reminded herself that she was, after all, an unwilling *and* displaced servant, with the man she loved far away and having no idea where she might be. These thoughts wiped away what should have been a pleasant outing and again brought tears to her eyes. Molly asked her why she was sad, a question the young girl seemed to be asking all the time lately.

****

It had been a harrowing trip for Hannah from Rock Creek Chapel to this elegant little port town in eastern Maryland.

When she had carefully folded and placed her note to Christopher in what the children called their "secret log," she was confident that the decision she and Christopher had made was the right one.

She had sat on the log and carefully wrote her note on a page in her copybook, using a stubby lead pencil which blunted the fine script intended in rendering the roundhand Missus Crabbe had tried to teach her. It was the difference between penmanship and scribbling, she had been told—and that didn't even factor in the spelling.

But the note was, she had thought, accurate in fact and full of good news. Her thinking was that the turn of events was happy in its own way, that being in Baltimore gave them a head start in getting on with their new lives. After all, going off to Baltimore as they wanted to do would not be nearly as easy as moving in with her new husband's family on the Leeke Forest land, to live a communal life until they could build a dwelling of their own.

Hannah's feeling of well-being changed shortly after her arrival in Baltimore.

The mood was much uglier there than in the remote areas from which she and the Crabbes had just come. Hannah didn't understand this, most likely because she had no understanding of "politics" as that word was explained to her. She understood it to mean "the art and science of government," something she would have sworn she had no interest in. However, politics in any guise seemed to affect everything she and Christopher wanted to do with their lives; and it was, she knew, the reason she was taken from her man, only to end up here in Chester, across a huge body of water that worldly people called the Chesapeake—but to her was an unimaginable expanse of water, which she could only associate with Noah and the Great Flood.

For a while in Baltimore, Hannah was happy and certain that Christopher would shortly join her and, together once again, they would see the fulfillment of their dreams. It was just a matter of time, and she was a patient person.

 She also met a young woman in whom she immediately saw a kindred soul.

Hannah was sitting on a stone bench in the church garden, thinking how pretty the marigolds and autumn crocus looked, when a young woman approached her. She was plump and pleasant looking, with dirty blond hair and freckles that covered her face like clusters of birdshot.

"Name's Alma Lynch and you must be Hannah, the bound woman."

Hannah acknowledged that that was so.

"The Reverend Johnson said you'll be staying awhile and helping me with chores around here."

"Aye, as long as the children are cared for. My name is Hannah and I'd be pleased to help ye out all I can."

Alma saw that Hannah was good natured about this and didn't act like she was uppity or anything.

"Hannah—pleased ta meet cha—and…well, my mother is caretaker here and is sickly, so I do most of her work—which I don't mind," the young woman said quickly. "I don't really need help doing chores," and she added shyly, "but I'd dearly love a girl friend…." Her voice faded self-consciously as she said "girl friend."

Hannah looked more closely at the woman. Her skin was so light it appeared almost blue. She was blond, blue eyed, and spoke with an accent—probably Irish. She was dressed in cheap clothing, a tick skirt and faded wool jacket over a chemise. It was hard to say if she was older or younger.

Hannah made an immediate decision. "Alma, I'd like to be your friend."

And for the short time Hannah was to remain in Baltimore, she and Alma became fast friends, confiding their deepest secrets and dreams with the other, and spending happy hours each day caring for the children and doing the daily chores. Even the drudge work became almost enjoyable.

They had a lot in common: each was not her own woman; each had certain expectations which the powers that be would not grant them; each aspired to be independent and mistress of her own fate; each was prepared to fight for what she believed in.

Though they did not acknowledge it, both were politically and socially radicalized by their respective condition; and, in fact, they had become revolutionaries without really realizing it.

Because of these undefined but heartfelt feelings, they were angered by the loyalist carping of the Reverends Johnson and Crabbe, both of whom spoke freely in their presence as if neither of the women could understand English. To Hannah and Alma, the two men obviously dismissed them as being so insignificant that they could brazenly discuss their anti-popular preferences right in front of them.

The unexpected announcement by the Reverend Crabbe of their departure from Baltimore caused a panic in Hannah. All of her dreams were suddenly letting her down. She gathered that they were going to Annapolis, but wasn't sure of even this. She had been waking each and every morning thinking that this was the day that Christopher would suddenly appear before her very eyes, but each day had thus far proved a disappointment. Now, she knew that she must get word to Christopher's aunt.

Hannah spoke to Alma. "Oh please, dear Alma, please visit Missus Jane Everett who lives at Lovely Lane. As ye know, she's Christopher's aunt and tell her my situation as best you can." Hannah was desperate. "Tell her to tell Christopher that I don't know where I'm going—I don't think it's to be Annapolis—" Her voice trailed off. "I just don't know, Alma."

In fact, they only made a brief stopover in Annapolis. It was long enough, though, to bring back so many memories. Hannah immediately recognized Church Circle and Saint Anne's Church, where she had first met the Reverend and Missus Crabbe and their two children some seven years ago. The rector was now a different man, aloof and dressed all in black.

They stayed down the street at Reynold's Tavern, with its double pitched roof which had angles like the hock of a horse's hind leg. Hannah remembered standing in front of this very tavern as a young girl in her tattered dress, sighing in admiration as she watched the comings and goings of beautiful ladies and gentlemen in their elegant carriages and colorful finery.

She took the children past the new State House, still unused because the roof had just blown off in a storm. Below State House Circle, they walked sharply downhill to the market house and city dock. Again, Hannah remembered the city dock and evenings sitting with her siblings in filthy taverns while her father gambled or argued over money with men who leered and went to touch her older sister. It was during one of these occasions that her father was killed.

The Reverend Crabbe had been very secretive about their plans. One morning, he gathered the family and they went by carriage to an estate on the Severn River, north of Annapolis. The house stood atop a cliff looking out over the river. A set of stairs led steeply down to a private dock, alongside of which Hannah saw a ship with two masts. Another guest told her that it was a shallow draft Bay schooner, a common conveyance on the Bay.

Following an afternoon buffet, attended by a number of well-dressed men and women and clerics, including the man in black, they descended to the wharf, the children hanging on to Hannah as they stared way down to the tiny ribbon of sandy beach below. They boarded the sloop and Hannah was surprised to see their baggage already on board.

Before she knew it, the sloop cast off and set sail, taking them past Annapolis and out into the great expanse of the Chesapeake Bay. They sailed into darkness, the twinkling lights behind fading into nothingness. The children were fascinated, hanging over the railing, listening to the ship's bow sluicing and slapping through the water. But soon even excited children fell fast asleep.

Exhausted and a little seasick, Hannah was finally able to catch a fitful nap, and awoke in the morning to see land.

The ship was navigating up a wide river and finally docked at a place called Chester. Some people called it New Town but Hannah soon learned that this was the old name and not the new name now in common circulation.

Was this to be her new home...?

The Crabbe family was provided a comfortable tradesman's house on Queen's Street, little more than an alley but within the hearing of a child's voice from both the green and the public dock. The house was provided rent-free by a prominent merchant and layman, who, the Reverend Crabbe proudly announced, was also a loyalist.

In fact, a good many people in Chester were loyalists. Unlike Frederick County or Baltimore, loyalists were outspoken about their politics and it was the patriots who seemed to have to talk softly. The Reverend Crabbe gleefully stated at dinner one evening that the rebels couldn't field a full militia company despite the ranting and raving of their committee because most of the able-bodied men had joined the nearest loyalist company!

The pastor of the Chester parish was the Reverend John Patterson, who was sponsoring the Reverend Crabbe, and who was in the words of the secretary of the local patriot committee, "the most provoking, exasperating mortal that ever lived."

****

All of their travels in the province of Maryland did not sit too well with Anne Crabbe. While the climate and wholesomeness of life in western Maryland had succeeded in suppressing her distemper, her symptoms had now become more pronounced: her dry cough, which she had had for years and which, so sadly, had put an end to her singing, was now accompanied by the spitting up of blood. Her night sweats had increased and she had increasing trouble breathing when prone.

The doctors ascribed these symptoms to bad, humid air and violent passions. The Reverend Crabbe ascribed them to a cruel and unjust rebellion against God and King. His dear Anne's condition had worsened solely because they had been physically assaulted and their home invaded by savages. Their subsequent need to flee that terrifying situation was obviously too much for her gentle constitution to bear, and it was poor Anne who ended up suffering for the evil of others.

Watching his wife grow weaker and weaker, Roger Crabbe became more and more enraged. His once accepting and forgiving nature had now been contorted by an unfair world into a hatred he could not previously imagine a sincere Christian possessing. Such a desire for revenge as he now had was not meant for man—"Vengence is mine sayeth the Lord." But, then, what was called revenge was actually punishment and *that* was reserved for the God of the Old Testament alone. It was *this* God, the Reverend Crabbe was now convinced, who had chosen him to join the righteous host in punishing these rebel sinners.

****

In her deteriorating condition, a pensive Anne Crabbe saw life in terms of being useful or useless, of being happy or unhappy, of being satisfied or unsatisfied. Spending more and more hours in bed, sleepless and in pain, she accepted her condition but wondered about why life was so unfair. And it came down to that, she concluded: no matter what was said, no one could adequately explain why life was so unfair.

As she confronted her own imminent death, Anne Crabbe put aside these weighty questions about the purpose of life and, instead, tried to make suitable plans for her children.

She worried a lot about her husband's growing anger. It wasn't healthy, she thought, and was definitely having a bad effect on the children. So, she worried the problem of how her children should be raised in her absence, and she came to this conclusion: One way or another, dear, sweet Hannah must continue to care for the children until they reached adulthood.

Now, this would require a great deal of finesse, which Anne Crabbe thought long and hard about. Following her death, Roger would, of course, remarry, and Anne made the decision that he would, if she had anything to say about it, marry Hannah Williams.

20

THE SECRET LETTER

Baltimore Town
Mid October 1775

THERE WAS NO TURNING BACK. In May, patriot forces had captured Fort Ticonderoga in the far northern reaches of New York. In addition to providing needed cannon for the on-going siege of Boston, it also opened the way for an American advance into Canada. Catering to the *rage militaire*, the Congress, on June 27th, directed Continental forces to invade Canada, considered by many patriots to be the "fourteenth colony." Feeling mightily put upon, the Crown saw no alternative but to respond with overwhelming military force, the gathering of which would take time.

"The calm before the storm, you say? Good Lord, madam, the storm has come and gone! Great waves of repression broke against the sturdy stone walls along the road to Lexington and Concord, and temporarily submerged the breakwater at Breed's Hill, but the storm tides have receded—receded, I say, madam!"

"Henry," intoned Aunt Jane, "I so enjoy listening to you pontificate, even when you don't know what you're talking about."

Henry Murray was a widower and a member of the town's literati, with whom Aunt Jane had an on-again, off-again relationship of an ill-defined nature. He was a sizable, florid-faced man who talked rapidly about any and everything.

"Why, the British are huddled in Boston and nowhere else. And they will be driven out of there before too long. So, they might send a few thousand more soldiers from England to land seasick and fearful on our shores—or more accurately, try to. So what?"

They were dining at Sarah Chilton's tavern, "The Sign of the Cup and Crown," on the corner of Market and Gay Street—Jane, Rachel, Christopher, and Henry Murray, whom Aunt Jane wanted Christopher to meet. Christopher found him wonderfully amusing.

The tavern was one of the more elegant ones in Baltimore, catering to "the better class" as Missus Chilton's advertisement in Missus Goddard's newspaper claimed. It also offered clean beds, and stabling with good fodder for horses.

"Now that we've won the war against Great Britain," interjected Rachel, "may we change the subject to more genteel subjects?" She forked a cube of meat and put it into her mouth, chewed the rather sinewy piece until it was soft enough to swallow, then took a sip of wine to wash it down.

Not to be waved off so easily, Henry had a quick rejoinder. "Did you know that the local players plan to give a performance of *The Tempest* at the Assembly Room in December?"

"You don't say!" All were enthusiastic about this. This would be the first play since public amusements were discouraged by the Congress in '74.

"I do, indeed. Though I think it's still illicit, people are so weary of political theater, they want to enjoy the real thing."

"How wonderful! You say December—around the holidays? I do hope they are planning a ball, or at least a dance following the play!"

From this point on the conversation became as varied as the food courses and the drinks served, which continued with increasing gaiety and loudness until it was time to go.

****

Later that evening, Chris joined Terry at one of their favorite coffee houses, hoping to hear that there had been success in deciphering the secret letter.

"Good news it is, Christopher. Charles was able to break the code."

Christopher thumped the table triumphantly with his fist. "That's great. Do you have the text?"

"I do, indeed, here."

Christopher studied the sheets of paper, while Terry sipped his drink.

Finally, Christopher looked up and said, "Terry, this is a conspiracy against *us* Americans, isn't it? I mean...I don't understand a lot of this," and Christopher put his hand on the sheets of paper which he had placed on the table, "but such things as 'must strike now,' a planned abduction, infiltrating our provincial governments—why, they *really* do intend to enslave us, don't they?"

Terry was all seriousness. "Chris, we know that there are loyalists out there who are plotting against the Cause. I suspect we really don't know much of what they're up to, or what they are capable of doing. This particular loyalist cabal appears to be most dangerous—and who knows what harm it could've caused had we not uncovered it. No doubt, there are other such threats."

"Well, it is exposed now and we should take this information to the committee so that these people will be prosecuted. You have a relative on the Committee of Observation, right?"

Terry hesitated, perhaps a trifle too long. "There is mention in this letter to receiving information directly from—let me see," and he searched the second page for the needed quote.... "Ah, here it is: 'We are now receiving information direct from committees with occasional but good news from the ecumenical council itself.' While I would never accuse my cousin of being a spy, I think it best at this time not to involve him in this matter. He is not exactly a sterling example of moral virtue, if you know what I mean, Chris, and I would not want to test his patriotism."

"Then who do we take this to, Terry?"

This required additional thought and a pensive pull or two on his drink.

Finally, "I think we should take this story to Mordecai Gist."

"That's the plan, then?"

"Yes," looking at his watch, Terry noted, "It's too late now. We'll see him tomorrow," and they agreed upon a meeting time and place.

Satisfied with their plan, they relaxed and this gave Christopher the opportunity to again read the deciphered sheets; which, in turn, raised a reasonable question.

"How did your friend break this code?"

"Ah, now that's interesting. Actually, Charles was a bit disappointed at how easy it turned out to be. Said he was looking forward to a real challenge.

"It turns out the code is what Charles calls a 'Caesar' or shift cipher. It's a lot like the example I showed you the other day—in this case, you have a key number which determines how far to shift the second alphabet when it's written under the standard alphabet. In this case, the shift is seven letters, meaning that "H" in the actual alphabet becomes "A" in the shifted alphabet. Here's the key," and Terry handed Christopher a piece of paper upon which was written,

A B C D E F G H I J K L M N O P Q R S T U V W X Y Z
T U V W X Y Z A B C D E F G H I J K L M N O P Q R S

"Charles was gratified to see that the conspirators knew enough not to use spacing between words; but in the end the alphabet was monoalphabetic and used an 'X'—which is a "Q" in the shifted alphabet—to mark the end of a sentence, all very helpful in breaking it."

Christopher was impressed, but persisted. "All that's very impressive, Terry, but just *how* do you figure out this key number business?"

"Trial and error. Charles said the author of this cipher was erudite but simplistic in his understanding of ciphers and fortunately settled for one of the most common varieties. If simple word substitution is being used, the English language itself provides damning clues to deciphering a secret message: E is the most often used letter, followed by T, A, O, and N; further, double letters such as LL, EE, SS, OO and so on, are dead giveaways. According to Charles, given these parameters, it's just a question of time."

Christopher grinned. "It wasn't too long ago that I considered myself an educated man because I could read the Bible without having to ask the meaning of a single word—a plain, ordinary word, I might add—and now I'm confronted with ciphers and shifting alphabets and...well, secret plots."

"Yearn for the simple life of a tobacco farmer?"

Christopher shook his head. "All I need is Hannah and life couldn't be better."

****

Mordecai Gist, dressed in a modish suit of navy blue serge cascading with crisp linen and sipping a cup of coffee, was in a pensive mood as he talked to Terry and Christopher.

"Needless to say, you're right about this being a dangerous enemy plot and not just the rambling threats of ineffective loyalists. Now, the intelligence on our military preparations, such as they are, aren't important—any damn'd fool can see what we're doing down at the Point and a public bid was let for the cannon several weeks ago. And this reference to building a coalition of Anglican clergy is failed before it begins since a good many of the clergy are with the patriot cause...."

"What does disturb me about the actions of this cell are the references to a plan to abduct someone named 'Matthew'—most likely a codename—as well as the indication that the conspirators have an agent in a high place, with reference to the 'ecumenical council.'"

Mordecai Gist looked at Terry, "Doesn't 'ecumenical' mean 'universal?'"

"From the Greek, meaning 'inhabited world'—yes."

Gist glared at Terry. "So, it's my guess that 'ecumenical council' refers to the Convention; but could refer to the Continental Congress."

Terry was silent.

"Well, what do you think, Mister Simon?"

"Sir, it could be either, of course, but the chances are, since this appears to be a local conspiracy, that the reference is to the Convention. Just my opinion, sir."

"And a good one, Terry."

Gist got up from his upholstered wingchair and walked over to the window overlooking Gay Street. Disturbed by his passage, dust motes swirled and danced in the beams of sunlight. Turning from the window, Gist returned to take a sip of his coffee before continuing.

"Mister Sims—may I call you Christopher? Christopher, then, you spoke to this woman...Missus—"

"Lynch, sir, Alma Lynch."

"Ah, yes, Alma Lynch. A reasonably intelligent woman? Can she be trusted to follow instructions and not get the vapors for the slightest of reasons?"

Christopher thought about this. "I believe she is a strong, trustworthy person, sir."

"Well, then, here's the plan I propose...."

21

PUTTING THE PLAN INTO ACTION

Fell's Point
Baltimore Town
November 1775

THE REVEREND JOHNSON HAD TOLD HER, "Alma, go to the tavern called 'The Sleeping Dog." He informed her that the establishment was located at Fell's Point, but he did not bother to caution her regarding the low nature of the place he was ordering her to visit on his behalf. "Ask the barkeep for Tom Skerrit and give Mister Skerrit this." He handed her a folded packet, sealed, with "Deliver to Saint Anne's Church, Annapolis" written on it. This was the packet given by Alma Lynch to Christopher containing the secret message later decoded by Terry Simon's friend.

Now, as part of Mister Gist's plan, Christopher would accompany Alma to the tavern, playing the role of chaperone and hopeful suitor. Gist's plan would continue to unfold as it adapted to the outcome of Christopher's meeting with this fellow Skerrit.

And it was a good thing Christopher *did* accompany Alma. The bar was located at Fell's Point down among the public docks. It was a rude, often violent part of town, and "The

Sleeping Dog" was one of the more notorious booze-dens serving sailors, whores, and local toughs out for a night (or a day for that matter) of carousing.

As Christopher and Alma approached "The Sleeping Dog," they could hear singing above the usual din. The singer's voice, a bass monotone accompanied by a harmonica and raucous laughter, was yelling out,

"Man, man, man
is for the woman made,
and the woman made for man."

Once inside, they were confronted by a scene of debauchery worthy of biblical damnation, and by an almost physical wall of dissolute odors: unwashed clothing, unwashed people, bad breath, whiskey breath, and a powerful venereal muskiness. The room was small and pulsated with dancing shadows in the orange-yellow light from the large fireplace in the back, its mantel blackened by years of leaping flames. Next to the fireplace was a large cask from which a rumpled little negro boy was drawing mugs of ale. In a corner of the same wall was a small slatted barroom from which spirits were dispensed and monies paid in.

The room was crowded with plank tables and rough benches, and wall-to-wall bodies. The patrons were mostly men; but there were also women aplenty, all of whom, at first glance, seemed to have hands down loose bodices or arms thrust under rising skirts. Only a woman holding a hot loggerhead for mulling drinks appeared untouchable.

Alma looked like she was going to vomit from disgust and made to run from the place. Christopher put his arm around her and motioned toward the barkeep behind the bar. He practically had to push her towards the man, who could identify Skerrit, so terrified was she of the people and sounds around her. As she squeezed between crowded benches, disembodied hands fastened on her private parts like huge ticks. Even the singing demanded that she gratify unspeakable desires.

"As the spur is for the jade,
As the scabbard is for the blade,
As the spade is for digging
So man, man, man is for the woman made."

The barkeep was in no mood to converse, but said the woman mulling drinks would point out Skerrit. Christopher, with Alma in tow, gingerly approached the woman and asked her to point out Tom Skerrit. She looked with obvious distaste at him for having such a foul acquaintance, but after he quickly said he had business with the man in a disapproving voice, she pointed her flip-dog at a little man actually sitting on a large woman's lap.

Good lord, Christopher muttered to himself, recognizing the misshapen man who had led the attack on Missus Goddard's establishment. *I'll have to give him an even slighter likeness of myself,* he realized.

****

"But he didn't recognize you? Are you sure, Christopher?"

Rachel wasn't convinced upon hearing Christopher's tale of meeting Tom Skerrit. She knew that sharpers, no matter how despicable or petty, survived only because they were as alert as a ship's rat to the world around them.

"No, he did not recognize me, Rachel. Why would he?"

"Oh, I suppose you're right, Christopher," Rachel said worriedly, "but this whole business seems to be getting out of hand."

Christopher was not so bold that he casually dismissed Rachel's concern; instead, "Terry and I will be meeting with Mister Gist day after tomorrow. I intend to tell him that dealing with Skerrit will go nowhere. Perhaps that will convince him that it is time to notify the authorities and they can put an end to this affair. Fair enough, Rachel?"

"Fair enough," she said happily, and gave him an affectionate hug and kiss.

Rachel and Christopher's relationship had evolved into an easy intimacy since they had first met back in August. Without thinking, they would casually touch each other; and would even kiss occasionally, each telling themselves that it was a sibling's kiss...or maybe a cousin's.

One day, when they kissed, it lingered, and it stirred their blood. Neither could pretend that it was merely another casual kiss. Rachel stepped back with a quizzical look.

"You *do* find me physically attractive, don't you, Christopher?" This was not said in an accusatory way, just matter-of-factly, and maybe approvingly...

Never one to make excuses, Christopher had to admit that he did, indeed, find her physically attractive.

"There is nothing wrong with that, Christopher." She gently took his hand and placed it on her breast.

Time seemed to stop.

With her hands she pressed Christopher's hand to her and covered her other breast, and whispered, "I haven't had a man touch these for...oh, God, I don't know how long...."

Then, reproaching herself, she sighed unhappily, "Ah, but I see that I have made you uncomfortable."

"Nay, Rachel, the problem is I'm too comfortable...."

"Coffee House"
Gist House in Baltimore City
November 16, 1775

After supper, Christopher and Terry walked to Mister Gist's townhouse on Gay Street, one of a growing number of fine brick structures appearing here and there about the city. Only purposeful people were out on this late fall day, but the men had to dodge carts and wagons clacking up and down the streets.

It was a cold November day with a bone chilling wind pushing down the unpaved streets, sending gold and russet leaves from the few trees in town somersaulting along, or scurrying like crabs along building walls, or becoming restless piles in corners. Streets which had been soft mud just the other day had hardened and were now brittle and cracked, which made walking treacherous. With the strong wind shoving them along these frozen streets, both men walked as if they were maneuvering over glass shards.

Earlier that day over coffee, Christopher had described to Terry his and Alma's meeting with Tom Skerrit. He did not make light of it to the extent he had with Rachel. He admitted to Terry that Skerrit and his hellish world scared him, plain and simple. "It would be best if we walked away from this now, Terry, and have the authorities deal with those devils," he concluded.

After hearing Christopher out, Terry was of the same general opinion. He did volunteer, though, "While I agree he won't ever confide in you, Christopher, I *could* see Skerrit boasting of his secret work to an artful Delilah possessing Alma's... um, attributes. See? Perhaps if—" Terry abruptly ceased this train of thought when he saw the amazed look on Christopher's face. "I guess that isn't very realistic, is it?

"I guess not," Christopher said dryly, remembering poor Alma desperately praying that she would not go to Hell simply for going to "The Sleeping Dog."

Backed by Terry, Christopher made his case with Mordecai Gist, who clearly saw their point. However, there were factors involved to which the two men were not privy, factors which argued against closing down this potentially effective operation.

"Christopher, Terry, understand that I must be circumspect in what I tell you because there are...well...shall we say sensitive matters involved. Or, I might just as well say egos, as well as fragile intellectual positions amongst our leaders.

"As a member of the Baltimore County Committee of Observation, I've had the opportunity to meet and discuss positions with most of our province's leaders. Good men all. *But,* the fact is only one, maybe two of them have come to grips with the simple fact that Maryland will be *forced* to choose between independence and total dependence. Simple as that."

Terry went to say something, but Gist cut him short.

"Hear me out, gentlemen. Now, that means that each of our delegates to the Continental Congress has a critical say in the coming months which way our province, and possibly all of British North America goes—either independence or dependence, either freedom or slavery.

"And the British and their touts know it. That's why I'm convinced that the man they call 'Matthew' is one of our representatives to Congress. If they kidnap one of the few men open to independence, then they might—just might—affect the Maryland delegation's vote in the Crown's favor!

"Gentlemen," Gist looked at each man carefully, as a good businessman would assess a potential partner. "We must identify 'Matthew' and prevent his abduction."

Terry interjected, "Sir, can we not begin by identifying those who are staunchly for and those against the cause and go from there?"

"No, we cannot, Terry. And I'll give you an example why not. It is common knowledge, for instance, that Mister Jennifer—ye know him?" Terry nodded yes while Christopher shook his head, indicating no. "Well, he's known as a proprietary man who abhors the very idea of independency; *but* it is now being bruited about that he is supporting revolution! Do you see what I mean? We cannot deduct who 'Matthew' *might* be. The traitors who know who he *is* must tell us themselves!"

Both Christopher and Terry now understood.

But Rachel didn't understand.

"Tell me, Mister Simon, what happened to your vaunted ability to beguile? If you can convince some sinless maid to loosen her corset, why can't you convince Mordecai Gist to put an end to this amateur affair?

"Stop grinning like a fool, sir," she mocked him. "And ye ought to be ashamed of yourselves"—she glared at both men—"for putting Alma Lynch in such a position. She is so innocent, you've likely destroyed any belief she had in the goodness of man." Cynically, she asked, "Should I try to explain to her that what she experienced at "The Sleeping Dog" was not by any stretch of the imagination the holy union of man and woman referred to in the Good Book?"

Christopher and Terry took their tongue-lashing in silence.

Fortunately, Rachel was so disgusted by this affair that she agreed not to bother Aunt Jane with any of the details.

****

The affair, as Rachel choose to describe it, was, however, deadly serious. Lives and causes would depend on the outcome. Or simply on the way it played out.

Low tide in the inner harbor gave off foul odors and bared the filth, rubbish and embarrassments of a busy port city. It also occasionally revealed the city's more violent side.

The Maryland Journal reported that on the morning of December 2, the white, bloated body of one Thomas Skerrit, alias "The Vulture," a common street raff much in trouble with the constabulary, had been exposed at low tide on the slimy floor of the harbor. His throat had been cut from ear-to-ear "as neat," it was said appreciatively by those who would know, "as if performed by a Philadelphie barber."

22

'TIS THE SEASON TO BE JOLLY

Baltimore Town
December 1775

THE KILLING OF TOM SKERRIT seemed to put an end to Gist's ambitious plans to counter the loyalist plot. While this might have been unfortunate, it did free the former participants to enjoy the holiday season.

This was to be Christopher's first Christmas and New Year in the city and he was looking forward to it with both longing and anticipation. He fondly remembered the holidays back in Frederick County, and how they celebrated the season in a happy mixture of piety and merrymaking. He particularly remembered the intimacies Hannah had shared with him "in the spirit of Christmas giving," as she innocently put it.

While he would give anything to relive those past times, Christopher needed an outlet and found it in the growing anticipation of everyone around him as they prepared to enjoy the holiday season.

"We are much enamored...so to speak, that is—with the little liberties of the old Roman December."

To everyone's amusement, Henry Murray was educating Christopher on how worldly townspeople celebrated the season. "You see, Christopher, the celebration of Christmas has historically been an overlapping of Saturnalia and the Feast of the Nativity. The Christian Church has long taken advantage of pagan festivities to make the heavenly afterlife worth waiting for by making the earthly here and now so much more enjoyable. So, ya see, the Church should make no effort to artificially separate the two."

"Nor should the Congress," laughed Rachel, "and it has finally consented to the performance of 'rude dramas,' as they put it, so Shakespeare will make his reappearance this holiday season!"

"And with parties and balls before and after, I hope," said Aunt Jane delightedly.

"Most assuredly, My Dear," stated Henry Murray with certainty. "This return to sanity must be celebrated in proper style."

A large warehouse at the corner of Baltimore and Frederick Streets served as the theater for a three-day running of Shakespeare's *The Tempest*. Gossip was that most of Baltimore attended the play, with the upper class happily sharing the Bard with the lower class, each enjoying their version of his play on words. Christopher was hypnotized by the action and guffawed at Henry Murray's richly bawdy interpretation of Shakespeare's lines.

Following the final play there was a dance at the Assembly room, a two-story public building at which were held various social events. The dance took place in the large room, with the two rooms at each end hosting high-stake card games of long whist.

The women and men were dressed in their best winter finery. Christopher made do with his brother George's old brown suit, sponged and pressed for the occasion, and a pair of old pumps.

"...I'd be too embarrassed to dance, Rachel," Christopher pleaded in near-panic. "Believe me! All I know are rude country dances, conducted in barnyards, stomping around in dung."

"Christopher," said Rachel in a reasonable voice and suppressing a laugh, "the most fashionable dances in this town *are* country dances, with perhaps a reel at beginning and end."

"Oh," he said. "In that case, Rachel, may I have the pleasure—"

And they danced lively to the music of three violinists and a flutist.

It was a lovely evening and Christopher enjoyed dancing with Rachel, who was very skilled in all the dances. But there was no glowing face or heaving bosom, or anything to suggest that dancing in a fancy city hall with an elegant woman could possibly match the excitement of capering in a barnyard in the light of a bonfire with a woman who would abandon herself just for you.

A Letter from Home
December 18, 1775

"Oh, Christopher, a letter has arrived for you. I do believe the handwriting is that of your brother George." Aunt Jane handed him a thin packet with a wax seal bearing an Old English "$."

Christopher ran his finger over the seal, feeling the impression. He remembered being a little boy and looking with fascination at the solid brass instrument as his father allowed him to press it into a wad of hot green wax, which when lifted, had left the impression he now gazed upon with so much affection.

"This was your grandfather's seal, Christopher," his father had said with great solemnity, "and is a symbol of the Sims family, which is a proud and respected family, mind you."

"Yes, sir," little Christopher had responded.

Christopher carefully tore the paper around the seal, preserving the seal itself, and opened the letter.

"Now, let's see... He was quiet as he read,

November 4ᵗʰ. 1775

My Dear Brother,

Am much surprised that we have recv'd but 1 letter from you since You left home—Your family and frends expect'd from your promise to have mor news

Looking up at Aunt Jane, he said, "Well, to begin with, they're not happy with my indifferent correspondence. In fact," he looked sheepishly at his aunt, "I've only just sent off a second letter." Aunt Jane clucked disapprovingly as he went back to the letter.

The letter we did receve left many more questions than answers; the unnowen wherabouts of Hannah makes all of Us here very Uneasy—We can't get any intelligence of her or the Crabbe family, good or bad: We pray for a happy conclusion:

This last brought back all of Christopher's frustrations...and he had to calm himself before continuing to read the letter.

"Ah, Aunt Jane, George writes that the family is well and Mary is engaged to will be married in June." He looked at Aunt Jane with a gleam in his eye. "Let's plan on both of us attending the wedding—what say you!"

"Marvelous idea!"

"George also writes that they won't be plantin' tobacco, he says, 'The tobacco trade has greatly decay'd. We will plant wheat and Indian corn from now on. Wheat is readily marketed in the West Indies and flour and corn is in need by our army,' and so on."

Christopher read some local news which he knew wouldn't interest Aunt Jane. George concluded with *We hear the Dispute with Gt Britain grows worse and worse   God knows,* he wrote, *how it may end—*

The letter ended with another mild rebuke, *We Shall be glad to hear from you per 1ˢᵗ Opputy   The mean time remain your affectionate, &c. Brother George.*

Christopher handed the letter to Aunt Jane, who after reading it, said, "Well Chris Sims, I guess you have some writin' to do! And do tell 'em that I'll be attending Mary's weddin'."

****

Much to Christopher's consternation, a crowd of masked intruders forced themselves into Aunt Jane's house on New Year's Day.

"What—?" as he went to resist.

"No, no, Christopher!" both his Aunt and Rachel cried out, as they rushed to the door.

They invited the masked men in and dispensed small cakes and mulled cider. Before too long, they pulled the leader aside and, after paying him a copper or two, obtained his cooperation in pushing the pack of mummers out of the house.

Laughing and wiping tears from their eyes, Aunt Jane and Rachel told Christopher that this was yet another odd form of city frolicking during the holidays. "Seeing some of the costumes they wear is worth having such beggars in your house."

There was another surprise visitor—and a beggar of a different sort—on New Year's Day who was not in costume.

Alma Lynch appeared with news that she had just been given new instructions from the Reverend Johnson.

23

"FOR THE DEFENSE AND PROTECTION OF THIS PROVINCE"

Baltimore Town
January 1776

MOMENTOUS DECISIONS had recently been made by the Provincial Convention. On January 1, it resolved "that this province be immediately put in the best state of defense," thus creating Maryland's first regular armed force. It also created military districts, each under the command of a brigadier-general, who would command a brigade. And, finally, it authorized the dispatch of Maryland troops outside the province to any point within the Continental Army's Middle Department.

"I'm afraid worse has come to worst," Mordecai Gist said. "The United Colonies, as we now call ourselves, are collectively at war with Great Britain." Gist rubbed his forehead. "Now we have to decide what we are fighting for."

Christopher, along with Terry, had come to bring Gist news of the latest activities of the loyalist intelligence network according to Alma Lynch. But first, he had an announcement to make.

"Gentlemen, I have been elected by the Convention to be Second Major in the Battalion of Regular Troops now being raised by the province."

"Congratulations, sir," exclaimed Terry. Christopher quickly followed suit.

Looking at Terry, Gist said, "I had hoped the Convention would accept the Independent Cadets into regular service; but as I told the company, that appeared unlikely. So, I volunteered my services to the Convention, and it saw fit to appoint me as second major.

"Now," grinned Major Gist, "I'm out recruiting for the Battalion. What say you men?"

Terry took on a serious look. "Actually, sir, I intend to enlist after taking care of some personal business."

"Good for you, Terry." They shook hands, warmly.

Christopher was surprised by Terry's announcement. "I wish you had talked to me about this, Terry, because I'm embarrassed to say to the Major that I don't know how to respond to his offer."

Gist smiled, saying, "Christopher, right now I am busy cajoling all of my former comrades in the Cadets into joining the regular battalion." Turning serious, he added, "I know of the situation with your young woman. Something to keep in mind, sir: if—and I say if because of our namby-pamby representatives—if we declare for independence, indentured bondage will be outlawed."

Christopher gave Gist a curious look, because he clearly did not recognize the significance of this.

"Christopher, if we win our independence, your woman will be free!" He gave Christopher an intense look. "*That*, sir, would be worth fighting for—don't ye think?"

"Aye, it would indeed, sir."

"Well, then, let that govern your decision on whether to campaign or not—But, Christopher, 'tis not a decision that needs to be made this instant."

He clapped Christopher on the back. "Now, in light of the Convention's decisions," Gist continued, "Alma Lynch's report to you, Christopher, is even more ominous. It's obvious that the tories will not be discouraged; in fact, they may be encouraged because the Convention remains resistant to the whole idea of independence. It's a critical time for the cause, but it is also a critical time for the British government—if they cannot defuse the situation now, they will be unable to stop the movement towards independence; and they will be forced to wage a continental war of unimaginable scope, a war many are convinced they cannot win.

"Now, what does this new mission given to Missus Lynch have to say for itself? What must they accomplish right now or risk losing everything? I'm open to suggestions, gentlemen."

Christopher hesitated, then said, "Sir, in speaking to Alma, I got the impression that whatever they are embarked upon now, it is much more urgent than their previous activities."

"How so, Christopher?"

"Well, to begin with, the business with the Skerrit fellow didn't seem all that important—in fact, the Reverend Johnson hardly referred to Skerrit's death and casually told Alma to deliver such messages to another man at his convenience. On the other hand, he was so involved with this new matter that he actually took her to the site where special communications would be placed for her retrieval...."

...Listening patiently to Alma's monologue on New Year's Day, Christopher idly noted that she was wearing the same clothes she wore on her first visit to Aunt Jane's house and to "The Sleeping Dog." He supposed that she had no other "proper" clothes. He made a mental note to mention this to Rachel.

Then her description of events suddenly became interesting.

"...And I'm tellin' ye, Mister Sims—er, Christopher, that the Reverend Johnson was very stern when he told me how important it was to check underneath this flat rock for a letter"—

"What?" Christopher wondered if he had heard her correctly.

"Aye, strange business indeed, but the Reverend took me there hisself and showed me exactly what to do. And I'm supposed to look under this rock *every single day*! If there's a letter there he told me to take it as soon as could be to Mister Stevens and to inform him immediately afterwards."

"He didn't want to see this letter? Christopher asked her.

"No, indeed not, Christopher."

Gist was mystified, as had been Terry when he heard the story. "He referred to it as a 'post office under the rock?'"

"That's what Alma said. She's to deliver all these secret letters to a Charles Stevens, a shoemaker over on Forest Street. She added that Reverend Johnson said that Stevens is taking the place of Skerrit, who, the Reverend Johnson mentioned, suffered an 'unfortunate accident.'"

Shaking his head, Gist admitted, "I don't know this Charles Stevens. And I don't know what this means. We *must* find out!"

"Let's consider this logically," offered Terry. "There are two matters of concern: one, there is the plot to kidnap a prominent patriot—we think to prevent Maryland from supporting independence. You, sir," looking at Gist, "believe this person is one of our representatives to the Congress. Question number one: who is this person?

"Two, there is evidence that a prominent patriot is actually allied with the British. Question two: who is *this* person? Perhaps his importance is not in the passing of high-level intelligence to the British, as we might assume. Perhaps he is an agent-of-influence, which means that he would have to be in a position to directly influence our delegation to the Congress. Which means—in my humble opinion—the traitor is *also* a member of the Maryland delegation.

Mordecai Gist was appalled at the suggestion. "Sir, that is *not* possible. I know all these men and they are the very best the patriot cause can claim!"

Terry was suitably humble but not dissuaded by Gist's outburst.

"Sir," Terry said reasonably, "No one person has enough power and influence in the Convention to sway Maryland's position in Congress—only a representative to Congress can do that."

"I have to admit it's difficult to dismiss your logic, Terry. And …well…simply because I find the idea so repugnant, doesn't mean I will refuse to consider it."

Wearily, Gist motioned toward the door. "Thank you, gentlemen. That'll be all for today."

****

A week later, Alma again appeared at Jane Everett's house and handed Rachel a letter addressed simply to "Saint Anne's Church, Annapolis."

"Same as the last one ma'am. Please tell Christopher it ain't one of those from under the rock."

Rachel smiled at the absurdity of it all. "I'll do that. Thank you, Alma."

Upon learning of the letter later that afternoon, Christopher immediately sought out Terry.

"I'll have a go at breaking it out this evening." Terry placed the packet on the table.

"Terry, has it really come to this? I mean, do we have to go to war?"

Terry thought a moment. "Yes, Chris, we do. The problem with the tories is that they have always had a negative approach to colonial politics and arrogantly disdained taking part. They thumbed their noses at legitimate grievances, blaming them on a few hotheads and radicals. Worse, they convinced an ignorant British government of this and have quite frankly misled the Crown into believing that the current crisis is the work of demagogues not supported by a twentieth part of the people."

"Well, that doesn't really explain the anger, does it."

"Oh, I think it goes a long way towards explaining the anger. While I don't subscribe to it, many consider this a cousin's war, which, like a rift between brothers or between father and son, can be the most vicious conflict of all."

Thinking back on his discussions with his brother George, Christopher could agree with Terry on one thing: this is not a family war. It is a war between America and England, between the new world and the old world.

Evening of the next day, Terry was knocking at Aunt Jane's door with, he said, important news. He happily accepted a whiskey from Aunt Jane, who then busied herself with her accounts.

Sipping his drink, "I would've been here sooner, but I had to inform Mister Gist of the intelligence I'm now telling you. It looks like we have a break in the investigation," he announced proudly."

"This comes from the secret message provided by Alma?"

"Aye, I broke it out last night. Same key, same everything."

"Let me read it," said Christopher, with excitement.

"Can't. I left it with Mister Gist, who wanted to study it some. Sorry. I can practically recite it to you, though.

"Most of the message discusses intelligence obtained from informants regarding military affairs and a true state of Baltimore, calling it, by the way, a 'seditious city' and the Baltimore Sons of Liberty the 'most pronounced rebellious and mischievous people in the province.' Mister Gist referred to this as mere gossip. 'Too bad,' he said, 'that these people won't confine themselves to such prattle—that way, we'd have naught to fear from them.'

"Then the message gets more interesting. After reference to the Chesapeake as an 'avenue of war,' it informs the reader that Lord Dunmore's flotilla is to be used to support espionage! It goes on to say that "C" has agreed to work clandestinely with them and this requires new courier procedures. In addition, the operation against 'Matthew' has reached a new stage. As a result, 'special communications' will go straight to Lord Dunmore. The signal will be a lantern on a hill overlooking the Chesapeake and one of Dunmore's lighters staked out offshore for that purpose will come to the beach to pick up letters and pass any instructions for the plotters."

Terry ended his report at the same time he finished his drink. "Mister Gist is studying the letter and will send for us. So, nothing we can do right now. Let's go out."

"Sure, let's go. But Terry, who do you think this mysterious "C" might be?"—continuing their discussion as they departed the house.

24

BREAKING THE BOND

Chester Town, Maryland
February 1776

HANNAH FELT a considerable amount of resentment as she realized that Missus Crabbe expected her to devote her life to the children and, by extension, to her husband—sadly, a widower-to-be.

Hannah felt differently: she was not a daughter, or a sister, or a wife to this family. She was an indentured servant serving out her time. And 'though it wasn't her time yet, she *would* have her own life to live.

She had been on edge for weeks now, wondering what was going to happen to her. There were a number of possibilities, all of them bad because each would be determined by ill-fortune.

Prospects were bleak. Anne Crabbe was wasted by disease and clearly failing; the political winds were clearly blowing against the loyalists and their known world; and the Reverend Crabbe was clearly unable to come to grips with either the inevitability of his wife's death, or America's rejection of British rule…or—it was becoming clear—to the possibility that Hannah might want to leave his family.

The Reverend Crabbe's moods would swing from an unrealistic optimism to a more realistic pessimism. None of his mood swings were reassuring to Hannah.

Reasonably, neither Reverend Crabbe nor any of his comrades could take solace in the small victories won by the Crown. As one of the more realistic tories put it, "it's sorta like counting the number of men struttin' 'round with red cockades in their hats opposed to those struttin' 'round with black cockades on muster days, and decide who might have the upper hand."

This past November, inhabitants belatedly learned that George III had declared the colonies in revolt way back in August of last year. This was cheered by those hate-filled tories who wanted to see rebels twist in the breeze; but, in truth, the British government had rejected the colonies' olive branch, so now bloody war was the only answer.

In early January, a pamphlet appeared entitled *Common Sense*, a reasonable sounding title for the most incendiary political diatribe ever to appear in the colonies. And even the most optimistic loyalist realized that the world would never be the same.

James Chalmers, a rich Chester Town planter, irascible loyalist, and a hero to men like the Reverend Crabbe, attempted to expose the cant of *Common Sense* by penning a more reasoned pamphlet in response.

Chalmers labored mightily over his pamphlet, which he intended to entitle *Plain Truth,* and occasionally brought pages of his draft to the Crabbe residence for the Reverend to comment upon.

Hannah would bring in biscuits and occasionally the cup of tea when whiskey had no appeal to the tiny sitting room where the two men were in deep discussion.

"It reads very well, sir," she would often hear the Reverend Crabbe conclude after laboring through Chalmers' flowery language. He was not one to bite a hand that might feed him.

On a day in mid-February, Chalmers visited the Crabbe residence to announce that his pamphlet would be published in March. "I chose the penname 'Candidus.'"

"—Ah, 'pure' in Latin. Good choice, James," said the Reverend Crabbe with much enthusiasm.

"Yes, I wanted to use an honest penname instead of 'anonymous,' which to me is the *alias* of a criminal, if ye get my drift."

"I do indeed," said the Reverend Crabbe in a disapproving tone.

"And it's to be published in Philadelphia, the hotbed of rebellion, by none other than Robert Bell, who published *Common Sense*! Delicious, isn't it?"

The truth was Chalmers' writing was too highbrow for the very people he needed to persuade. Unlike the author of *Common Sense,* Chalmers had no idea how to write to the common masses. Even the Reverend Crabbe, having spent so many years in western Maryland, realized this weakness in Chalmers' too sophisticated argument. Many others did too, but none of them would say so.

In addition to the political atmosphere which affected the quality of life for all of them, the Crabbe family had to deal with Anne Crabbe's impending death. The children would miss her terribly, but they had been prepared. And frankly, they would likely miss Hannah more if she were to leave them.

How the Reverend Crabbe would deal with Anne's death was terribly important to Hannah. Her place in the family would be in flux: her departure would, no doubt, be resisted with tears and entreaties—or would it be prevented? Hannah hoped that wasn't the way it would be. The Reverend Crabbe had always been a gentleman and treated her respectfully. But how would he act towards her as a widower, needing both a mother for his children and presumably a woman to take his pleasure with?

For not only had Hannah become a capable housekeeper for a gentleman's family, a skill much in demand, but she had grown into a lovely young woman. Still taller than a good many men, she long ago accepted the fact and vowed that one day she would wear dresses that actually fit her! Her smile was still tight, not because she remained aware of the gap between her two front teeth, but because she had little reason lately to practice a smile. She did appreciate the fact that men were now taking notice of her. She enjoyed the approving looks after so many years of feeling ill-designed for her role as a woman; now she was tall and slender, with a decent waist and a noticeable bosom. Her eyes were still remarkable, her hair was still a soft brown, her demeanor was still sweet and open. Best of all, Hannah Williams was still a good person.

****

The Reverend Crabbe never confided his plans to his family and certainly not to Hannah, and it was only through casual comments made to her by some of the townswomen that she learned that the Reverend Crabbe was entertaining the idea of moving to the Bermuda Islands.

Every day, Hannah would go about her errands, dressed for the weather, this time of year wearing a warm kerchief over her mob cap, with her splint oak shopping basket in hand. Her first stop would be the baker's, where she would drop off the meat or fish dishes for the day to be cooked; then she would usually visit the vegetable and fruit stalls; perhaps purchase ham or other meats at the butcher; have her pitcher filled with cider; she would return to the baker, pick up the cooked dish for the day's meals; then perhaps buy some sweets if visitors were expected; and, finally, snatch a loaf of fresh, hot bread, her fingers burning as she quickly dropped it in the basket.

She would always hurry home then, and she and the children would treat themselves to slices of hot bread slathered in butter.

On one of these daily outings, Hannah was purchasing winter apples and chatting with Missus McPherson when the latter made an odd comment.

"Well, Hannah, are ye hopin' maybe ya won't have to shiver through another winter in Chester?" Missus McPherson mentioned in a casual way, as if Hannah was privy to the Reverend Crabbe's plans.

"I beg your pardon, Missus McPherson?"

"Why, *if* you go off to those Bermuda Islands like folks are sayin'."

Hannah was nonplused. She politely told Missus McPherson that she was perfectly happy here in Chester, but the Reverend had his calling. A few more comments over the next several weeks alluding to a Crabbe family move to the Bermuda Islands convinced her that here might loom just one more threat to her happiness.

It took Hannah a little while to figure out where Bermuda was, and once she did, she realized that if she was forced to go there, she would never return to Baltimore to be reunited with Christopher.

Reaching down her bodice, she pulled out the Spanish dollar, remembering what Christopher told her as he had gently tucked it between her breasts. "Save it for the worst of times...."

Clutching the coin as if it was a religious medal, she vowed then and there to run away and take her chances in flight rather than travel one step further away from her goal....

Fortunately for Hannah, influential people sought to dissuade Reverend Crabbe from leaving Chester Town. The activists spoke passionately of important work to be done and practically begged him to stay. Indeed, it reminded Reverend Crabbe of his once enviable position as Curator of Rock Creek Chapel—the need of the populace for his services, the respect given him and dear Anne...and the happiness—and for the first time in many months, Roger Crabbe made an effort to remember the good times.

One of those who spoke strongly on this subject had become an occasional, as well as something of a mysterious visitor to the Crabbe residence.

He appeared one day in March. He was introduced to Hannah as Mister Benjamin Harvey. He was a handsome young man, well-dressed, with an upper class English accent. After his initial visit, Hannah was told by the Reverend Crabbe that she was not to interrupt them as they met in the future. In fact, she was forbidden to acknowledge his presence and was never to mention his visits to anyone.

"Merely politics, Hannah—nothing to interest you—but we do not want an honest subject of the Crown abused by the likes of the local Sons of Liberty, do we? Of course not!"

Avoiding Mister Harvey proved difficult. It was clear from the beginning that he found Hannah attractive. He would seek her out to the point that Hannah was fearful that the Reverend Crabbe might suspect her of putting herself in Mister Harvey's way!

Harvey, who insisted that she call him Ben, was relentless in his attempts to impress Hannah. Finally, he confided to her that he was a British naval officer who was also an amateur secret agent. Having told her, he seemed to feel that she would be so impressed that she would allow him a small liberty.

"I can't discuss the details, of course," he said conspiratorially. To say this, he drew close enough to whisper, his lips almost touching her ear.

Hannah drew back in exaggerated surprise. "Sir, I'm sure you should not be revealing such things to me."

"Oh, not to worry, my dear Hannah, I'm sure I can trust you with my most important secrets."

"I'm sure you can, but why would you?" she looked curiously at him.

Almost impatiently, he said "Why, because I'm attracted to you, Hannah, and hope that you might feel the same."

There was a silence which Benjamin Harvey did not expect.

"Well—?" he finally asked, in exasperation.

"Well—what?"

He sprang towards her, saying "Oh, surely you won't deny me a kiss, Hannah," and before she could respond one of his hands was on the back of her neck forcing her face towards his, even as his other hand pressed demandingly against the small of her back.

"Mister Harvey" she said in a controlled voice, as she pushed him away—

"I insist that you call me Ben—"

"No, I will not call you Ben." She smoothed her skirts but really felt like wiping her mouth.

She then said, *"Mister* Harvey, if you dare do such a thing again, I will inform Reverend Crabbe. Do I make myself clear, *sir?"*

Benjamin Harvey understood, but even as he apologized as a gentleman for the "misunderstanding," he seethed. Scenes like this were humiliating for both parties, and unnecessarily so, since he'd get his way one way or the other.

She'll learn the value of pleasing her betters, he thought, contemptuously. *They all do.*

Hannah later regretted her improvident outburst. If she had good-naturedly tolerated his tepid advance, she could have learned more about his business with the Reverend Crabbe. Was he really a "secret agent" for the British? Could she use this to her advantage if her situation turned ugly? Just as importantly, Benjamin Harvey might have become an unwitting ally in keeping the Reverend Crabbe *and* herself here in Chester Town.

An opportunity missed, Hannah supposed. *It might be politic to ingratiate myself the next time I see him,* she thought.

She hoped that everything would work out for the best. Just in case they didn't, though, Hannah would prepare herself body and soul to run away at a moment's notice.

25

THE POST OFFICE UNDER A ROCK

Baltimore Town
Mid to Late March 1776

AFTER WEEKS of anticipation, Alma finally found a secret packet hidden under the flat rock. With a feeling of awe, she quickly picked it up, pinching it between two fingers just as she used to pick up the crawfish she and her little friends found under rocks in the creek.

It was a flat packet wrapped in painted canvas to waterproof it and then tied with twine. As quickly as she could, Hannah took it to the house at Lovely Lane and handed it over to Christopher.

"Now, you've been instructed to take this to Charles Stevens right away—correct?"

"Aye, and then inform the Reverend Johnson of the delivery."

"Good. Come back tomorrow, Alma. We'll deliver it to this Stevens fellow together. In the meantime, don't say anything to Reverend Johnson. Understand?"

"It doesn't have a seal," Terry said, in confusion.

"Well, isn't that good? That way we can read the letter without risking being found out. Isn't the whole purpose of seals to thwart people like us?"

Terry had untied the twine and carefully unfolded the wrapper, only to find that the pages contained within were not sealed.

"The question is, why isn't it sealed?"

"Possibly because putting a letter under a rock is considered security enough? Then again, maybe the spy doesn't want to use a unique seal."

"All good points, Christopher,' Terry grinned. "And aren't you becoming quite the conspirator!"

Terry opened the pages and, looking over the sheets, said, "Of course, it's in code. I'll make a copy right away, and, later, have Charles decode it."

Days later Terry met with Christopher and he had a glum look on his face.

"Charles can't break the code in the letter Alma retrieved from under the rock. He said it's different from the other code. He's not even sure of the method. He suspects it's also a substitution cipher, like the other; but so far he hasn't been able to discover the key. He's working on it, like the man happily digging to China, but that doesn't give us much to go on."

Christopher thought about this. "Terry," he began slowly, trying to find just the right words, "Could this be the 'friend' at the highest level? And if that is a possibility, isn't there something significant about this—this spy, passing his reports, or whatever, here in Baltimore—?"

"—Meaning...could he be from Baltimore? Of course! Let me look into this. It might be worth discussing with Major Gist."

Terry had taken to referring to Gist as major. In his new military capacity, Major Gist had been put in charge of inspecting military equipment and he had an office here in Baltimore. Busy as he was with his military duties, he was still very much involved in this on-going loyalist plot to subvert the cause.

"What if we're wrong?"

Terry shrugged, "Then we have no chance to solve the mystery. You make the best guess you can, Chris."

"The best guess you can," repeated Christopher, thinking *'tis the cane we use as we stumble through life.*

"Oh, and Terry," he threw in, "we still need to have a talk about joining the battalion—"

****

After listening to their theory, Major Gist shook his head in perplexity, saying, "Gentlemen, I have to admit that I do not have the temperament for intrigue." Looking at Terry and Christopher with a smile, "I am thankful the two of you do.

"I offer a short list of possible suspects, who are among our representatives to the Congress with a Baltimore connection. They are John Carroll of Carrollton, and Samuel Chase. Each could be the elusive Mister "C." I also include Thomas Stone—but only because he is from Charles County, which is somewhat close to Baltimore," he said lamely. "Those are all of the possibilities, if we stick to your premise.

"John Carroll? Absolutely not," stated Terry, vehemently. "Our families have been very close for years...and Mister Carroll sponsors Catholic Masses every Sunday at the Carroll mansion. It's simply not possible."

"I'll certainly agree with that, Terry," said Gist.

"Now Samuel Chase is—" Gist absent-mindedly rubbed a finger over his lips before finishing, "well, Sam is 'self-indulgent' and one who will use confidential plans for his own profit. I suspect he has the mind of a profiteer and not that of a traitor.

"And finally, Tom Stone makes no sense."

Terry was thoughtful. Always one to analyze a situation, he took his time, before suggesting, "What we can do is check to see if these men were present in Baltimore on those dates packages are delivered, beginning with the current one. Also, is it not possible to determine who is in Philadelphia and in Annapolis—or, in any event, determine who *is not* in Baltimore when a package is put under the rock?"

Major Gist and Christopher agreed that could be a method for identifying "C." All of them admitted that it was a long shot.

"After all, Mister 'C.' could have a lackey to do the labor."

"And, unfortunately, we are no closer to discovering the identity of 'Matthew,' which could be even more vital to the cause than uncovering the traitor 'C.'"

****

Christopher appreciated the sign of the "Blind Eye" every time he saw it, with its carefully painted pirate's head and black eye patch, signifying one of Terry's favorite watering holes. He entered the tavern and spotted his friend sitting near the fire on this cold, damp March afternoon.

Joining Terry, the two of them watched a barmaid as she squatted down to place a footed kettle on the side of the hearth, her petticoat tight against her buttocks, both appreciating the teardrop shape of her haunch.

She rose, adjusted the roast on the spit string, giving it a good twist, then swished over to their table. Smiling at Terry, she indifferently asked Christopher for his order.

"I'll have an ale and the ordinary if it includes that roast."

Christopher had to admit that she had a coarse attractiveness about her, and, as he turned to Terry, noted, "Terry, you do have a good eye for slatterns, don't you?"

"Down to earth women with down to earth needs, all of which I understand and much of which I can provide for! As opposed to your spoiled bitch, who won't sell her inexperience for less than a man's entire fortune.

"But enough of that. Charles...," Terry hesitated, building drama, "has broken the new code!" Terry sounded ecstatic; but then, "Well, not all of it," he added with somewhat less enthusiasm. "Actually, he was able to break only the first two lines of the message."

Christopher was baffled as usual when it came to codes and ciphers. "Two lines?"

"Yes. They read, 'Please advise if you can read this. I am uncertain of how I receive your communications.' You have to understand, Chris, secret codes and such are meant to frustrate those who are not meant to read the message."

Before long, the barmaid brought them the prepared meal—a trencher with a slab of roast beef surrounded by potatoes, succotash, wheaten bread with butter, a salad of seasoned cabbage, and some fried eggs.

Terry forked some cabbage into his mouth, noisily grinding the crispy leaves even as he began his report. "According to Charles, it is indeed a substitution cipher. He could guess by the number of double letters; but it was very sophisticated. He found that it started with reversing the alphabet for two lines; then the substitution key changed. He hasn't been able to figure out the pattern and has to break the code line by line. 'Slow work,' he said."

They continued to eat and drink and talk late into the evening, until Terry excused himself to "escort" the barmaid home.

Ten days later, Charles had managed to decipher four additional lines and, upon reading these, Terry realized that the author had made a terrible blunder.

"The writer substitutes false names for real names. But fortunately for us, he used the same false name, 'Matthew,' for the man they plan to abduct. This time, however, he has provided information which should help us identify this person. Here, this is Charles' transcription:"

Please / advise / if / you / can / read / this / x / I / am / uncertain / of / how / I / receive / your / communications / x / Same / rock / questio n / x / how / often / question / x / Matthew / very / ill / past / month / be dridden / x / Postpone / plan / until / he / able / to / travel / to / coach / t o / Rock / Hall / x / Will / . . . .

After reading the sheet of paper, Christopher smiled. "Terry, thanks to your friend Charles, I think we're going to save 'Matthew.'" Then he asked, "Where is Rock Hall?"

"Oh, Rock Hall is on the eastern shore, near Chester Town. It's along one of the main routes to Philadelphia."

****

"By God, this is the break we've needed," exclaimed Major Gist. "Terry, Christopher, I can't tell you how important your work in this regard has been…and the young lady, of course," acknowledging Alma's contribution. "We are so near a decision on independence and so deeply divided on the matter that the slightest shift can mean the difference!"

Gist paused to collect his thoughts. "With this latest intelligence, it is my opinion that this plot is more than the three of us can deal with effectively. I trust you agree?—good. Well then, I intend to approach Matthew Tilghman, President of the Convention, explain the situation to him and ask for his discreet support. I'll travel to Annapolis within the week to meet with him and will let you know the results."

Gist looked fondly at both men. "You've done a great service for the cause, gentlemen."

26

THE CRISIS

Baltimore Town
April 1776

UPON MAJOR GIST'S RETURN from Annapolis, he sent word for Terry and Christopher to call upon him at his residence. He received them in the dress uniform of the new Maryland Battalion of Regular Troops, a handsome red coat turned up in buff.

"Ah, gentlemen, you find me wearing my other hat in honor of my distinguished visitor. May I introduce The Honorable Robert Alexander, one of our representatives to the Continental Congress. An important assignment, but to me his true value lies in his genius for procuring military supplies for the province's troops.

"Ah yes, powder, plates for paper money and cartridge paper, not necessarily in that order!" Alexander said this in good humor. He was an elegant if not handsome man, dressed in a colorful suit, sparkling with stone buttons, and an overflow of scalloped linens.

He added, laughing, "And I've already told the Major that I do like the uniform. Unfortunately, gentlemen that is one expense of war I have been unable to squeeze out of a miserly Convention!"

Major Gist pretended to look crestfallen. "Why 'tis true. The Convention declines to accept the Cadets into provincial service, and now it chooses the hunting shirt over our 'red and buff' uniform—because of the expense, you know. But the officers have elected to outfit ourselves thus at our own expense."

"As elegant a uniform as ever there was," said Terry, with a hint of injured pride since he had not been offered a commission; and, thus, would not have a chance to parade in front of the ladies in his own very fashionably-cut Cadets uniform.

The men talked about the raising and equipping of the province's regular forces, a daunting task for an agrarian society, until Mister Alexander, looking at his silver pocket watch, announced that he must leave.

"Unfortunately, I really must excuse myself, gentlemen. I'm accompanying my family to our home in Cecil County before I continue on to Philadelphia. I've been appointed—or I should say sentenced to the Marine Committee because Sam Chase is in Canada on a special commission."

"Oh," exclaimed Gist, ignoring the information about Chase, "I thought your family was already in residence at 'Friendship.'"

Robert Alexander shrugged. "Of course, it's more convenient for them to be at Head of Elk as I travel between Philadelphia and Annapolis, but they do enjoy living in Baltimore Town."

With that, Gist walked Alexander to the door. Returning to the sitting room, he remarked, "A fine patriot. Robert Alexander is a man of firmness tempered with moderation."

Terry, his mind on another matter, sounded disappointed as he stated, "Well, Mister Alexander has helped us to rule out Samuel Chase as the elusive "C."

"Have a drink, gentlemen," offered Gist, who pointed to the array of decanters and deeply carved fluted glasses on the side table.

Pouring drinks, "Now, to business. I spoke to President Tilghman about our local tory plot. He was much concerned, to say the least, and interrogated me at some length on what we knew or surmised.

"He recommended vigilance and patience. 'Await another message,' he advised. He also authorized my use of one of the regular companies from Baltimore should the need arise. I've already spoken to Captain Samuel Smith, an old friend of mine and commander of the Eighth Company, in regards to this.

"So, there it stands at this moment, gentlemen," Gist concluded. He looked inquiringly at Terry and Christopher.

"I think we've done all we can for now," stated Terry. "One question, though: how might 'C' communicate with the Reverend Johnson—or does he? Something to think about."

"That's a good question," noted Christopher. "This 'C' did ask questions in his letter, didn't he? Presumably he also has a way of receiving a response," he ventured. "I'll ask Alma."

Gist was pensive. There was something on his mind and Christopher and Terry knew enough to be patient.

Finally Gist said, "Gentlemen—Terry, Christopher," he looked grimly at each man. "Let's not forget what this is all about.

"We know that a continental war is now just a question of time. The Crown government will, I fear, decide the time … and, no doubt, the place. But it is up to us Americans to decide *why* this war is being fought. Are we to be free or not? Whatever the answer, gentlemen, we cannot allow this plot to play the spoiler."

A Reason to Enlist

The British army had evacuated Boston by ship on March 17 and was feared to be headed for New York; there, this force would combine with an even larger force coming from England and, thus reinforced, attack New York City.

While the Continental Army hurried south, the middle colonies were being called upon to have troops readied to come to New York City's defense should the British fleet appear there. Maryland's regular battalion, intended for just such an emergency, was still woefully short of men, and captains were anxious to fill their company's ranks.

"And so you feel an obligation to enlist in the regular battalion," Rachel asked curiously, "because Terry Simon has done so?"

"No, Rachel, I don't—nor is it because of any idealistic obligation I might feel towards the cause. But the idea that independence would mean an end to indentured servitude ... and allow Hannah to return to me—isn't that worth fighting for?"

"It could be, Chris." Rachel was not so easily convinced. "And I'd agree with you that winning your woman's freedom two years early is worth soldiering until the first of December. In fact, I'll go further and say if half the things the independence-minded folks say will happen upon independence actually do happen, then I would believe every man, woman and child in America ought to pick up a musket and join the fight. But that'll never happen.

"My difficulty," she continued, "in sorting through all this is deciding why we have to fight in the first place. Oh, you can quote Mordecai Gist, who asks theatrically whether we're to be free or enslaved; but, Christopher, that's not the issue. The issue is do we live our lives as British subjects or American democrats? And which will provide us and future generations the better life?"

Rachel looked hard at him and asked, challenging him, "How will mothers and wives be made better off by this war, Christopher Sims?"

Christopher played Old Harry's advocate. "Well, the author of *Common Sense*—who, by the way, is an Englishman named Tom Paine—claims we Americans have the opportunity to begin the world all over again."

"Whoa there, sir, that's heady stuff for a nation of God-fearing rustics!"

"Is that a reference to the likes of me, Missus Jones?" grinned Christopher. Rachel gave him a playful slap.

As a way of concluding this argument, Christopher said, "Missus Goddard called *Common Sense* the 'perfect argument, at the perfect time, for the perfect crisis.'"

****

In fact, discussions raged all day long at Missus Goddard's publishing house. Even as Christopher busied himself with his work, he either overheard or participated in the political discussions among those patronizing the establishment, who included not only the brightest minds in town, but also the most combative.

"Sentiment for separation is certainly swelling. Does the Convention want it? The answer is no. They fear it will lead to anarchy. The populace, however, is now swaying towards independence. The whole business has become too irresponsible and democratical." This from a delegate to the Convention, who was a patriot, but clearly not a democrat.

Another man, a middling sort who favored independence, said accusingly, "So you're sayin' the ruling class will let this fizzle out."

"I'm not saying anything of the sort," retorted the former, clearly irritated by the man's reference to the patriot leaders as the ruling class. "How can it? No, the Convention is, or soon will be, in the position of deferring to the public's desire on this matter, and then it'll try to salvage whatever authority it can."

"Hardly a heroic approach," Missus Goddard said wryly, "but certainly a step in the right direction. Now who said our leaders don't favor democracy!"

And so the discussions went....

Christopher also asked Missus Goddard for her opinion of his joining the regular battalion.

"If war will do away with slavery of any kind and give women, Catholics...and aye, even negroes, equal treatment under the law—" She interrupted herself, "Now, I'm not sayin' equality in everyone's opinion—just according to the law—now, that would be worth the fight!"

Aunt Jane was not quite so enthusiastic, but she did agree with Rachel that if a victorious campaign would win Christopher's woman her freedom two years sooner, it would be worth the hardship—"assuming you don't go and get yourself killed, Chris Sims...."

Christopher realized he could spend countless hours going around collecting peoples' opinions one way or the other regarding reasons for and against enlisting.

What likely made the decision easier for him was the almost unendurable pain of having waited almost a year now without seeing Hannah, or knowing when he would see her again—and, after all that, knowing she was still bound out for two more years....

So, there it was.

He would enlist.

To free both of them.

27

GONE FOR A SOLDIER

Headquarters, Eighth Company
Stationed at Baltimore Town
April 1776

"We whose names are hereto Subscribed do voluntarily Enlist ourselves Soldiers to Serve as Such during the present dispute between Great Britain and America unless Sooner discharged by Order of the Convention or Council of Safety of Maryland for the Time being hereby Subjecting ourselves to Such Rules & Regulations as are or shall be made by the Convention of Maryland for Regulating & governing the forces in the pay of this Province, Witness our hands."

CHRISTOPHER CAREFULLY WROTE out the date, *April 15th, 1776*, and signed his name under that of David Deane. He surrendered the pen to Captain Samuel Smith who, after refreshing the nib in ink, handed it to the next man in line, with the interesting name of Walker Muse, who laboriously signed his name below that of Christopher's. In all, nine men on this day enlisted themselves as privates in the Eighth Company of the Maryland Battalion of Regular Troops, more commonly referred to now as Smallwood's Battalion, after its colonel, William Smallwood.

In less than four months, one of these men would desert, two would die in battle, two would become prisoners of war and suffer lingering deaths in the Hulks—those prison ships which lay stinking and rotting, like their cargo, in Wallabout Bay; two others would eventually succumb to camp fevers, while only two would survive the war to grow old and live out their lives as Revolutionary War heroes.

After all nine men had signed their enlistment papers, their new commanding officer spoke to them, and, after a stirring speech congratulating them on joining the company, turned them over to the company's senior sergeant.

Sergeant Jonathan Older was a tall, refined looking man in an unbleached hunting shirt, unmarked by any insignia of rank, although the Convention allowed him to distinguish himself from the privates by "different feathers, cockades, and the like, as fancy may direct." Sergeant Older's fancy had directed him to act like an officer rather than just appear to look like one.

His usually soft voice was deceiving. "All right, soldiers, stand up straight, in line if you will, and I'll take you to the clothier and armorer to get you outfitted. Following that, we'll march down to Whetstone Point to join the company. Do you understand?

"*I said.*"—the hard authority of his voice surprised the recruits—"*Do you understand? I want to hear 'yes, sergeant!' whenever I ask a question.* Do you understand?"

"Yes, sergeant!" They all said in unison.

Satisfied, Sergeant Older walked out, expecting them to follow.

This was just the beginning of their military indoctrination.

The recruits were issued clothing from the supplies available, which consisted of a military hat with black ribbon, a plain smock of tow cloth, and a thin blanket.

At the armory, they were issued a military musket, bayonet and frog, cartridge box, and shoulder belts of buff leather. Fascinated, Christopher looked over his issue musket, which was marked on the lock with the initials "MBG" and a crude "MB." This wasn't a Crown musket, which was referred to variously as a brown musket or a Brown Bess. Christopher later learned that the muskets were surplus French army arms, obsolete but serviceable, which Colonel Smallwood had arranged to be bought in the French West Indies in return for good Maryland flour.

Thus equipped, Christopher and his comrades were marched down to Whetstone Point, where fortifications were being constructed to defend a log boom and huge iron chain stretched across the channel to prevent access to the harbor by the enemy flotilla prowling the Bay.

Here at the encampment, amidst black workers with glistening ebony torsos digging earthworks, and formations of soldiers drilling on the parade ground, all laboring under a grey haze from the nearby ironworks which coated them with fine particles of soot, the recruits were introduced to their drill master.

"Hullo, *Gentlemen.*" He looked over his new charges unenthusiastically.

Corporal Smith had a hard angularity about him and, to the new recruits, looked ferocious enough to beat the martial arts into them. He wore a light infantryman's leather helmet which sat on a thatch of reddish-brown hair. His clothing was of the best quality but worn and spotted from both his duties and his indifference; his hunting shirt was stained with sweat and salt rings, his leather breeches scratched and blotchy, while the white silk stockings above his splatterdashes were soiled and had runs in them.

Jeremiah Smith was the third son of a Catholic family of successful merchants who had no interest in becoming a merchant. Intense and prone to action rather than thoughtfulness, Jeremiah Smith was a natural warrior. Born to gentry, but given to the rough and tumble ways of common brawlers, Jeremiah Smith found his true calling in the army, where his natural lack of self-restraint was in complete harmony with the rigorous demands of a military life.

Staring sourly at the men standing nervously in front of him, Corporal Smith prodded one of the recruits to align himself with the men on both sides before continuing. "Welcome to the dance, gents. I'm your dance master. Corporal Smith to you—don't ye dare go calling me 'sir'—and you're goin' to dance to my tune, you are! Shall we begin?"

"Yes, corporal!"

Following drill, Christopher and Walker Muse were ordered to follow a bantam rooster of a corporal, who assigned them to a mess, and curtly introduced them to their new messmates. Christopher was surprised and delighted that one of them was Terry Simon; but just as the smile appeared on his face and he was about to give a happy "hullo," another soldier, hanging his sweat-dampened hunting shirt on a tent line, said without ceremony, "Do ye see that pile of wood over there? Get a goodly supply for cooking…and you, Muse—is it? Fetch some water," and handed him a large kettle.

While the new men went off on their errands, Terry went over to the kitchen, a large open tent with women and negroes fussing about, and drew their rations, while another member of the mess, who was introduced as Private Hayes, got the fire started.

Terry soon returned with the day's rations, which consisted of a hunk of beef, peas, vinegar, a pound of bread, and cider. Back at the cooking fire, the man introduced to Christopher as Private Lynn, dumped the peas and beef into the kettle, to which he added salt, a couple of pinches of spices, and some vegetables.

Looking at Christopher and Muse, Lynn pointed at the kettle. "Now, gents, that's camp stew. We'll cook enough for dinner now, supper tonight and breakfast on the morrow." The new men also learned that each member of the mess contributed one-third of a dollar each month to pay for such items as salt, spices, produce, and dairy products.

"Issue is beef or pork, pork or beef…day in, day out," said Private Lynn, in a matter-of-fact tone which avoided endorsement. "But most usually it'll be marsh beef. What! Ye never heard of 'marsh beef?' Why, that's meat from beeves which are left to forage on the grasses growing near brackish water. As opposed to stalled beeves," he added. "Marsh beef ain't unsavory—just peculiar tastin'.""

The third member of the mess was named Caleb Hayes, who finally joined in the conversation by asking the new members if either one of them could cook better than Private Simon. When neither Christopher nor Muse admitted to any such talent, he went back to cleaning his musket.

Daylight faded and darkness came on like a rush of relief because it meant the end of another long workday. They formed up as the drums beat The Retreat, the roll was called, orders of the day read, and fatigue parties and guard details called out. Those not assigned duties usually drank at the sutter's tent 'til The Tattoo was beat which sent all of them to bed.

For a week now, Christopher had been sleeping in a six-and-a-half-foot tent with four other men, whose noises and sleepy migrations were far worse than sleeping in the same bed with his little brother.

Rolled in his thin blanket, using his felt hat as a pillow, Christopher tried to stake out a claim to some hard ground. Tattoo had sounded, and whether he felt like sleeping or not, he was a prisoner in this tent until daybreak. He tried to ignore the snoring and sleep-talk, as well as the body odors strong enough to burn nostrils.

What on earth have I gone and done?

Major Gist's Headquarters
Baltimore Town
April-May 1776

Fortunately for both Christopher and Terry, they were assigned to "other" duties, meaning they were assigned to fatigue duties at company headquarters or at Major Gist's office. This was intended to ensure that they were on hand for any developments regarding the spy ring, but for Christopher and Terry, it was a reprieve from the unbearable boredom of garrison life.

As for developments in the spy plot, there was more bad news than good news.

Despite his contacts, Major Gist was unable to quickly identify "Matthew" based on his reported illness alone. None of Maryland's representatives to Congress were known to be so incapacitated that they could not travel to Philadelphia. "But I will continue to pursue the matter."

Discouraged, Christopher also reported, "Alma does not know how "C" communicates with his handlers."

The only good news was that Alma had retrieved a second and even a third message from "C."

"Could there be a new sense of urgency on their part, which seems to correspond to the Convention's increasingly sharp discussions of independence?"

Obviously, they were hoping for more mistakes which would shed additional light on the tory plan. But even this "good" news was mitigated by more bad news. Of course Terry would see that his friend tried to break it; but, "The trouble is he's still laboring on the first message and has only succeeded in breaking out eight sentences." He read the latest transcription to them:

Will / be / out / of / touch / with / Matthew / until / he / arrives / x / A m / leaving / for / F—here Charles had indicated a possible garble, but noted that it could have been meant as just a capital letter—and some more garbled letters, then *Be / assured / plan / will / work / inform....*

"But this is important information in its own right," Gist quickly pointed out. "Breaking out this first message in its entirety is vital."

Terry agreed, but added, "We should immediately check to see if the second message uses the same method of shifting from sentence to sentence as the first. It may help in breaking the entire code."

****

The loyalist sense of urgency was well-founded, and so was that of the patriots. While there was support for a declaration of independence among many, it remained a contentious issue in Maryland.

Thomas Stone, one of their representatives to Congress, while visiting Missus Goddard's shop, was chatting with her and Christopher and informed them, "Just the other day, the Convention unanimously renewed its hesitant instructions to the delegation in Congress, even as that body wants a vote on independence."

"Well, that doesn't surprise me, Thomas. Neither the province of Maryland nor you delegates, except for Matthew Tilghman, Samuel Chase and William Paca have been very forward in promoting it."

Stone sighed unhappily. "As you know, Mary Katherine, I don't count myself an independence man. I will, however," he added, clearly angry, "prepare for it as an absolute necessity—but *only* as an absolute necessity."

So both loyalist and patriot alike had reason to hope that the Maryland Convention and its representatives to the Congress in Philadelphia would do the right thing....

On the other hand, hard-liners on both sides looked forward to a decisive war.

"County committees and militia units throughout the province are clamoring for a decision," Major Gist said with grim satisfaction.

"My sources have told me that Tilghman, Chase, and Paca will soon leave for Annapolis hoping to return to Congress with support for independence, and," he hesitated..."and an alliance with France!"

Christopher was stunned. He grew up on stories about the great war against the French and their savages. "I can't fathom an alliance with France! How could such a thing be acceptable to the populace?"

Gist understood. "Ye know, Christopher, my uncle, Christopher Gist, fought the French for years along the frontier and actually saved the life of General Washington during Braddock's lamentable campaign. Yes, indeed, he did! So I can see why many of our comrades will not understand why we must truck with the French...but we must—to win this war."

About this time it also became common knowledge among Americans that their king had hired thousands of German mercenaries to punish his recalcitrant subjects.

"Hessians! Barbaric Germans spawned to kill and offered for hire to any prince who could pay the price to brutalize *his* subjects. *Our* sovereign has done this to us."

"Well," added Terry, with finality in his voice, "this is no longer a family squabble, is it?"

And all the while, a growing number of armies and navies were being fielded, to be moved and counter-moved like tokens in a game of checkers.

A British fleet had appeared in New York harbor last February, throwing that city into a panic, then went to Norfolk in March. Around the same time, the Continental Army had marched from Boston to New York City. The patriots had intercepted a letter from Lord Germain to Maryland's own Governor Eden, dated December 23, 1775, which revealed that the Crown would send naval forces and seven regiments across the Atlantic with orders to strike South Carolina or Virginia. Enemy sails were sighted off Charleston just recently. Maryland's military forces were being readied to meet any threat in the middle colonies.

And people feared that the British government was prepared to burn and pillage any and every town in British North America in angry response to its rebellious colonies.

All of this, the political and the military hardheadedness, gave a new and horrible dimension to this conflict. The effect this had on Americans was to push enough of them over the edge to send all thirteen colonies plunging, now out of control, into the caldron of revolution.

28

RACHEL'S NEWS

Lovely Lane
Baltimore Town
May 9, 1776

R ACHEL HAD GONE OFF to Annapolis on personal business—she had said it would be for a week or more—so Jane Everett was surprised to see her bursting into the house barely two days after her departure.

The reason for this was evident when, hurrying over to Jane, she said with unusual impatience, "Jane, Where is Chris? He must see this immediately," and thrust an issue of the *Maryland Gazette*, dated May 12, at her, pointing to a column.

It took a moment for Jane to focus on the paper and realize that Rachel was stabbing at an advertisement. She began to read,

20 DOLLARS REWARD

———

R AN A WAY from the subscriber, on The 4th inst.White Female
HANNAH WILLIAMS,

Jane looked at Rachel. "Hannah Williams? Is this Christopher's Hannah?"

"Read on, Jane," Rachel ordered impatiently.

> About 18 years of age, slender, very tall, 5 feet 8 or 10 inches high ; large brown eyes, fair complexion with no marks, brown hair ; had on when she went away, a light-ground calico gown, an old striped linsey quilted petticoat, and a blue linen handkerchief, and wearing a white linen cap ; She may have other clothes carried in a reed basket ; She lived with Rev. Crabbe and family in Chester Town, from whom she ranaway three days ago ; she is serving a bond with St. Anne's Parish, in Annapolis The above Reward will be paid by Securing her with Officials of St. Anne's Church, Annapolis or of St. Paul's Church in Chester Town, and if brought back to Chester Town, All reasonable expenses.

> **REV. SCOTT,**
> St. Anne's Parish
> Annapolis, May 6 1776

Jane was nonplussed. "Oh, my. Christopher must be with his company at Whetstone Point. What do we do?"

"Damn the military! I'll see if Major Gist is in town—no, I'll see Mary Katherine first, to see if she's received a similar advertisement...then I'll go see Major Gist."

Looking intently at Jane, Rachel carefully told her, "Jane, *I* want to discuss this with Christopher. Understand? I don't want him running off half-cocked, which is his reaction when it comes to this woman. I'll be back shortly. Should Christopher return, tell him I must talk to him regarding an urgent matter."

Rachel turned to leave, then turned back. "And tell him, Jane, that I did not discuss the subject with you."

Jane looked relieved.

Christopher was home when Rachel returned several hours later.

He looked concerned. "I'm going to be late in reporting to Major Gist's office, but Aunt Jane said there's an emergency?"

"Yes, there is, Chris. And don't worry about reporting to Major Gist. I've just spoken to him and he's given his permission for you to stay the night here and report to him first thing tomorrow morning. He's sending an order to Captain Smith as well. All's taken care of in that regard."

"Good lord, this is serious, then."

Rachel told him of the news and then showed him the advertisement, adding, "Fortunately, Mary Katherine told me that no such advertisement has *or will*," she said emphatically, "appear in her newspaper."

Stunned, Christopher knew he should be concerned—and was—but he did not know if he should also be happy that Hannah had now forced the issue.

He looked at Rachel, the panic welling. "Damn, we have to do something *now!*"

"You mustn't do anything rash, Christopher...I know this won't be easy, but—"

Christopher cut her short. "Rachel, ever since Hannah was taken away from me, dear friends have prevented me from doing anything—always, there's been good advice, which, in the end, cajoled me into doing nothing—*nothing!*"

Christopher took a deep breath and looked at both Rachel and Aunt Jane. "Well, now is not the time to do nothing."

And he walked out of the room.

Thinking about it later, he realized that, based on his outburst, Rachel and Aunt Jane would stay up late into the night to prevent him from doing something "rash." So he returned to the parlor and sat with them for some time, admitting that there was little he could do on his own, and inviting their assurances that things would work out.

****

It must be early morning by now, he reckoned. Sure that Rachel and Aunt Jane had finally fallen asleep—both must be as exhausted and distraught as he was—he quietly let himself out of the house.

He would be a deserter and a disappointment in the eyes of so many; but he had to do this. He thought of Jeremy and Constance asking him what he had intended to do had he gone after Hannah back in June of '75 and—truthfully, he couldn't say …well, right now he couldn't say either…but he felt…well, that he was doin' something, at least. Tomorrow, he would consider just what that might be.

Glancing back at the house he now considered home, he began to walk down Lovely Lane to Main Street and the road to Annapolis, suddenly feeling very alone.

"Ah, Private Sims," the voice, reverberating down the empty street, came out of the darkness like clarity itself.

"Major Gist knew you to be a fine soldier who would want to get an early start to this day! And so he sent me to accompany you to 'Coffee House,' where he's lookin' forward to speaking with you."

Christopher was dumbfounded as Terry Simon casually appeared out of the darkness and into what little light the street afforded, to confront him.

Terry came up to Christopher and looked very hard at him.

"Actually, Chris, Major Gist sent me to make sure you did not make the mistake of your life. You can thank Missus Jones for that. She thought you might 'panic'—that's the word she used to describe how you'd react to the news of Hannah's plight.

"*Panic*…" Terry let the word hang in the cool air. "Now, that's not a particularly manly word, is it?"

"It surely isn't," Christopher admitted wearily. "Terry, let's go talk to Major Gist."

They were standing in Major Gist's office at "Coffee House." On this occasion, they did not gather in the parlor, a social room full of color and softness and light, which people said remained unchanged since the death of Gist's beloved wife, Cecil, going on eight years now. His office, on the other hand, was oiled mahogany and cracked leather and had the smell of serious business and fine brandy.

"...and if I were a young man with my woman running for her life, I'd damn well be on the road looking for her, too. And if I did that, *sir*, I would be behaving just as selfishly as you. Do I make myself clear?"

"Yes, sir."

Gist was upset with Christopher. He had the temper of a redhead, so he had every intention of punishing him. At the same time, he was fond of him and knew him to be a good man.

"Now, since you did, in fact, report to me as instructed," there was no smile on his face as he said this, "I'll ignore the obvious and will expect nothing less than exemplary service from you 'til the first of December, if not beyond. May I count on that, Corporal Sims?"

"Yes, sir," responded Christopher, in his best parade ground voice.

"And I will talk to Captain Smith about appropriate punishment. I will not tolerate lack of discipline in my command."

"I understand, sir," said Christopher, contritely.

"Very well. Now, on to other matters." He went over to the sideboard, where a servant had just placed a coffee service. "Men." It sounded like an order as he motioned to the tray.

Gist took a sip of coffee, and with the clatter of china, placed cup and saucer on the table, and announced, more with relief than anything else, "We have, I feel certain, finally identified 'Mathew.'"

Both Christopher and Terry were surprised and delighted by this news.

"He is none other than William Paca, one of our most outspoken advocates of independence in Congress."

"You're sure of this, sir," asked Terry.

"No doubt in my mind—and 'twas purely by chance. During a conversation someone mentioned that our delegates to the

Congress were returning to Annapolis to receive directions from the Convention concerning the province's vote for independence. Interesting enough, but then it was mentioned that poor Paca was too ill to travel and several of our representatives had decided to delay their own return until he was well enough to travel."

"Ah," exclaimed Christopher, "So our sickly 'Matthew' was in Philadelphia and not here in the province as we assumed. Well, sir," looking at Gist, "you did say that we could only learn the identity of 'Matthew' from the enemy."

Gist gave a shrug which indicated that he accepted no credit for this deduction. "Paca and the other representatives plan to travel overland from Philadelphia to Rock Hall on the eastern shore, then by boat to Annapolis. Such an itinerary is fraught with peril because the tories are so strong on the eastern shore and in the lower Delaware counties. We believe this is the logical place for any attempt to abduct Paca.

"So militia companies in Delaware and eastern Maryland have been ordered to meet and escort *all* our congressional representatives, and our naval vessels will transport them from Rock Hall to Annapolis."

"Why not arrest the plotters and put an end to the threat?" asked Christopher.

"A reasonable question," replied Gist. "Ignoring the legal evidence against them—which is insufficient—we don't know the extent of the conspiracy. In addition, we would lose all hope of uncovering the traitor 'C.'

"So there's the plot as best we can interpret it and our own response. Now for some additional information which will interest you, in particular, Christopher. In addition to the Reverend Johnson in Baltimore and the Reverend Scott in Annapolis, we have identified a Reverend Patterson in Chester Town, who is allied with the infamous James Chalmers, as a member of this conspiracy. There was also mention of another Anglican minister, a Reverend Crabbe as being associated with this cabal. It is thought that he provides sanctuary to spies from Lord Dunmore's pirate fleet."

Gist looked knowingly at Christopher.

"The Reverend Crabbe! But that's the man to whom Hannah is bound out!"

"Yes, we know all that...just as we now know that she has been residing in Chester Town.

"Now, Christopher...we have all these suspects under close watch. Should your Hannah fall back into their hands, we no doubt will learn of it.

"In sum, Christopher, above and beyond defense of the cause, I believe we are doing everything in our power to protect Missus Williams and deliver her to safety. What think you, Corporal?" Gist purposefully emphasized his military rank.

Christopher could not express his gratitude. With tears in his eyes, he asked, "What can I do to help, sir?"

"Join your company and learn alongside your comrades how to fight like the Redcoats. If we win this war, we'll all have the new world we're seeking. Sound reasonable, Corporal Sims?"

Christopher understood. "Yes, sir!"

29

OUTSIDE THE LAW

Chester Town
Eastern Shore of Maryland
May 4-21, 1776

IT SEEMED A LONG TIME AGO, but the instinct for survival sent a familiar shiver through her. She felt the same fear as she fled…and the same terror at the thought of being caught.

It all came back to her. How the fear had propelled her even as her long, skinny legs grew wobbly; and how the terror had addled her mind as she began to think everyone was reaching out accusingly to prevent her escape.

Back then, her crime might have been just filching an apple from a basket or, perhaps, something really brazen, like grabbing a loaf of bread. Whatever it was, her life depended upon desperate wiles.…

…Just as it did now.

As children, their phrase for it had been "stayin' smart," which described their ability to avoid or manage one threat after another, day after day, until their luck ran out. Street justice their only warden, Hannah and the other children who risked a crime generally fended for themselves until they died or were confined or simply disappeared. She couldn't remember any of the older children ever making their own way to adulthood.

"Stayin' smart" is what Hannah had to do now.

First, she had to outguess the Chester Town authorities, who would look for her in all the usual places: around the ships at the public dock, of course, and the road to Rock Hall, in case the idea was to escape by ship; they would also quickly seal off the overland road to Philadelphia through the Delaware counties and the road up to Head of Elk, at the very head of the Bay. From Chester Town, these were the established routes to Baltimore, Annapolis, and Philadelphia, all places which beckoned to the runaway.

Hannah understood this, and trying her best to think like her pursuers, decided she would go *east*, taking the road along the river towards Bridge Town, cross south into Queen Anne's County, putting the daunting width of the Chester River between her and any pursuers; then, she would reverse her direction and make her way down to Queen's Town, which was at the mouth of the Chester River, but on the opposite bank, south of Eastern Neck Island, and near the Bay itself.

She made the best plans she could. Telling the children that she would be late returning, Hannah took her shopping basket, in which she had hidden a change of clothing, and dressed in a drab outfit which would be hard to describe, set out as if she was on her usual errands. She couldn't even think about the children. She did allow herself to feel guilty about the few shillings she would, in truth, be stealing; but this was, she concluded, the lesser crime, as she briskly walked up High Street to the river road, and turned east—to begin a fugitive's life.

****

Hannah had first thought seriously about running away as soon as they left Baltimore. But she was a cautious woman and felt most comfortable when she erred on the side of caution, which in this case meant waiting until her situation was intolerable. Even their flight across the expansive Bay to Chester Town was not enough to cause her to abandon her responsibilities.

What caused her to finally break the bond was Anne Crabbe's death…well…not exactly Anne Crabbe's death—but rather the social pressures which followed—and it wasn't the Reverend Crabbe who was really to blame.

Anne Crabbe died following a period of quiet, a blessed change from the weeks of wracking coughs and spitting up of bright red blood. But as quiet as she became, she never seemed to be at peace, and she looked frightful…like "a stalking ghost," who terrified even her own children.

A lovely ceremony was given for her at Emmanuel Church, with those attending bathed in a rich light from the stained glass windows as they sat in the high-backed pews. She was then laid to rest in the elegant cemetery out back. Mister Roberts, the stonemason, was already working on her headstone, which would feature a cherub, who represented heavenly reward:

> *Here cease thy tears, suppress thy fruitless mourn*
> *her soul—the immortal part—has upward flown*
> *On wings she soars her rapid way*
> *To yon bright regions of eternal day.*

Roger Crabbe tried to think of her death this way; but in the end he could not control his anger at the unfairness of it all. She was murdered by rebels. And this finally possessed him.

Almost immediately after Anne Crabbe's death, people began to talk about the Reverend Crabbe remarrying. This was natural, but in his state of mind he had no time for meeting eligible women, much less act the sensitive suitor. After a while, people started to think that maybe Hannah was seeing to his needs just as she was seeing to the children's needs. So, talk of a proper state of cohabitation between the two of them became a common topic of discussion.

To make matters worse for Hannah, the Englishman Benjamin Harvey reappeared. Not only was he not apologetic for his earlier crassness, he was even more outrageous than before.

"…After all, Hannah, you're in a compromising position. I've heard the rumors!" He made a gesture as if acknowledging how unfair it was. "What will you do? Marry the Reverend? Of course you won't! But please me, and I will become your guardian. Who would question your relationship with the Reverend if I, your 'betrothed,' approve the living arrangements? That would make your life so much easier, and mine," he laughed gaily, "so much more pleasurable when I visit Chester."

Hannah, in her desperation, said as convincingly as she could, "I shall describe this conversation to the Reverend Crabbe, sir, and we will see who has the last laugh."

Benjamin Harvey sighed dramatically. "My dear Hannah, the Reverend Crabbe has been made quite mad, you know, by his wife's death. He has no passion but that of avenging his wife's 'murder,' as the poor man puts it. And I, as an agent of the British Crown, am here to help him do just that.

"*You,*" and he delicately ran his finger over the buttons securing her bodice, noticing that she did not flinch at his touch, "you…do not want to be an impediment to this…grand design," and he gave an airy wave. "I can assure you of that, Missus Williams."

He saw the sudden realization in her eyes.

"Now, what do you say, my sweet? I'm not unattractive, am I? And I would be the happiest of mortals if you would give me just a little encouragement in my pursuit of you. Is that asking too much, Hannah—under the circumstances?"

She shuddered—imperceptibly she hoped. "No, Mister Harvey, it isn't. And I'm willing to consider the changed circumstances."

Remembering their last conversation, the insult still burning, he pointedly requested, "Please call me Ben, Hannah." He carefully brushed her breast with his hand.

She understood. "No, *Ben,* it isn't asking too much."

"Well, then," he said, his smile becoming a smirk.

****

Now on the run, her journey initially took her east along the river road, past large houses with splendid views of the Chester River, to Collister's Ferry. Here she was able to cross by agreeing to mind a well-to-do family's three rambunctious children during the crossing, in return for her fare.

As the parents, Jacob and Sallie Seth, sat comfortably in their coach enjoying their wine, and some cheese and bread, Hannah played with the children on the ferry, a flatboat large enough to carry the stagecoach, a chaise and numerous people on foot.

Once on the south side of the Chester River, in Queen Anne's County, both Hannah and the Seths, chatting gaily, realized that their destinations would take them on the Church Hill Road in the direction of Queen's Town.

"Missus Williams," suggested Sallie Seth, who had thoroughly enjoyed her brief reprieve from mothering, "would you be interested in accompanying us as far as the road to Wye Mills? It's quite close to Queen's Town."

"I would, indeed. Thankee, ma'am."

Missus Seth was not interested in talking to this young woman, being perfectly content to have her entertain the children; while Mister Seth enjoyed covert glances at such a pretty woman, letting his imagination ramble. Hannah and the children spent their time looking for wild fowl flushed out of the brush by the noisy carriage, and counting terrapins basking in the sun along the road.

The countryside sloped gently southwest towards the Bay as they passed occasional estates, with manor houses of brick. Long dependent upon the sot-weed, the land looked farmed-out, with many fields reverted to sedge or scrub pine, though a few were seeded with corn or wheat. *Looks a lot like Frederick County,* Hannah mused. Between estates, there were also vast stands of oak and loblolly pine, great tall trees much in demand for shipbuilding. Underneath these grand trees, were dogwood and holly, the former now bursting with white blossoms.

They stopped over at Church Hill, named for Saint Luke's Church, already ancient and made from brick carried as ballast all the way from England. They spent the night at a nearby tavern, with Hannah sleeping with the children.

Next day, Mister Seth actually had the carriage go all the way to Queen's Town, where, at a crossroad to Wye Mills, the Seths and Hannah said their goodbyes. The children cried, which made Hannah, against her will, think about the Crabbe children.

Saddened, she set out to find passage to Baltimore.

But first, Hannah intended to visit Saint Peter's Catholic Church. She had heard about this church from one of the few Catholics in Chester Town, who referred to it as a "mass house." Now that she was here in Queen's Town, she couldn't wait to visit it. She had never been to a Catholic church.

Actually, the church was a little outside of town. And it didn't look like a church. In fact, it looked like a miserable old wooden house. Disappointed, Hannah entered and found a little old lady busily dusting.

"Hello, ma'am."

The little old woman turned to look at her, surprised.

"I'd like to see the priest, if I might," Hannah said.

"Why, young lady, there's no priest here. Once in a while, one comes from Kent Island and gives a mass, but that isn't very often."

When Hannah looked confused, the woman smiled and said, "Miss, this is God's house, no matter what it looks like, and you don't need a priest to pray. I need to do a few things outside, I do," and she left with a smile.

Hannah looked at the plain table with a little vase holding a few fresh wildflowers. Behind the table on the wall was a crucifix.

Awed, Hannah went to her knees and for the first time in her life prayed as a Catholic.

Hannah had supposed that her Spanish dollar would easily buy her passage on a ship crossing the Bay over to Baltimore. After a few inquiries, however, she realized that she would have to negotiate passage, and it would not be on a comfortable ship.

She finally found a captain who agreed to transport her to Annapolis for her silver dollar. His was a filthy old bay schooner which carried produce and bulk cargo. Such a vessel was not tied up at the town wharf, but anchored, almost furtively further up the river.

"...No, sir! I will give you the dollar as soon as we arrive at Annapolis."

"Well, all right," the captain said sourly. "We leave in a coupla hours. Ye can wait here." And he pointed to a bench near the boat.

It couldn't have been an hour later when the captain reappeared and approached her.

"We'll be leaving sooner than planned, ma'am." He was smiling. "And now, we have cargo goin' to Balimer, which is where you want to go, right?"

Hannah couldn't believe her good fortune. "Oh, that would be wonderful, captain."

"Glad to oblige ya, Missus—?" and he looked questioningly at her.

Without thinking, Hannah blurted out, "Oh, it's Williams—Hannah Williams."

"Well, now, Missus *Hannah Williams*, it appears people are lookin' fer you!"

Hannah was dumbfounded.

"An' they're willin' to pay twenty dollar to see ya again!"

"Sir," she said in her best condescending voice, "I do not know what you are talking about *and* I do not like your tone," and she went to leave.

"No ye don't, missy." He blocked her way, as two grinning sailors also surrounded her. "You'll be our guest for a spell."

"I demand you let me go—immediately, or I'll yell for the sheriff. Do you hear!"

"Why, yell away, missy, because it'll be the sheriff, hisself, who'll vouch fer yer re-ward."

They enjoyed restraining her, their hands roaming at will, as they propelled her through a door.

And the next thing Hannah knew, she was locked in a dingy building smelling of marsh mud and stinking oyster shells.

30

SOLDIERS, RASCALS, AND SPIES

Baltimore Town
Mid May 1776

CHASTISED but still on the verge of insubordination in his desperation to see Hannah safe and in his arms, Christopher reported as ordered to his company at the Whetstone camp. Following the embarrassing meeting with Major Gist, he threw himself into his military duties. In the rigorous demands of military life, he now sought escape from his constant concern for Hannah's welfare.

But Christopher soon learned that all the days in the Whetstone camp followed pretty much the same routine, and would offer him little reprieve from his worries: Reveille was at first light, they would breakfast at about eight o'clock before forming for morning roll call, then drill for two hours; following a variety of fatigue duties, dinner, then drill some more before being dismissed for supper and camp chores; finally, there would be Retreat at sunset, and drinking at the sutler's wagon for those who had money or credit, and Tattoo to end the day.

The mind-numbing life of a common soldier in cantonment proved not to be the narcotic he sought. He needed not just physical but mental diversion. The soldier's life did not provide him with relief for a mind which refused to succumb to the oblivion of wine and forced him, for too many days now, to stay wide awake worrying about Hannah.

What did keep Christopher occupied was their secret observation of the tory espionage plot, particularly now since it involved the Reverend Crabbe, and might—just might—include news of Hannah.

Even though it appeared that the attempt to abduct one of Maryland's patriot leaders, William Paca, had been foiled, they had still not been able to identify the traitor referred to as "C." As a result, both Christopher and Terry continued to be assigned to duties at company headquarters, just in case there were new developments involving Alma and the secret messages.

And new developments there were; but not developments that favored a resolution of this affair, and which, in fact, did more to confuse the situation.

Christopher and Alma had established a means by which she could alert him to the need for them to meet. Alma would place a little bouquet of wild flowers on a certain grave in the church graveyard on any morning. Christopher would pass by the graveyard every afternoon, and if he saw a bouquet he knew to meet her late that afternoon at the New Bridge over the falls.

Checking the graveyard one afternoon, Christopher saw that Alma had placed her bouquet on the grave. He gathered up the flowers, and that evening, he went to meet her at the appointed time and place.

He waited and waited, but she never came. Worried, he went and stealthily observed both the church and the parsonage in the hopes of seeing her. To his dismay, she was not to be seen. Thinking that she might be sick or otherwise unable to meet him this evening, he decided he would check the graveyard again tomorrow.

Tomorrow came and went, with no bouquet on the grave. Very much concerned now, Christopher, though sorely tempted to call on Alma's mother, held his impatience in check and forced himself to check the gravesite one more time.

The next afternoon, he passed the graveyard, holding his breath as he glanced at the gravesite. A small cluster of ox-eye daisies, the flower rays stark white against the green grass, lay in front of the headstone.

With a tremendous sign of relief, Christopher couldn't wait to see Alma at the meeting site, and, in fact, was there an hour before the scheduled time.

"Alma!" Christopher rushed up to her as she approached the bridge. "We've been so concerned for you." He stopped his jabbering, and asked "Is everything all right, Alma?"

Alma shrugged. "Appears to be, Christopher, but the last two days have been worrisome."

"How so, Alma?"

"Well, first of all, no sooner did I find the most recent letter under the rock and leave the flowers for you like we agree'd, then the Reverend Johnson ask'd me if I check under the rock every day and immediately deliver it to the shoemaker over on Forest Street, as I was instructed to do. Then he ask'd me if I ever told another soul about our holy secret.

"I assure'd him I always did what he said for me to do, and he seemed to accept that. But it scared me, Christopher, and I just couldn't bring myself to meet with you, thinking the Reverend might be watching me, ya know."

"I understand perfectly, Alma."

"So, then, he tells me when I next find a letter under the rock I'm to take it direct to a Mister Harvey, who's staying at Fite's Inn, over on Baltimore Street—which I did, yesterday. I couldn't risk holding the letter—I'm sorry."

Christopher looked fondly at the young woman. "Alma, you did fine. Now, do ye know who this man was?"

"Nay, but he was a proper English gentleman—handsome, too. Said he wish'd he had time to fete me, but he was obliged to go to," she hesitated, thinking.... "Annapolis, I think he said."

Christopher immediately reported Alma's information to Major Gist.

Gist checked with Henry Fite but learned little more about the Englishman Harvey, except that he had departed immediately after a young woman visited him. He also confirmed that the shoemaker and covert courier, Charles Stevens, was in town and continued his business, as usual.

By then it was the first week of June, and there had been no further secret letters, or any other developments in the plot

"Could they have realized their plot has been uncovered?" Terry asked after hearing Gist's news.

"Why? Because of the measures we took to protect our representatives?" Thoughtful, Gist shrugged and said, "Could be—I suppose we might have been a little less obvious about our concern for their welfare...."

Christopher was thoughtful. "Even if they only suspect a breach in security, that alone might be enough to endanger Alma."

Gist dismissed this. "Christopher, I think that may have been Reverend Johnson's purpose in interrogating Missus Lynch the other day; and it appears, to me at least, that she is not under any real suspicion."

About this time, too, William Paca and the others elected to represent the province in Congress arrived safe and sound in Annapolis hoping to return shortly to Philadelphia with authorization from the Convention to vote for independence.

"As I am sure they will," stated Mary Katherine Goddard, speaking to a few visitors to her shop.

"We have what?—eight deputies, of whom three or four will be empowered to represent us in the critical vote in Congress."

Old John Freelon, a fixture at the shop, said, "Aye, and I think it will be Chase, Paca (of course), Alexander, and Carroll of Carollton. That's my opinion."

Mary Katherine shook her head sagely. "Nay, I know for a fact that Robert Alexander excused himself from participation in the Convention *and* the Congress move to vote for independence due to a disabling injury to his ankle.

"Oh, 'tis true, John," Mary Katherine continued, "Robert can't travel due to his injury, and, in fact, is still here in Baltimore."

Another of those present shook his head, sympathetically. "What a pity! After all that he has done for the cause. To depart from the most famous assemblage ever to meet in America; and to miss participating in the creation of a perfect society...."

31

HELD CAPTIVE

**Queen's Town
Eastern Shore of Maryland
Late May 1776**

IT NEVER OCCURRED TO HER that word would travel so fast. She had counted on a week at least before broadsides would be distributed, and even longer before the province's two newspapers would be circulating with advertisements for her apprehension. By then, she expected to be safe in Baltimore.

Hannah paced the interior, which appeared to be a shed of some sort. It contained nothing but a dozen or so empty baskets, some caked with mud and containing a few oyster shells, others with the withered stalks and leaves of produce. Fortunately, they had thrown her basket in as they closed the door, so she had a little food.

Light showed through gaps in the riven wooden boards of the shed. She was able to peer out and saw other rough wooden buildings—warehouses, she thought to herself. She had seen such rude structures in Chester Town; and they lay along the river edge outside of town, as did these—unfortunately, she sighed, for she knew proper people were not to be found around such places. She also saw boardwalks cutting through various marsh grasses, reeds and arrowhead leaf, and beyond some buildings, the shimmering gray of a tidal river.

Sometime later, she heard voices outside and yelled for help, banging the door as hard as she could, the rough splintered wood scrapping her fingers and palms.

The talking outside stopped and the door flew open with a bang, and in stepped the man who called himself Captain Fellows.

"Quit your clamoring, woman!" he ordered.

"I demand to be taken to the sheriff. This is outrageous treatment."

The man leered, looking her up and down. "Why, missy, sure, I kin hand ya over to the sheriff, and he'll put ye up in his little jail, where the drunken and brawlin' sailors you'll be sharin' a cell with will be more than happy to entertain ya!" He looked contemptuously at her. "You're jest a runaway and a slattern, and deserving of no special treatment in most anybody's mind."

Hannah was silent, her outrage changed to fear.

Captain Fellows nodded knowingly. "I thought you'd prefer my choice of quarters for ya, missy. Now, no more noise outta ya, do ye hear?" Without waiting for a reply, he turned to leave, then stopped and faced her, adding, "Oh, there'll be guards here all the time." He then left, shutting the door behind him.

As the hours passed, Hannah rolled her extra clothing into a pillow and, despite the heat, fell asleep.

She was awakened by Captain Fellows.

"Sorry 'bout the accommodations, missy, but as I explained earlier, it's this or the jail. So this'll have ta do 'til we see someone about our re-ward. In the meantime, I'll take that silver dollar you promised me and with that maybe I kin arrange fer water and food. An' a course, ye could make it easier on yerself if you'd care to share me bed."

Hannah thought about all the insults she had absorbed, and she finally exploded. She walked over to the man and slapped him as hard as she could on the cheek.

Before he could collect himself, she was in his face. Speaking through clenched teeth, her voice loud and threatening, she stabbed him repeatedly in his chest with her finger. "Now, you listen to me, little man. The people who will pay you your twenty damn dollars are not kind people. They are not religious people. They are members of the S.P.G. If they find me in this hellish place, half-clothed, crying that I had been ravished by *you*...they will surely kill you. Do you understand?"

She could sense that the man was unable to cope with this situation.

She looked at him and said, "Well *mister* captain, what are you goin' to do?"

The man had made up his mind but tried one last stratagem. "Well, maybe if ya give me that silver dollar ya have, I'll let ye go and we'll forget about all the rest. How's that?"

Hannah laughed contemptuously. "Filthy liar! Let's you and me wait for your 're-ward,'" which she pronounced exactly as he did. "As for the silver dollar...I don't have a penny to my name. If I did, I wouldn't have had to truck with a scrub like you."

He couldn't help himself. He hit her. It was a half-hearted blow, half a slap and half a balled fist, because he wasn't sure if he should have allowed himself the pleasure; but, nonetheless, Hannah stumbled and fell to her knees, cupping her face in her hands. She tried not to cry, even when he put his hands on her.

Enraged, he forced his hand down her bodice, wanting to humiliate this woman. Seeking her naked breast, to squeeze, to hurt, he felt metal.

Grasping it, he pulled it out and realized it was a coin. Why, he grinned, it was the Spanish dollar the bitch claimed she didn't have.

He pulled the leather thong roughly over her head and took her Spanish dollar.

"Bitch." He pushed her so that she crumpled on the floor. He went to hoist her skirt, but suddenly froze, remembering her threat.

"Bitch," he said again, and already thinking of the explanation he would give the woman's masters for her treatment, the man who called himself captain quickly left, locking the door behind him.

****

Days went by. Occasionally someone would open the door and a young black girl would quickly place water and food on the floor. She would retreat, and quickly as the door opened, it closed.

Because of the heat and the boredom, Hannah would frequently sleep, so the passage of days and nights became confused. She had no idea how long she was imprisoned.

The heat of day, the chill of night, never enough water, never enough food. The air in the shed became fetid.

One day, the door was opened and, instead of the young black girl, a man entered. He was not her captor, but someone else.

"Ye must be Hannah Williams," he said politely. He was dressed like a gentleman—or perhaps like a British officer in civilian dress, like Benjamin Harvey.

"You *know* I am Hannah Williams, sir," she said wearily. "And I apologize for not being presentable to receive visitors." During the day she felt like she was in a bake oven and would strip down to her chemise. That this man found her so immodestly dressed didn't bother her a bit. Then abruptly, "What do *you* want?"

He looked at her, a filthy, disheveled young woman, who was trying hard to maintain her pride. He couldn't tell if she was attractive or not. But she stood straight and unvanquished, challenging him. He liked that.

"Well, immediately, some sunlight and fresh air...." The stench of human waste was powerful, "and perhaps you would care for some cool water? How does that sound?"

"Better than living in a shed that might as well be a necessary house, sir, and this has been my home for I don't know how long."

Staring at the man, who then looked away, she dressed.

"If ye please, ma'am," and he escorted her out into the light of a beautiful day. She took a deep breath and did not gag. She smelled the salty breeze and water grasses and—what was that smell? It was, she realized, the clean smell of the outdoors.

Walking only a few steps, Hannah became unsteady on her feet and felt faint.

"Easy, Missus Williams, easy…" The man quickly grasped her from behind by her elbows to make sure she did not collapse.

"Do ye need to sit on this bench for a bit?"

Hannah shook her head, saying "No, thank you," even as she disengaged herself from his grasp.

She put her hands up chest high with her palms facing out as if to ward off further contact. She stood like this for a few seconds and began to feel better. Shortly thereafter, now revived, Hannah asked, "Sir, would you introduce yourself? I assume you have some association with my masters, the S.P.G, and that I will be returned to them." She looked accusingly at him.

The gentleman looked with amusement at Hannah. "I beg your pardon, ma'am, my name is Hyman Cohen. And no, Missus Williams, I have no association with the S.P.G., an organization which I, a Jew, detest."

There was a silence during which Hannah realized that Mister Cohen did not intend to add anything further concerning her status.

"Am I still a prisoner, then?"

"Not really. I am responsible for your welfare. And so far it appears I have not done very well. I notice you have a nasty bruise on your cheek."

"Oh, compliments of my host. Small cost for what he really had in mind. I told him if he put his filthy hands on me he would be killed." Hannah laughed. "It was a bluff which worked."

Mister Cohen did not laugh. "Captain Fellows was paid five gold joes to deliver you uninjured and in good spirits. I apologize for putting it in those terms, Missus Williams, but I have my responsibilities. Captain Fellows has cheated my employer."

"He also stole my Spanish dollar, which," she sighed, "meant more to me than just money."

"Ah, then I have a number of issues to raise with Captain Fellows. Enough for now. I'm taking you to an inn, here in Queen's Town, owned by Missus Crabble—you'll find it very comfortable. You'll have a negro maid to take care of you and we will obtain some new clothes for you. In return, I ask that you do not try to leave—quite frankly, you won't be allowed to. Can you sit a horse, ma'am?"

"Yes. I suppose you won't answer the questions I want to ask."

"Let's leave your questions for later, Missus Williams. Right now, I think you need a day or two to recover from your ordeal."

"As you wish—Mister Cohen."

"Ma'am," the negro woman pointed out, "it's almost June and time for a good spring bathing anyway."

With this introduction, Hannah was coaxed into the soapy tub. Immersed, she was scrubbed and her hair washed. Out and wrapped in a huge towel, her hair was combed and set, her nails clipped, and, then dressed *a la robe*, her measurements taken for a comfortable traveling outfit.

After two good nights' sleep, marvelous meals in her room, and two days spent being doted upon by manteau-maker, hairdresser and cosmetician, among, it seemed, a host of others, Hannah was transformed from wretched prisoner to decent woman.

On the second day following her release, all was finished, and Hannah appeared in the downstairs sitting room beautifully remade, wearing a simple raw silk dress consisting of a low-cut bodice over a linen chemise with a flowing skirt gathered around the waist, topped off with a mob cap and a rakish straw hat.

"Good lord," said Hyman Cohen, splashing his coffee as he hastily rose to greet his protégé. "I'll need an army to protect you from every male in the province—including myself!"

Hannah laughed, delighted by the effect she had. Then sobering, said, "This is all very nice, Mister Cohen, but what is in store for me, if I may be so bold to ask?"

"Ah, of course, you are interested in your future, Missus Williams. I will explain as best I can. Let's do so in a civilized manner, shall we? A glass of wine, perhaps, and a nice dinner?"

"I find your offer irresistible, sir."

Mister Cohen walked Hannah to a pleasant arbor and seated her at a table with two comfortable chairs. A manservant brought them both a glass of red wine, and a plate of pungent cheese and hot bread.

Relishing the wine's fruity taste and its earthy, ripe plum bouquet, Hannah wanted to savor the wine and feel its heady effect.

She put her glass down. "Now, I am in an awkward position, sir, and I would appreciate the courtesy of your honesty. What is my status?"

"Your status? I work for...well, let us say a very powerful person, who owes a debt of gratitude to someone who has your best interests at heart."

Hannah was incredulous. "A powerful person concerned about *me?* I don't understand."

Mister Cohen chuckled. "I see you are confused. Please, have some cold beef—the sauce is excellent—while I try to explain."

He took a sip of his wine. "There are circles within circles, my dear. I have been told that a Mister Christopher Sims is most concerned about your safety and I have been instructed to do everything in my power to return you to him." Mister Cohen looked quizzically at Hannah. "He must be a very important man. You know him, of course."

Hannah gasped and almost laughed at the absurdity of it all. "Mister Cohen, to me Christopher Sims is the most important man in the world, but why he is important to your powerful employer, I know not."

"Nor do I, Missus Williams, but I am sure we will learn in good time."

"How did you find me, Mister Cohen?"

"Not terribly difficult. After all, Captain Fellows knew who you were when you fell into his hands. *Our* business, Missus Williams, is the making of money which we do by knowing what is going on in the ports and warehouses up and down the Bay. We have an extensive network of informants." Mister Cohen smiled.

"Oh," was all Hannah could say.

"And I have something of yours to return." Mister Cohen was suddenly holding Hannah's Spanish dollar in his hand. It was on a silver chain.

"Unfortunately, the leather thong broke under…stressful conditions. I hope this chain will do."

"Oh, dear, it's beautiful; and Mister Cohen, you don't know how much this coin means to me."

"Perhaps I do, Missus Williams. Let's drink to—a good luck charm? That, and to a happy conclusion to this adventure of yours."

All of a sudden, Hannah looked as if she was going to cry.

"Mister Cohen, please, may I ask a favor of you?"

"Of course."

"I'd like to visit Saint Peter's Church, which is not too far from here, to say a prayer and leave a little offering….

32

REUNITED

Lovely Lane
Baltimore Town
May 25, 1776

CHRISTOPHER LET HIMSELF IN, the door as usual open. Either Rachel was home, or Aunt Jane, as she often did, forgot to lock the door upon her departure. He entered the sitting room and was surprised to see a strange woman quickly rise from the settee. As she turned to look at him, he saw that she was tall, with swirls of shiny brown hair, and was dressed in a light blue dress which complemented her slender figure.

The woman turned to face him, looking at him in a hopeful way....

...She was fourteen then and he was seventeen when she had first asked the question, and then asked it again and again at important moments in her life, always seeking an answer that would reassure her: "Do you think I'm—

"—too awkward to be attractive?" the woman asked, standing very tall and looking at him with her great brown eyes, and a shy smile that showed a gap between her front teeth.

Christopher was spellbound, barely able to respond. But with a catch in his throat, he managed to remind her, "Didn't I pretty much say, 'if you stood tall and wore the look you're now wearing, Hannah Williams, you'd be about the most beautiful woman in the entire province?'"

"Pretty much, Chris—*but*," she couldn't resist adding, "ye still wouldn't dance with me!

"By the way, your Aunt Jane and Rachel have been wonderful. Oh, and your aunt," Hannah giggled in embarrassment, "assured me that they had engagements which would keep both of them away until this evening!"

Until this evening, Christopher smiled, knowing what Aunt Jane had in mind. That Hannah would mention it, knowing how suggestive it was, he knew, was meant to break the ice.

They gave each other a tentative hug, much like cousins would when meeting for the first time since a childhood which had been close.

Then both stood back, holding hands at arms length, to look at the other. Both saw changes, because both were more worldly now.

She stood tall, and still slender; but at first glance, it seemed to him that she had filled out, perhaps because this was the first time he had ever seen Hannah in a dress that seemed to perfectly fit her girl-woman figure. He had never seen her hair looking so soft and curly.

Hannah's face, though, while still pleasant, was different. It took Christopher a few seconds to realize that this difference was caused by her eyes, always big and brown and looking as if in wonder at the world…now, however, that wonder was gone, replaced by a depth and intensity that was a little unsettling to him.

As for Hannah, she was not interested in any physical changes in Christopher—he was still attractive without really being handsome, his outward appearance better now, dressed as he was in a town suit. But what caught her attention were the worry lines on his face. She was sure these lines weren't there a year ago. No, these new lines were caused by worry for a loved one and not by a farmer squinting into the sun.

"Hannah, I can't believe we're here, together, and needing no one's permission!"

Hannah had been brought to the house on Lovely Lane by Mister Cohen, who introduced her to Jane and Rachel. Very business-like and politely declining refreshments, he quickly departed, leaving the three women to themselves.

"Missus Williams—may I call you Hannah? I'm Jane, but Christopher calls me Aunt Jane, of course—"

"And I'm Rachel," the other woman laughed. "Welcome to Baltimore and freedom!"

Jane and Rachel prepared afternoon tea, light fare of hot bread and butter, and Rachel's "whigs," explaining to Hannah that these were round cakes upon which she spread sugar icing and nuts. "Some people are calling them 'buns,'" noted Rachel, as she took a sip of wine.

Hannah had looked oddly at Jane when offered wine, but accepted the latter's explanation: "What's left? We can't have tea."

The two women were eager to have Hannah tell them all about her adventure, and sat enthralled as they heard the young woman describe her escape, her capture, and then her liberation.

Having completed her tale, Hannah looked at both women and said, clearly mystified, "but I don't understand the involvement of Mister Cohen or his 'employer' as he described the man who was responsible for my freedom. Do either of you know anything about this? I do so much want to thank my benefactor. Do ye suppose Christopher would know?"

Both Jane and Rachel professed ignorance of the matter, with Jane saying, simply, "Just thank the Lord."

Rachel was a little more vocal. "If Mister Cohen was unwilling to provide additional information about his employer, perhaps you should leave it at that. I suspect whoever this 'benefactor' is, the gratitude you expressed to Mister Cohen will be sufficient."

Hannah cocked her head as she looked at Rachel, hearing something in her voice that seemed to discourage further inquiry.

"I'm sure you're right, Rachel."

They then insisted that Hannah tell them about life in Frederick County and how she and Christopher came to fall in love with each other.

"How romantic!" exclaimed Rachel after hearing Hannah's version of their love affair. "Christopher tried to describe this to me, but men simply don't have the gift of gab!"

Hannah asked about Alma Lynch and learned that both Jane and Rachel had met her on a number of occasions and liked her. Jane intimated that Alma was cooperating in a sensitive political matter, but Rachel politely cut her off with, "We best let Christopher discuss that, Hannah."

Finally Jane and Rachel claimed that they had important errands to do. Rachel showed Hannah to her room, which they would share together. "...and please, Hannah, feel free to consider anything in this room as yours." Rachel gave Hannah a hug, and stepping back, said, "Christopher and you will make a wonderful couple!"

They descended to the sitting room, where Jane and Rachel then excused themselves, talking happily as they walked out the door.

Christopher and Hannah, after the initial shock of seeing each other for the first time in a year, and after tentatively touching and hugging each other in ways that became more familiar as their awkwardness dissipated, were eager to rekindle the flame that was reduced to an ember in May '75.

So many things had changed since they had last seen each other back in Frederick County. Neither knew what effect this would have on the other. Each realized they had explanations to give, gaps to fill, moments of weakness to wrestle with...and, perhaps, to explain—who could tell?

But for now, they just wanted to be as comfortable with each other as they once had been.

Christopher poured glasses of wine and making themselves comfortable on the settee, each with a firm hold on the other's hand, Christopher said, "Hannah, there is so much I want to ask you, and so much I want to tell you—but right this minute, you have to tell me about your escape. I couldn't believe it when Rachel showed me the advertisement. Did they show it to you?"

"They did, Chris, an' you know something...the advertisement for my capture was smack between those for negro runaways—people who will never have the chance I got to be free."

Christopher was not sure what to say.

"For the rest of my life," she went on, "I will fight to put an end to slavery—because I know what it's like to be treated like a slave, and I wouldn't wish that on anybody, not even negro people. An' you'll support me in this, Chris Sims." It was obviously not a question.

"Aye, Hannah, I will."

Both were momentarily quieted by Hannah's intensity.

After a pause, Christopher kissed her hand, and repeated, "I will, Hannah." Then gently redirecting the conversation, "Back to your escape, Hannah," he asked, "What caused you to flee? How did you cross the Bay? How did you get here? What—"

Hannah put a stop to his cascading questions by suddenly kissing him.

"Now," she said primly, "would you like to hear my story?"

She began by explaining why she felt compelled to flee. In describing what drove her to this, she did not include those ugly incidents with Benjamin Harvey. She had already worried this to distraction, and finally concluded that what is done out of desperation does not require a confession. She just prayed that her reluctance to discuss this with Christopher did not represent unfaithfulness.

So, she emphasized the atmosphere after Anne Crabbe's death, which she said became unbearable.

"...and it wasn't the Reverend Crabbe's fault—I guess... well, I guess people just want to think the worst, for whatever reason. It got to the point where people thought the Reverend Crabbe should marry me. I didn't want that, but, then, neither did the Reverend Crabbe! So, I ran away."

"The advertisement said on the fourteenth of May. We received the news on the eighteenth. Missus Goddard refused to advertise it in her newspaper, and we did try to do more. Major

Gist," and Christopher briefly described him to Hannah, "Major Gist had word sent to the various Committees of Observation to be on the lookout for you, because you had fled from a tory who was involved in a plot to sabotage the patriot cause."

Hannah was surprised. "Ye knew this about the Reverend Crabbe...here in Baltimore?—really?"

"Indeed," Christopher said with passion. "We knew that he was involved in a conspiracy that included loyalists here in Baltimore, but also in Annapolis, and beyond.

"But I've gotten us off on a tangent. You fled—"

"Well, I thought I would fool them by going 'round to Queen's Town, but it didn't work." Hannah shrugged. "I talked to this captain and thought I had arranged passage across the Bay, but he caught on to who I was and held me until he could get the 're-ward.'" Hannah pronounced it the way her captor had. "I'll likely say it that way for the rest of my life," she laughed with a hint of embarrassment, remembering....

"And your imprisonment?" Christopher asked.

"Unpleasant, and that is all I would like to say about it."

"All right, Hannah. But how did you escape?"

"I didn't, Chris—"

And so it went for more than two hours until....

"...We crossed the Bay in a beautiful boat. Mister Cohen called it a 'bugeye.'" They both laughed. "What a name for a boat!"

"Anyway," Hannah continued, still laughing, "He said the 'bugeye' was designed as an oyster dredger; but this one was converted to a pleasure cruiser for 'his employer,' as Mister Cohen always referred to him. I had the owner's cabin, which, I have to admit, can certainly spoil a woman.

"We docked in Baltimore this morning and here I am, not having the faintest idea how or why it happened. Mister Cohen was a lovely man but unhelpful in explaining who masterminded my salvation. I thought it might be you, Chris, who was directing all these powerful forces—" Her voice trailed off, and she could only shrug, happy but confused.

Christopher, too, was mystified. "Hannah, I wish I could claim to be the 'power' behind your freedom, but, truthfully, I have no idea…There were a lot of people looking for you, I can assure ye of that, but until we greeted each other this afternoon, I had no idea that you had actually been rescued days ago.

"Somebody, though, thinks enough of you and me to have gone to such great lengths to bring us together. I want to do everything I can to deserve the trust you and others have placed in me—not to mention…well, the affection," he ended, not as eloquently as he wanted.

Hannah smiled happily at Christopher. "I'll accept that as a commitment, Chris."

By the time Jane and Rachel returned that evening, Christopher and Hannah, needing to catch their breaths, were ready to go out on the town.

33

MEMORIES OF A PAST AND FUTURE LIFE

Baltimore Town
May-June 1776

AT THIS POINT IN THEIR LIVES, the most important thing for Christopher and Hannah was to reaffirm their feelings for each other, and then get on with their new lives. In the backcountry of Lower Frederick County, they had dreamed of living in a real city like Baltimore or Annapolis; but the harsh realities of city life, the compromising circumstances—for both of them—surrounding this last year apart, and a looming revolution were all obstacles to their dreams.

Did they see a change in each other? Though so far unexpressed, the answer was yes. So, what effect would this have on their relationship? They needed to find this out, and they didn't have a lot of time to do so.

Not wanting to dispel the joy of being reunited with Christopher, Hannah had been side-stepping a matter which now had to be dealt with.

"Chris, you've joined the army. We need to talk about it."

Christopher looked downcast. "Aye, I did, Hannah. Now it's apparent that it won't work out exactly as I hoped—which was we would defeat the British in one swift campaign, win our independence, and I would come to liberate you—the gallant hero, no less!"

"How romantic, Chris!" Hannah exclaimed, actually excited by the thought.

"Romantic?" Christopher gave a self-deprecating laugh. "Well, I wanted it to be like that, Hannah; but, seriously, we do need to talk about it. I have an obligation.... " He explained his rash decision to go off to rescue her and how common sense was restored only through personal humiliation.

I really have to see this through, Hannah."

"Chris, we'll see it through. It'll be only a few months of campaigning while so much rides on the outcome. Remember that I've been living amongst those who have lorded it over us and would do so for all time if given the opportunity."

Hannah looked at Christopher, her eyes a little watery. "I'll be a soldier, too, Chris!"

He looked fondly at this marvelous woman. "We must all be soldiers."

They still had a lot of catching up to do.

Hannah eventually started at the beginning, that awful day in early May '75 when she learned that she and the Crabbe family would abandon the house and chapel on the hill above Rock Creek and flee—that was the word the Reverend Crabbe used with great bitterness—flee to Baltimore.

"You obviously recovered my note in our 'secret log.'" Having said "our" Hannah again thought of the Crabbe children, feeling guilt but also a sense of loss.

Christopher sensed her sadness but could do nothing about it.

"As soon as I learned of your leaving, I wanted to chase you down, but cooler heads prevailed. Jeremy and Constance both asked me what I intended to do when I had overtaken you—"

Here, Christopher stopped himself, showing the same indecision he felt at the time.

"Then Jeremy said to me, 'Why, anything you'd do, Chris, will be unlawful.' And then Constance weighed in, saying I shouldn't do it."

"Oh, my good friends!" Hannah clapped her hands, thinking of more innocent times. "Do you hear from them?"

"No, not directly. They really aren't much for writing, you know. But George occasionally includes news about them. They're doin' fine by the way."

"How are things back home?" Hannah still thought of Lower Frederick County as home.

"Good, generally. I've been getting letters from George and Susan from time to time. They're not happy with my letter writing," he admitted sheepishly. "I just sent off only my third letter to 'em last week."

"Oh, Christopher, shame on you—and you can write so well."

"I know, I know. Aunt Jane has been all over me for that. Anyway," he said, hoping to change Hannah's frown to a smile, "Mary and Mike are finally getting married! And she's not even with child yet," he said. "But then—"

"Now, stop that, Christopher!"

"Oh, speaking of bread in the oven, this will interest you: the Hungerford's Sally—I know you two were friends...well, Sally went and got herself with child. According to Doctor Wootton, who I saw a while back, the man responsible for her condition didn't come forward, and Sally refused to name the scoundrel.

"Doctor Wootton said that Mary Hungerford decided that Sally would marry any man willing to buy her indenture, and that turned out to be old Matt Fraser."

Hannah was horrified. "Matt Fraser? That old cooper who was always too drunk to work?"

"That's the man. Doctor Wootton said though old man Fraser complained that she'd cost more than a milk cow, he was still willin' to buy her paper for hard money."

Hannah was about to explode when Christopher added, laughing, "But then none other than Doctor Tylor—if you can believe this—steps forward and claims responsibility for Sally's condition."

Hannah looked hard at Christopher. "Chris, you know it wasn't Doctor Tylor—"

"Of course it wasn't—"

"It was James Bayley...." Hannah stated quietly.

"Why, that little bastard," exclaimed a surprised Christopher. Then after a pause, he opined, "Well, most say that Sally ended up with the husband of her dreams."

"Could do worse than Solomon Tylor," Hannah said, sort of nodding in agreement. "Doesn't make it right, though," she concluded.

"Well, anyway," Christopher wanted to end this conversation, "they up and went off to North Carolina."

And they continued to put missing pieces together.

"When I got to Baltimore, you were gone!"

"It was the lowest point of my life." Hannah was thinking back, and shuddered. "Leaving Baltimore, not knowing our final destination, I truly thought I might never see you again, Chris Sims." Hannah looked at him with tears in her eyes.

"Hannah, I promised you that I would find you no matter where you were."

"And I thought of that many times, Chris, believe me, I did—"

She continued, glossing over her painful memories of Annapolis, spinning a wonderful story about the trip by boat to Chester Town, and what she did there until she felt compelled to flee last month—all of which brought Christopher up to date on her activities...as far as Hannah was concerned.

They finally got around to the future.

"I want to be a printer, Hannah, and publish a newspaper." He then told her about Missus Goddard and her newspaper, and working for her for a good part of the year he had been in Baltimore. "I came home in clothes splattered with ink spots and stinking of the same stuff. But the satisfaction in holding a newspaper, or a pamphlet, or...whatever, is so satisfying, Hannah. Missus Goddard refers to it as the broadcasting of information, and I'm certain that's what I want to do."

He went on to tell her that Missus Goddard promised him work as a printer's devil to learn the trade. "It doesn't pay much, but we can make do."

Hannah was enthusiastic. She knew the drawbacks to finding work in town, but what she had seen so far seemed to suggest that there were enough good people around who wanted to support them.

Buoyed by Christopher's telling of his plans, which seemed sensible enough, Hannah offered hers: "Rachel asked me if I could read and write and I told her I could. She mentioned that she could use a helping hand with her academy for young women. Now, I know how to run a household and it seems to me there's not much difference between the two. What do you think?"

"Hannah, I think—no! I *know* we have a future here in Baltimore."

34

ALL IS NOT WELL

Baltimore Town
June 1776

EARLY ON, Hannah had stated that she wanted very much to see Alma. When Christopher made awkward noises about her meeting with Alma, Hannah made it clear that she was aware that there were some sensitivities involved in her request.

"Rachel said you would explain it to me. Please do."

Christopher did so, explaining the tory plot in general terms, and noting that Alma was playing a crucial part in their efforts to thwart this plot.

"... so you can see, Hannah, that visiting with Alma is not without its risks. In fact, I have no easy way to contact her. It just wasn't necessary."

"Please, please, Chris, I do so want to see dear Alma."

"Hannah, I'll go to the rectory and if I see either Alma or her mother, I'll arrange something. No! You'll not go with me, Hannah. Please be patient."

That afternoon, following his duty, Christopher went to the church and set himself up at a spot on Crooked Lane near the main road which gave him a good view of both entrances to the church and the rectory. *Surely*, he thought, *I'll be able to spot Alma from this vantage point.*

But hours later, he still had no sightings of either Alma or her mother.

Late afternoon, and Christopher finally called it quits and went home to tell Hannah that he did not see either Alma or her mother. He assured her that he would try again tomorrow afternoon, duties permitting.

He followed the same pattern for the next two days with no success. He had told Hannah that Alma's mother was sickly and from time to time required that Alma spend long hours in the rectory, often at her mother's bedside.

But finally, Christopher had to admit that something might be wrong and sought a means of checking on Alma.

Aunt Jane came to the rescue, volunteering to contact a member of the St. Paul's women's group, using the excuse that she had heard that Missus Lynch was bedridden and she wanted to help as a member of the Anglican community.

A Night on the Town
"The Sign of the Cup and Crown"
June 9, 1776

A couple of weeks after Hannah's arrival in Baltimore, they all went out to dine, a party which included Mary Katherine Goddard, Terry Simon and Henry Murray.

After the usually filling midday meal, evening supper was "a simple repast" to quote Henry Murray. In this case, it included batter-fried oysters garnished with breadcrumbs and lemon slices; a salmagundi of minced veal and chicken with pickled onions and boiled eggs, all chopped and served with oil; bread, butter; a good, sharp cheese; fruit; and a light dessert which was Sarah Chilton's "fine ice cream," a rarity which all enjoyed.

Sloshing down some wine, Henry Murray continued his lecture. "A declaration of independence would be a secular confirmation of God's Great Design that we Americans have been chosen to be the Defenders of Liberty for the rest of mankind."

"To which I can only respond, Mister Murray, that tracing such a partisan event back to Jesus Christ is a bit presumptuous!"

"But, Mary Katherine, how else can you explain the miracle of thirteen quarrelsome colonies being of like mind on the issue of independence, even while gathered together in the same room, when they can't even agree on why they disagree with England?"

Hannah looked at Christopher as if to ask if Mister Murray was serious. Christopher mimed that he had no idea. Not even Aunt Jane could tell if Henry was serious.

It was true that most Americans had now accepted the fact that this unfortunate matter with England had come down to self-preservation, if nothing else. Without thinking ahead, Americans now generally viewed a declaration of independence as a last ditch effort to reclaim English democracy from the clutches of...well...the English.

Then again, there were those Americans who believed that America was the promised land. With a religious fervor bordering on the fanatic, these people were visionaries who disdained the very nature of English democracy for the absolutism of a perfect nation under God's rule.

"Or perhaps it is just weariness on the part of those in Congress," Missus Goddard suggested spitefully, "who no longer have the vigor to arrive at an English solution to what we all assumed was an English problem."

Rachel did not enjoy this repartee. "So, out of—what?—spite, do we seek the perfect world? Who was it who wrote, 'They wander in the dark because they prefer lightening to light?'"

Later that evening, Mary Katherine said her goodbyes, wanting to finish an article for the next issue of the paper. Henry and Jane also excused themselves, citing old age as an excuse for calling it an early evening. Commenting naughtily, the others decided to go to a popular coffee house.

As they approached the coffee house, a man and a woman were dismounting from a carriage. In the yellow light of the two gas lamps standing as luminous sentinels in front of the entrance, a very attractive couple could clearly be seen.

Hannah stopped dead in her tracks, and quickly turned away from the couple. Her motion was so abrupt that the strangers even seemed to notice her awkward movement—but only for a moment, as they continued into the coffee house.

All in the group looked curiously at her, and then Christopher asked, "What is it, Hannah? Is something wrong?"

Feeling almost physically sick, Hannah whispered, "I know that man. His name is Benjamin Harvey, and he's a secret agent for the British. He told me so himself once when he visited the Reverend Crabbe in Chester Town. We *must* leave!"

Christopher looked at her, alarmed. "Ye say his name is what?—Benjamin Harvey? Why, Alma met a man by that very name here in Baltimore not more than two weeks ago. He accepted a secret letter from the Reverend Johnson. Good lord."

The group quickly left and returned to Jane's house.

Hannah described how she came to know Harvey, and described his relationship with the tory clique in Chester Town. She said nothing about her more personal involvement with him. She had hoped against hope that she would never have to explain this particular episode in her life to Christopher, or any one else for that matter. Now, she might have to consider doing so sooner rather than later.

After hearing Hannah's story, Terry hurried off to inform Major Gist.

Hugging Hannah, who was literally shaking, Christopher said,"Let's get a good night's sleep and see what tomorrow brings."

****

Tomorrow was even more ominous. The very next afternoon, Jane brought home disturbing news.

" ...I'm just tellin' ye what I heard from Missus Whiteman, Jane insisted. "She said that Missus Lynch is very ill, likely on her deathbed, and her ungrateful daughter just up and left."

"That isn't possible," Hannah said heatedly. "Alma would never, ever leave her mother."

Christopher tried to calm her. "Hannah, we know that, and we'll make that very point to the authorities. I'll see Major Gist and insist that he take action."

Rachel looked at him with what could only be called tolerance, but she was adamant as she said, "No, Christopher, you are a private soldier and will not—nay, cannot, speak plainly to Major Gist. But I certainly can, and I intend to take this up with Major *Mordecai* Gist in the strongest of terms." Turning to Hannah, "and I assure you that the Reverend Johnson will be made answerable!"

True to her word, Rachel raised such a ruckus that Major Gist ordered Captain Smith to personally take a detail of soldiers to Saint Paul's and confront the Reverend Johnson, even threatening arrest if he did not provide a satisfactory explanation as to the whereabouts of Alma Lynch.

But Captain Smith reported back that the Reverend Johnson had departed suddenly for "consultations" with Church authorities in Annapolis. A young minister, newly arrived from London, was in temporary charge and, according to Captain Smith, "knew nothing useful."

Major Gist sent a request to the Annapolis Committee to interrogate the Reverend Smith. Missus Goddard placed an advertisement in her paper, as well as printing and distributing broadsides, offering a handsome reward for any information leading to Alma's safe return.

In the meantime, all that could be said was that Alma Lynch had gone missing.

35

NO CERTAIN FUTURE

Baltimore Town
June-July 1776

WEEKS LATER and there was still no word of Alma. Foul play was widely suspected among the patriot community. Patriot authorities in Annapolis called on the Reverend Johnson in Annapolis but were informed that he had departed for England due to "poor health."

The Reverend Scott, the subsequent report referred to him as "a sinister man appropriately dressed only in black," was arrogantly dismissive, assuring his inquisitors that he was a man of God and loyal to the Crown, then asking them in deadpan fashion, "Surely, sir, you are not accusing me of disloyalty?" And smiled at their discomfort.

Attempts to track down Benjamin Harvey met with failure. By the time Terry was able to talk to Major Gist, Harvey was long gone; and despite a Committee warrant calling for his detention to answer questions concerning the suspicious disappearance of Alma Lynch, there were no leads to his whereabouts.

Frustrating as it was, Major Gist was able to identify Harvey, which might help one day in capturing him. "Our spies inform us that Harvey is Lieutenant Harvey of His Majesty's Navy.

When he is not acting the spy, he serves on the armed sloop *Otter*, which is terrorizing the Bay under Lord Dunmore."

"In other words, this Harvey is a pirate," said Captain Smith disgustedly.

All of this was disturbing in itself, but then it occurred to Christopher and then others that Hannah might also be at risk.

"Major Gist," Christopher said with great concern, "I haven't raised this because I want to make sure I'm not creating unnecessary fears; but *my* fear is that Hannah, through no fault of her own, while only an innocent spectator, could be confused as a player in this whole drama."

Major Gist looked blankly at Christopher, then suddenly grasped the significance of what he had just heard.

"Damn! How true. Not only is your Hannah a runaway, but she is associated with," and Major Gist enumerated her associations as if listing charges in a court of law, "the Reverend Crabbe, Alma Lynch, James Chalmers (the infamous 'Candidus'), and this Lieutenant Benjamin Harvey."

Continuing, Major Gist admitted, "We should have realized this immediately, and not have left it to Alma's unfortunate disappearance to bring it to our attention.

"If nothing else, there is a handsome reward out for Hannah, and those involved in this intrigue certainly want to know any part that she may have played in their exposure."

Christopher looked hopefully at Major Gist. "What can we do to protect her, sir?"

For a military officer with an entire company already assigned to him by the President of the Provincial Convention for this very purpose, Major Gist knew immediately what could be done.

"For the time being, and until we can come up with a permanent solution, I'm going to order your commanding officer, Captain Smith, to provide a detail to guard Missus Williams twenty-four hours a day. *And* I'm going to recommend that you, Private," looking at Christopher, "and Private Simon stand the night watch. How's that?"

Christopher was elated. "Yes, Sir!"

****

"Listen to me!"

In her exasperation, she felt like throwing her wine glass at the intricately carved gold-leaf mirror which reflected both of them. *Not in the best of light,* she thought looking at herself, before continuing.

"She'll forever be missing…because that's the desired result of assassinations such as these. There's no reason to be coy about this with you. I can assure you that Alma Lynch is dead and no doubt food for our delectable blue crabs."

She was angry. "People will be enjoying eating their crabs at the stands down on the Point this fall and commenting on the uncommon sweetness of the meat."

Disgusted by what she had just said, she added, "I say that with tremendous sorrow."

"You say that with tremendous venom—which you spit at me, and I admit that I deserve it. I ill-used the young woman. My only excuse is that it was necessary for the cause." He, too, was angry, but he was equally firm in his righteousness.

She looked hard at him. "Mordecai, fanatics care less about people than they do about their perverted ideas. I know you're not like that."

"Rachel, you're a hard woman—"

"Why do you say that? Because I'm a survivor and have suffered enough at the hands of fools and knaves?"

"You know, it wasn't until I heard the name Hyman Cohen that I realized you—and by extension Robert Levy, had become involved in this—" Mordecai Gist waved his hand, "This business. I was going to seek your advice, since I am so ignorant in these matters—neither I, nor the politicians are much good at intrigue—but I shrank from doing so, believing you would bite my head off!"

Rachel shrugged. "I had hoped those days were over, Mordecai, but good citizens like you seem to cause more harm than good; and right in front of my eyes, of course, so I'm left to clean up the mess."

He could only laugh at that.

"So what do you think we should do about Hannah Williams? I feel so damn'd guilty about Alma Lynch. I do not want to be in any way responsible for something happening to this young woman. And," he announced, "I just hope I have found a solution."

He went over to his desk and picked up a copy of the *The Maryland Journal,* folded in quarters, and pointed to an advertisement. It read,

> WANTED IMMEDIATELY
> A DISCREET and capable Woman to officiate as Housekeeper in a Gentleman's family on their Estate near Head of Elk. Such a Person, upon coming well recommended, will hear of a good Encouragement by Applying to the office of the Maryland Gazette on Market Street.

Rachel looked at him, quizzically.

"I know the gentleman in question to be none other than Robert Alexander. We discussed his need for a domestic manager some time ago. With her experience, I am sure Missus Williams is exceptionally well-qualified."

Rachel was pensive. "No doubt she is, Mordecai. But why condemn her to Head of Elk?"

"Because she's not safe here in Baltimore, and will be even less safe when the great majority of law-abiding men in this town go off to war in a few weeks; *and* because Head of Elk is the province's military depot for our troops who will be serving in New York—we *are* going to New York to fight, you know."

"I had supposed so," Rachel responded wearily. "Perhaps a position with the Alexander family is the answer." She sipped her white wine, savoring its chilled fermented fruitiness, thinking.

...Finally, putting the glass down, "In fact, it does seem a good idea, Mordecai. Now all we have to do is convince Hannah and Christopher."

Gist grinned. "No, Rachel, we don't have to do anything of the sort. I'm a major and Christopher Sims is a private."

****

In effect ordered by Major Gist and more gently urged by Rachel, Christopher and Hannah agreed that she should accept the position with the Alexander family. Hannah was not happy about going off to Head of Elk, whose very name suggested wilderness and nosey wildlife.

"Actually, it's not bad at all," Rachel assured her. "It's an attractive little town of brick houses on hills above a pleasant river.

While both accepted the fact that Hannah would go to Head of Elk to work for yet another family, while Christopher would go off to campaign against the British, neither course of action sat well with them.

Hannah was disappointed. It was enough to allow Christopher to go off to war while she remained at home, but she had hoped to mitigate this ordeal somewhat by working for Rachel in her new academy.

As she pointed out to Christopher, "I can read and write well enough, and that I know how to operate a household would be very helpful in running a school for young women. Rachel said so herself."

"Aye, Hannah, and it will come to pass sooner rather than later. And as ye know, I have my own hopes that are to be found here in Baltimore." Christopher had already told Hannah about learning the printing business from Missus Goddard and his desire to become a newspaper publisher, and a printer of any and everything to make a decent living.

"Well, these are the kinds of plans we were just dreamin' about a year ago, Chris, and now they're on the verge of comin' true. It might be a little disappointing to have to wait a few months or so longer, but it's also exciting, isn't it!" Hannah said this not as a question, but as an exclamation, with those wide eyes of hers and an unselfconscious smile.

Christopher wrapped Hannah in his arms, gave her a fond kiss, and smiling, said, "You are absolutely right!"

Hannah insisted on another kiss, this one she made far more passionate than the first, which spoke for itself.

And in their ensuing happiness, they promised to thoroughly enjoy their remaining time with each other and not dwell on once again being separated.

Towards the end of June, Rachel and Mordecai Gist introduced Hannah to Robert Alexander.

"I have heard such wonderful things about you, Missus Williams. And I am certain you will like Missus Alexander—Isabella—and our brood of children!"

They chatted for sometime over tea in the Coffee House parlor, the ladies and gentlemen in comfortable settees or armchairs, and the servants discreetly there with more coffee or wine, and dainty cakes and tarts, just like Cecil used to serve on such occasions.

Following Mister Alexander's departure, Hannah was in a good mood and assured both Rachel and Major Gist that she was sure both parties would enjoy the arrangement.

Looking at Rachel, she added, "And to have six children of such varying ages will, I'm sure, add to my qualifications as a teacher's assistant, don't you think!"

Later, as she told Christopher about her interview with Mister Alexander, Hannah mentioned that she had already met Robert Alexander in Chester Town eight or nine months ago:

"Oh, not met him exactly, Chris, but I was present when he was introduced to Mister Chalmers and I also saw him speak briefly to the Reverend Crabbe. No, I don't think he remembered me from that occasion."

Christopher wondered if it was not odd for a prominent patriot to socialize—not so much with well-meaning loyalists, but with meaner-minded tories, such as these men. Worried yet again about Hanna's welfare while he was off campaigning, Christopher mentioned this to Major Gist.

Gist thought about this for a minute. "Oh, yes, of course. I do remember him as a member of the Council of Safety which visited Chester Town back in October '75 to arrange for the manufacture of saltpetre in an extensive manner. I know that because of my responsibilities for contracting supplies for the battalion."

Gist looked gently at Christopher, remembering with ineffable joy his unabashed protectiveness towards his wonderful wife, Cecil. He said confidently, "Robert Alexander is one of our staunchest patriots, and Head of Elk is, for all intents and purposes, an armed fortress. As for being civil when in the presence of one's political enemies, a gentleman must act like a gentleman." Gist then laughed, cynically, adding, "Not long ago I considered Jim Chalmers a friend, and would certainly not cane him if I saw him this very day!"

Clapping Christopher on the back, "Your young woman will be fine, Christopher. Undoubtedly the greater concern should be the need to bring you home safe and sound!"

36

RUMORS OF MOMENTOUS EVENTS

Baltimore Town
Early July 1776

ON JULY 7, Hannah said a tearful goodbye to Christopher, and to Aunt Ruth, Rachel and her other new friends, then climbed into the Alexander family's personal four-horse coach, which would take her to "Friendship," the family estate at Head of Elk. It was a wonderfully comfortable coach, completely enclosed with a door and windows, even padded benches, and a rear rack covered by a tarpaulin for bulk luggage—of which there was considerable since a number of people had contributed happily to Hannah's new wardrobe.

There were final yells of goodbye through cupped mouths and waving arms, and the elegant coach, with a lurch and the grating of wheels across sun-dried ruts, haltingly set out for the main road to Philadelphia.

And once again, Hannah was gone.

The previous afternoon, Hannah and Christopher had dinner with all their Baltimore friends at "The Sign of the Cup and Crown," their favorite dining room.

It was a bittersweet gathering, but also a happy one in the sense that all considered this separation of the two lovers to be the final sacrifice in a remarkable saga of love and revolution.

Days earlier, on July 2, the same day that thousands upon thousands of seasick British troops had landed on Staten Island, making certain a decisive battle for New York City, the Continental Congress took a deep breath and voted in favor of American independence. Two days later, a slightly amended declaration was approved without dissent and sent off to the printer.

Rumors of these momentous events had touched down in Baltimore on July 6 with the impact of a twister, picking up people, their lives and futures and spinning them off in every direction.

So, despite the purpose of this event, personal as it was, it was understandable that much of the conversation was taken up by the great events of the day.

Looking terribly earnest, Terry stated, "I do believe America has the opportunity to create a far better constitution than that of England. But first we need to obtain the liberty which the declaration of independence claims for us…and there's no doubt we'll have to fight for it."

"No doubt, sir," intoned Henry Murray, "and soon you and Christopher here will be off to secure that independence by force of arms. So, war will determine America's moral and physical survival. But it is, I maintain, also a test of our holy mission!"

"I think independence will be enough," suggested Rachel. "Once that is secured, then we can worry about an even greater design."

Christopher was thoughtful, even as he clutched Hannah's hand in her lap. "Well, the British have a great fleet and huge army before New York City. It appears they're puttin' all of their eggs in one basket…and will risk all in one great battle for North America."

"But why New York?" asked Rachel, asking no one in particular.

Henry Murray, as usual, was quick to offer an explanation. "My dear, having failed to douse the fires of liberty which raged in Boston before it ignited all the colonies, the prime British objective now is undoubtedly to separate New England from the rest of the colonies. New York City occupies a position at the mouth of the Hudson River from which the British army can effect this strategy.

"Besides, the city is on an island surrounded by navigable water fit for the Royal Navy and also provides excellent winter quarters for the troops. Defeat them here and we've won!"

Missus Goddard questioned this rather simplistic explanation. "Mister Murray, Boston used to be the key—liberate Boston and we've won. Now, it's New York City. Has anyone bothered to ask the British how our assumptions play with them?"

Nonplussed, Henry Murray hurriedly took a less omniscient position. "Well, after their rude comeuppance at Charleston, the British don't have much choice but to invite a decisive engagement," he noted. "With the exception of Canada, an unfortunate but inconsequential setback, I've been assured, we've thoroughly beaten the regulars on every occasion. It would seem that New York is a suitable place for their final stand."

"Tens of thousands of regulars," Aunt Jane uttered in awe. "I simply cannot imagine our poor men standing up to such a host."

"Bah," exclaimed Henry Murray, airily dismissing the numbers. "We can gather fifty thousand, a hundred thousand men, or more. *And,*" he paused for effect..."and the American citizen-soldier is not your European peasant who passively offers himself up as cannon fodder for the British regulars."

"Why, Henry, I didn't realize you were a military thinker!"

"I most certainly am not, my dear Mary Katherine, but General Charles Lee is, and he has written in the New York papers of his confidence in the 'zealous citizenship' of Americans 'as an alternative to Prussian discipline.'"

General Lee was a former British officer who had convinced most patriots, including General Washington himself, of his military genuis—to the point where many thought he should be the commander-in-chief of the Continental Army; therefore, his confidence in the American soldier carried great weight—not even Missus Goddard would question the marvelous General Lee.

"Well, let us pray that you and General Lee are right," she said earnestly. "Because we will soon be sending forth the flower of Maryland's youth to do battle with both the regulars and their Prussian hirelings."

Mary Katherine looked at Christopher and Terry with a mixture of pride and concern. "I know for a fact that our heroic Battalion will be marching to New York within days, and with it go our husbands, and sons, and brothers, and fathers."

So, both Rachel and Christopher would be leaving their new home, reluctantly going off to war each in their own way, but for the same compelling reason: to defend their right to be free and independent—and, to be together.

That evening, they were left to themselves at Aunt Jane's. They sat on the settee in front of a small fire, sipping wine and talking. Christopher ran his finger along the delicate blue vein on the inside of Hannah's wrist. She smiled, wistfully.

So many emotions vying for attention as the day of departure was practically upon them.

"Our situation seems to pale in the face of these recent events." Hannah said this with great sadness, as if accepting the fact that henceforth the desperate struggles of everyday people would be overwhelmed by history ... and, epic stories.

"No, Hannah, no, it doesn't!" Christopher said emphatically. "And that's just the point. With so much happening, it would be easy to dismiss our lives as unimportant in these times. But truth is, Hannah, in trying to live our lives as God Almighty intended, we—aye, you and me!—have taken a stand which will change the world—just as Thomas Paine, who some say might be a modern prophet, ordained!

"We're not victims, Hannah, or innocent bystanders. *We are the revolution!*"

A little later, Christopher pulled out the card table from its place against the wall and unfolded it to serve as a dining table for a light supper. Hannah had prepared a salmagundi of leafy greens, sharp white cheese, veal, onion, boiled eggs, pickled red cabbage, and nasturtium flowers. She artfully arranged this mixture over inverted bowls to create a dome effect, placed a heart-shaped pat of butter on top, and served them with an oil and vinegar dressing. It was a perfect summer snack—crisp and tart and light, perfect with a chilled wine.

They turned to the future. Idly twirling his wine glass on the table, Christopher repeated his plans to become a printer and newspaper publisher, more to reaffirm Hannah's support for this ambition than describe any firm plans. Hannah, though disappointed that she would once again assume the role of domestic servant (never mind the fancy title bestowed upon her by the Alexanders), also wanted to have plans. For both of them, these plans represented a real future and not just an imaginary one.

They talked about the future in confident voices now. All the things they did talk about were not really important, being merely an attempt to get the feel of what a normal life together might be like; something to think about during the next six months when they wouldn't be together to talk about it. And it also brought temporary relief from the ticking clock.

When their small talk ran out, Hannah reached down her bodice and brought forth a silver coin, which she displayed in the palm of her hand. Christopher recognized it immediately as the Spanish milled dollar he had given her so long ago.

"You still have it," he exclaimed in wonder.

"Brought me good luck—have to give it that. I almost gave it away to a scoundrel, thinking it was buying my way to you, and then he actually stole it from me, but Mister Cohen returned it—" Hannah fingered the silver chain. "Mister Cohen said the leather thong broke, so he put it on this silver chain."

Christopher looked at Hannah much as he had looked at her that day when she was just fourteen and had won his heart.

Now, he realized she was also someone to be looked up to: she was his hero.

Deep in thought, he vaguely heard her say, "But now, you need it for your trial." She had risen from the table and all of a sudden was standing over him, carefully placing the chain over his head and gently letting the coin hang on his chest.

Christopher lifted the coin and holding it in the palm of his hand, took Hannah's hand and placed it over his.

Looking at her, he asked, "What adventures lay before us this time, Hannah Williams?"

They found themselves once again on the settee. Christopher was rubbing Hannah's neck with the pads of his fingers, feeling the warmth and moisture. Her hair was soft and a little damp as he twisted soft curls between his fingers and then scissoring a thick strand of hair, dragged his fingers down its length. Soon he was nuzzling the nape of her neck, excited by her scent and the taste of her sweat. Staring at the clock on the mantle, Hannah held his hand tight between her breasts, rubbing it hard. She looked at him, her mouth a little crooked, and he knew what she was thinking.

"Yes, Hannah, we'll be parting once again. But this time nobody is abducting you, and so I don't have to chase after you. When this campaign is over, I will come for you. You know I will, don't you?"

Hannah nodded.

"Well, then—" Christopher was at a loss for words. "We'll see each other at Head of Elk soon, and…well, when this is over— Oh, Hannah, it will be all right! I promise."

Neither would ever remember how they ended up in the attic pressed together on Christopher's mattress. It was quiet and he dreamily watched Hannah remove her clothing down to her lawn chemise.

Wet, the gauze-like material molded her breasts and nipples.

As she settled next to him her dampness felt cool to his touch.

He cupped her breast, feeling its heft and pliancy in his hand. As he fell asleep, he felt her warm breath on his neck, and inhaled the sweet smell of her hair even as it tickled his nose.

By the time he awoke the next morning, she was gone.

****

After seeing Hannah off, Christopher and Terry collected their belongings, said their own goodbyes, and reported to the company at Whetstone Point, where they would remain in camp until the battalion marched to New York.

That first evening as they sat outside their tent, Christopher and Terry joked about being just common soldiers now. The other members of their mess, tolerant throughout of their comrades' special status, now enjoyed the two complaining about their onerous details, and uncomfortable sleeping conditions.

"...but we did destroy the plot, or at least crippled it," Terry proclaimed proudly. "And Mister Paca was one of those who voted for independence. Imagine if he had been snatched by the plotters! History might have been rewritten."

"Aye," Christopher agreed, "*but* we still have not identified the traitor 'C.'"

Having said this, he was thoughtful. "You know, Terry, Alma Lynch may have died because of the very fact that we were not able to uncover the traitor."

Terry looked at Christopher, his expression solemn. "Aye, Chris, it could be. Regardless, 'tis a shame that such an innocent young woman was made to suffer."

"Terry," Christopher said impatiently, "All of that is true, but you miss the point: Hannah may be in danger for the same reason."

"I don't know why she would be, Chris. She wasn't really involved in this matter. But, in any event, Hannah is in safe hands with the Alexanders, and at Head of Elk she is surrounded by our troops. The loyalists and British won't be able to touch her even if they wanted."

"Well, Terry, I have to believe that ..."

****

By order of His Excellency, General Washington, on July 9, the Continental Army was paraded and the Declaration of Independence was read in full to the troops. Following this lead, the Maryland Convention ordered that all Maryland troops in Continental service celebrate the Declaration on the same date. Lieutenant Colonel Francis Ware, Deputy Commander of the Battalion, officiated at the ceremony held at Fort Whetstone, which had become a proper little star-shaped earthen fort in the rear of the shore batteries.

The three Baltimore companies were drawn up between the fort and the battery, and the declaration was read by the acting adjutant. Since the battalion chaplain was in Annapolis, Major Gist had arranged for the minister from his home town to offer a prayer, rich in quotations from the Eighteenth Psalm.

> *He delivered me from my strong enemy,*
> *and from them which hated me: for they were*
> *too strong for me.*
>
> *He teacheth my hands to war, so that a bow*
> *Of steel is broken in mine arms.*
>
> *Thou hast also given me the shield of thy*
> *Salvation: and thy right hand hath holden me up,*
> *And thy gentleness hath made me great.*

Finally, the companies rendered a *feu de joie* with a credible attempt at a rolling volley, accompanied by a salvo from the eighteen-pounders at the battery, the dirty gray smoke from the cannon mixing with the black smoke from the ironworks, casting a shadow over the festivities which did not go unremarked by those who disagreed with independence.

The men were given a double ration of whiskey to celebrate this great event, but the liberating effects of drink had hardly worn off before they were back at work again. This time it was preparing for the campaign in earnest. The men were sized and graded and accordingly assigned to the first or second rank, with the tallest in the rear rank in order to fire over their comrades in the first rank. Each man was also assigned to a file, or firing, given a number—Christopher's number was forty-seven, then they were drilled incessantly.

Cartridges were rolled and stored in tinned-iron ammunition boxes, tents were struck and loaded on wagons, and weapons and personal equipment were inventoried, attended to, and inspected daily.

Preparations for the march also meant culling out the lame and sick, those unfit for the rigorous campaign ahead. Some of these men were shirkers, others were good men who just weren't up to it. Among the latter, sad to say, was Walker Muse.

Walker and his constant companion, Caleb Hayes, had been set upon several weeks ago by a gang of rakehells as they left their favorite booze den along the waterfront. Both were badly beaten, but while Caleb recovered to the point where he could accompany the company on its march, Walker, though he was up and about, sloughing like an old man and doing some useful chores in the hospital, was not fit for the rigors of a campaign.

Public Wharves
Fell's Point
July 11, 1776

On the evening of July 11, the three Baltimore companies of Smallwood's Battalion marched to the public wharves at Fell's Point, where they would embark for Head of Elk. The departure of the battalion on this date happened to coincide with the town's official celebration of the Declaration of Independence.

Just as they were marching through town to the shouts and pumping arms of Baltimore's citizenry, the town exploded with the sounds of fireworks as the sky over the town was bathed in crackling cascades of green, red, and white embers in a grand illumination the town had never before seen.

The display was a fitting finale to the day when the town of Baltimore welcomed the arrival of independence, even as it bid farewell to its finest young men.

****

They climbed the swaying gangplank and jumped down on the deck of a rickety schooner named the *Harmony*. Christopher immediately noticed the differences between being on water and being on land: the pleasant swaying, which Terry poetically compared "to our innocent stay in our mother's womb;" the smell of open water, which seemed different to him—more powerful—than at the water's edge, and of pitch and new hemp and waterlogged oak; there was also the redolence of grain, rum, perhaps spices, and a dozen other ancient cargoes carried by this creaking vessel, with its lines resonating like a bowstring.

Christopher was excited by this new adventure, and a little nervous.

"Have you ever been sailing on open water, Terry?"

"Oh, sure. Not much to entertain you. But of course we're sailing at night, so you won't see anything. C'mon, let's get comfortable. I've got a little of the 'good creature' with me to ease our passage," and he pulled a flask from his waistcoat.

Their vessel seemed ungainly as it was coaxed away from the wharf. The schooner slowly headed out to the Northwest Branch; beyond was Whetstone Point—now seen from a different perspective, then the Patapsco River, and finally the Chesapeake Bay. The winds on the Bay were southwesterly and fair; but winds were peculiar during this time of year, and, at best, the voyage, as short as it was, could still take until early morning, or beyond.

They stood along the rail, which was lined with men gawking just like them, pulling from the flask, listening to the slap of the hull as it hit wavelet after wavelet. The canvas above fluttered or screeched as it swelled and surged according to the vagaries of the wind. The wood, long unvarnished, felt soft to the touch.

The flickering lights of Baltimore Town faded to a thin white line. Clouds hid the moon and stars. Except for the ship's little lanterns and the glowing bowls of tobacco pipes, all was complete darkness as Christopher and his comrades set out to recreate the world all over again.

ABOUT THE AUTHOR

JOHN CONRADIS learned his love of history from his father who was a published author of local Civil War history in Montgomery County, Maryland. He has been a student of the American Revolution since his teens and has spent years researching Maryland's role in the Revolution. He is a member of the Company of Military Historians. He saw active service in the U.S. Army in Vietnam and was a career intelligence officer serving overseas for thirty years. He lives in Bethesda, Maryland with his wife Hazel and son Brandon.

www.ingramcontent.com/pod-product-compliance
Lightning Source LLC
Chambersburg PA
CBHW070516030726
47503CB00004B/1284